# FATED PACK

## THE HYBRID WOLF SERIES: BOOK FOUR

CIARA DELAHUNT

DUBHLUNA
PUBLISHING

Fated Pack
*The Hybrid Wolf Series: Book Four*
© 2025 by Ciara Delahunt



**Cover art by Anna Spies of Atra Luna Graphik Design**

Contact information:
www.ciaradelahunt.com
ciara@ciaradelahunt.com

ISBN: 978-1-7391785-4-3
First Edition: March 2025

# CHARACTERS

Eve O'Connor *(hybrid)*

**CRESCENT PACK***
Luke Whelan – *surname pronounced 'wee-lan'*
Tom Whelan
Max Whelan
Helena Whelan (*human*)
Alice Whelan (*hybrid*)
Darren Donohoe
Paula Donohoe
Dylan
Joshua
Liz
Sorcha
Maggie
Áine

**FAOLCHÚNNA PACK***
Ryan McKenna – *surname pronounced 'mac-ken-ah'*
Damien McKenna – *pronounced 'day-me-en'*
Rebecca McKenna
~~Nick McKenna~~
Mary McKenna
Fiona – *pronounced 'fee-own-a'*
Nadine

** Werewolves unless otherwise indicated.*

## OTHER

~~Kate~~
Craig (*vampire*)
Béibhinn (*witch*) - *pronounced* 'bae-vee-n'
Cadhla (*witch*) - *pronounced* 'kai-luh'
Jonas (*vampire*)
Darius (*vampire*)
Alec (vampire)
Larissa (*witch*) – *pronounced 'la-ris-ah'*
Henry Edmonstone (*werewolf*)
Maya (*witch*)
Gabriella/Gabi Patel (*witch*)
Ezra Patel (*hybrid*)
Valeria Patel (*witch*)
Cassandra (*witch*)
Russell Stewart (*werewolf*)
Callum Stewart (*werewolf*)
Lawrence (*vampire*)
Jeremy Walker (*werewolf*)
Lila Walker (*werewolf*)
Leanne *(psychic)*

# BEFORE YOU READ

I write paranormal romance and as such, my books are aimed at adults. *The Hybrid Wolf Series* includes themes of an adult nature, and violent scenes typical of the paranormal romance and fantasy genres. This book contains certain subjects that some readers may be sensitive to.

Please stay safe and visit my website to check the content warnings for my books before reading:

www.ciaradelahunt.com/content-warnings

# IRISH LESSON

Class is in session. By the end of this series, you're going to be fluent in Irish slang.

***Mam* is not a typo!** We don't say mom over here.

I know our names have too many vowels, but revert to this when you get stuck and enjoy the ride.

- **Boreen:** a narrow lane in the countryside
- **Cert:** certificate
- **Chips:** fries (we call chips 'crisps' here)
- **College/university:** interchangeable
- **Craic:** fun/entertaining
- **Faolchúnna:** wolves
- **Flash drive:** USB stick
- **"For fuck's sake!":** exclamation of frustration, similar to 'What the hell?'
- **Fresher:** student in their first year at college in Ireland *(approx. 18 years old)*
- **Garda:** police officer *(Bán Garda is a female police officer)*
- **Gardaí:** police plural
- **Garda station:** police station
- **In the nip:** in the nude
- **Keeping sketch:** view the area for approaching authority
- **Lie in:** to stay in bed later than usual in the morning
- **Lift:** elevator
- **Lose the plot:** lost their mind, to no longer be able to act normally or understand what is happening

- **Luas:** name of the tram service in Dublin
- **Mam:** mom/mother *(the Irish don't use mom)*
- **Path/footpath:** sidewalk
- **Piss:** to pee
- **Puke:** vomit
- **Punter:** your average paying customer
- **Runners:** trainers (shoes)
- **Snug:** a small room or area in a pub where only a few people can sit
- **Strop:** a bad mood
- **Tracksuit bottoms:** joggers
- **Twig:** to suddenly realise something
- **Wing mirror:** side-view mirror on a car
- **"You're taking the piss":** you're pushing it or you better be joking

It's highly possible I've missed something here. If you're ever confused, check my reader groups, or drop me a message on social media!

*"Without your past, you could never have arrived—
so wondrously and brutally,
by design or some violent, exquisite happenstance
... here."*
— *Taylor Swift*

# CHAPTER 1

LUKE

**B**reathe.

Stars danced in my vision—not the kind I stared at every night, willing my mate to find me. No, these constellations were accompanied by white, hot pain shooting through my jaw as the palm of Larissa's hand connected with my face. But Eve was there in my mind; my mate tethered to my soul by an invisible string. Her voice echoed in the darkness as she called to me, begging me to hold on and fight. It was the ghost of her, mere memories, my mind playing tricks on me. Deep down, I knew she was too far away to be using the mind link, but the bond endured. A constant reminder, a reason to live. Her memory spoke to me as I drifted in and out of consciousness, demanding me to force air into my burning lungs. Urging me to fight. To fight for her. To fight for myself. To fight for us.

Another stinging slap landed, sharp nails slicing into my cheek.

The stars faded, darkness receding to reveal Larissa leaning over me. An all too familiar sense of dread settled as I found myself in the same make-shift cell, surrounded by a bed of straw in a converted stable. Beyond the steel bars blocking my escape, I could see the red-hued sunrise bleeding into the sky. Another day dawning. Another day trapped. I'd lost count, but every night, I caught a glimpse of the moon on the cusp of her first quarter, warning me how much closer she was to her full phase and how little time I had left to complete the mating bond with Eve.

The exposed brick was cool against my back where I was slumped, the silver shackles binding my wrists hindering my ability to heal. The chains attached were just long enough for me to crawl to the other side of the cell to relieve myself like an animal. That was the extent of my freedom, and the sick bitch had punished me for not being grateful for it. The plastic dog bowl in the corner that was so generously topped up daily was another twist of the knife.

The mask of rage contorting Larissa's features morphed into one of twisted pleasure as I blinked back into consciousness, her ruby-painted lips framing a hungry smile that sent chills down my spine. "Oh good, I was worried we'd have to stop for today. And I'm not done with you yet."

She was never done with me for long. Her thirst for pain and power was insatiable, and unfortunately, I was her favourite toy. She made an appearance most days, twice on the worst ones, and her torture depended entirely on her mood. Today was not a good mood day. She'd interrogated me that morning for hours before I'd blacked out. Always the same questions, mainly about that elusive dagger. The last piece of the puzzle I was slowly putting together. Or at least I was trying. My brain seemed to shut down during her sessions, the memories blurred and broken as if my mind was trying to protect me. But I cared more about retaining information that might save Eve than protecting myself from the witch's violence.

Larissa crouched by my side, curled her fingers around my throat as if she could sense the lump of emotion rising there, and drew my attention back to her. She stabbed her thumb under my chin as soon as my eyelids shuttered, forcing me to look up. "I'm not in the mood for games today, so don't even think about playing pretend."

That was a lie. She loved games, but much like a spoiled child, she only enjoyed the ones where she was in control. One thing I'd learned was that she didn't want me dead. Whether it was because she needed me for the ritual or because I was leverage, I wasn't sure. So I often pretended to be out cold. It worked, sometimes. But today was not one of those days.

"I would never dream of it," I rasped, my throat raw from screaming.

She increased the pressure on my windpipe, her upper lip curling in displeasure. "Weeks with me, and yet you still haven't learned to control that tongue. That bitch of yours might enjoy it, but I'm not a fan."

Magic charged the air, and the chains binding me suddenly pulled taut, the silver shackles around my wrists scorching the flesh as my arms were pinned against the wall above my head. I gagged as she pressed down so hard I thought my windpipe might collapse. My back arched, my lungs burning as they strained for air. My pain only spurred her on, the image of her leering over me flickering until I felt like my chest was going to explode. My fingers clenched around air, her grip silencing my roar.

"Much better," she purred, squeezing one more time for good measure before releasing my throat. "You're wide awake now."

Air scorched my throat as I fought to catch my breath. My heaving chest, covered in angry red marks that were struggling to heal from her last torture session, seemed to draw her attention.

"Back to business, we're running out of time. *You* are running out of time. You know what I want. Just give me the answer, and we can end this."

My scoff came out as a pathetic wheeze. "By 'end' you mean killing both me and my mate in some fucked up ritual. It's not much of an incentive."

"There may be an alternative."

She trailed her hand down my bare chest, and I stiffened. While she'd never overstepped that particular line, being used as her plaything still took its toll. Tracksuit bottoms two sizes too big hung loosely round my hips, the only scrap of clothing I'd been allowed to cover my modesty. I'd been stripped, whipped, stabbed, and endured her magic tearing into my skin so many times I'd lost track. Sometimes I wondered if she got off on my reactions, my pain. And then there was always the threat that she *could*. We both knew I was completely at her mercy, and she loved to flaunt her power.

The disgust that writhed in my gut must have been written all over my face because her knuckles connected with my jaw, my head cracking against the brickwork at the force.

"I'm not making any deals with you, witch," I spat, a metallic taste filling my mouth.

She snatched my cheeks between her forefinger and thumb, jerking my head to the side. "It seems no matter how many times we go through this, you never learn. Surely your mate is more important than the secrets you're guarding?"

I refused to meet her eyes, focusing instead on the brightening sky beyond my cell as I tried to empty my mind. Switching off and going to another place, making myself numb, was the only way to endure her little interrogation sessions.

"I know the Edinburgh pack don't have the dagger. My researchers have informed me that it was last given to an Irish pack in Leinster. Damien doesn't have it. That leaves your father."

Guilt hit me like a freight train at the mention of my dad, my alpha. I didn't have long to dwell on the disappointment that washed over me.

Just when my lungs felt like they were starting to inflate properly, pain lanced through my body as she released me from her grip only to poke the wound healing over my heart. She didn't stop there, my skin splitting open as she dug her fingernail into the wound.

I jerked against my restraints, gritting my teeth and fighting to breathe through the pain.

"Perhaps you are an alpha in the making," she mused, her violet eyes sparkling with violence as she removed her finger, watching droplets of blood roll down my chest. "You're healing well enough despite the silver and the nightshade." Her lips spread into a malicious grin, my only warning before she gouged her nails through my wound. "I thought I could use Damien's son, you know? I thought maybe I could entice you to take over one of the English packs, and we could work together. But unfortunately for you, this prophecy doesn't have any loopholes. Him loving her isn't enough. I need her *mate*—moon bound and all that bullshit."

Witches usually had extreme respect for ancient magic and prophecies. But the way she spoke, it was as if she only cared about what she could gain. Power.

The light in my cell dimmed, the lone light bulb dangling from the ceiling guttering out.

There was a sickening, wet sound as she tore the laceration wide open once more. I cried out, pain searing through my body. My stomach heaved as a fresh wave of blood gushed down my chest, and I turned my head to the side just in time to retch bile onto the straw.

She wrinkled her nose in distaste. I would have happily puked all over the evil cow if I'd had anything in my stomach.

It didn't stop her though, no. She kept digging into the wound, twisting her fingers like the blade of a knife. My cries echoed off the bare walls of the stall, beads of sweat coating my body. It was as if she wanted to remind me she could claw her way to my heart and rip it out. Her movements became more erratic, her eyes closing as she released an otherworldly cackle.

"Life-source of the undead, the true heart of a hound." Larissa's voice took on a childlike singsong as she recited the prophecy. She drew the element of fire, the scent of burning flesh filling my nostrils as her nails not only cut into my flesh but seared through it to accentuate the lines. "Ancient magic spilled, bloodline and moon bound."

*In.*

I sucked in a shallow breath, the movement of my diaphragm expanding triggered another jolt of pain through my body.

*Out.*

All I could do was breathe—fight.

Her face was inches from mine, and I could feel her breath on my lips as she whispered the final line of the prophecy like a spell. "Trinity tied by the blade of magic intertwined."

The air shifted, straw rustling as wind whipped through the cell. The hairs on my neck stood on end as magic stirred around us, much like when Eve and I had found the prophecy in the library. My heart twisted, the memory of our little research session adding another layer of pain. How I'd teased her, the mischievous glint in her eye, and how beautiful my girl looked when she came apart.

Larissa sent another charge of magic straight into my chest, tearing me from the sanctuary of my mind back into my torturous reality. My body convulsed, each movement of her hand or my own straining against the silver cuffs setting my body alight in an unrelenting cycle of agony.

"No smart response?" Venom laced her words, and it wasn't the first time I wondered what forged such a hateful being. Or was she born evil?

After what seemed like an eternity, a sickening squelch made my stomach drop as she retracted her fingers from the wound on my chest.

I collapsed. My wrists still scorched by the cuffs, but it was a constant ache rather than the unbearable pain she liked to deliver by hand. When I finally met her gaze, my tortured heart stuttered. Swirling pools of silver white had replaced her lilac irises. The way they moved like mist conjured images of the old crone who had stopped Eve in the London Underground. As magic simmered in the air, I realised why it reminded me of the library we had explored. Gone was the sour taste of Larissa's powers, this was something ancient.

Something about how the witch moved felt wrong. She straightened, dragging her tongue across her teeth slowly as her hungry gaze drank me in. Were her cheekbones sharper? Had her hair darkened? I could no longer see the rising sun outside, not even the bars on the stable door were visible. Shadows had filled the space, shrouding the cell I had memorised in darkness. I could feel them snaking around us, as if they were alive. Dread coiled in my gut, and somehow I knew that the woman staring down at me was no longer the bloodthirsty witch, but something worse.

She cracked her neck before a slow, sinister smile curved her lips. The voice that finished the prophecy was not Larissa's.

"Wielded by the blessed can history unbind."

# CHAPTER 2

The waxing crescent moon was hanging low in the purple-hued sky as dusk descended. Taunting me. A ticking clock. A reminder I didn't need because I was all too aware that we were running out of time.

Two weeks. We had spent the last fortnight camped out with the Edinburgh pack trying to follow leads while we failed to crack that damn flash drive. Weeks with no real answers. No one we could track on Edmonstone's or Damien's payroll would spill anything. The longer we spent getting nowhere, the more the fear that we wouldn't get to Luke in time mounted. And if I lost him, I could lose my pack, my friends. The only semblance of family I'd truly had, and it was close to being ripped away forever. It was a fear I couldn't face, let alone speak into the universe. So, I focused on the hunt.

Rain ricocheted off the cobbled streets of Edinburgh, masking the sound of our steps. The streets began to blur into obscurity as my alpha led the way, closely followed by Josh and Mary. Craig kept pace with me while Dylan stayed one step behind at all times. A lump rose in my throat at the way they flanked me, the same way everyone had gathered these past few weeks. Protecting me in Luke's absence.

"Are you sure about this?" Craig's head whipped from side to side as he scanned our surroundings, damp strands of red-tipped hair peeked out from beneath his hood plastered to his forehead.

Tom glanced over his shoulder, the dark circles under his eyes accentuated by the shadows we clung to. "I trust my source. Cassandra said this is the last known location of the book, and it's our only lead."

I didn't miss the tick of Josh's jaw at that comment. He'd been relentless in his pursuit to crack the flash drive, and no one was more frustrated about the lack of progress than Josh. He didn't need any added pressure; the guy beat himself up daily for not making more headway. Reminding him that fixing his laptop had taken time or that he was doing his best didn't help. On the nights where sleep eluded me—which were most—I often came downstairs to find the telltale sign of the blue light filtering out from beneath the living room door. He'd managed to crack some of the encrypted files, but nothing contained information that brought us any closer to finding Luke. Alice had reluctantly stayed back to monitor while his latest attempt ran, knowing he needed this outing more than anyone.

Tom noticed it too, reaching out to clasp Josh's shoulder in a silent show of support.

None of us blamed him. If anyone was to blame for this mess, it was me. Luke had thrown himself at Larissa's mercy for me. My mate had traded his life for mine. The bond was growing weaker as the lunar cycle progressed, another twist of the metaphorical dagger in my heart. Except the pain was entirely real. I felt like I was walking around with my chest cleaved open. Raw, exposed, vulnerable, and broken.

I must have been wearing my feelings on my face again because, after one look, Tom was changing the topic. Driving us forwards, trying to focus on our purpose. His positivity was admirable, but I was clinging to frayed threads of hope by my fingernails.

"This guy is meant to be one of the biggest collectors of

magical artefacts," Tom explained, dropping back to fall into place beside me. "Even if he doesn't have the dagger anymore, he would know where it was. I'd rather skip the face to face on this one, but we'll get answers one way or another."

There was no mistaking the promise: Tom would stop at nothing to get his son back.

He had jumped straight on a plane once he heard the news and lived up to every facet of being a true alpha since his arrival. I wished Luke could have seen it, how much his dad was fighting for him. Maybe then he'd finally realise what he was worth.

I swallowed the lump rising in my throat and fisted my hands deep in the pockets of my hoodie, focusing on drowning out the noise of our shoes slapping the soaked pavement to scan for any threats. This wasn't our first attempt at finding information. One or two leads had turned into interrogations that came to bloody ends. I wasn't in the mood to confront the evil bitch that was holding Luke captive, but from the way my entire body was tensed and my fingertips tingled, I was ready for anyone who wanted to try me. My mental health was balancing on a knife's edge, but I wouldn't hesitate to defend my pack at a moment's notice. It's funny how quickly I'd gone from a normal human living a mundane life to being okay with clawing someone's eyes out. The mate bond tugging on my heart, along with the pack that had claimed me as one of their own, meant more to me than anything else. My world had changed—I'd changed.

"I think this is it." Mary signalled for us to halt behind the silhouette of a van parked on the side of the pavement.

I didn't stop with the same grace as my vampire bestie.

The narrow street was identical to many in the city, lined by rows of terraced Georgian houses standing four stories high. The exterior brickwork and sash windows lent character to the street that belonged on the movie screen. Iron railings cordoning off the small front gardens were well kept, except for one property Mary pointed to.

If you didn't pay much attention, the last house on the row

to our right almost blended into where the cul-de-sac ended, tall tree branches draping over the garden wall. Unlike its well-kept counterparts, its railings were coated in flaking paint and rust, the woodwork around the window frames worn by the relentless Scottish weather. As if it had been unloved by generations it passed through, left to fall prey to the elements.

If our information was correct, that was the truth. We'd found the dragon's den.

"I thought they'd live in some fancy palace or something," Craig mumbled, flinching as a raindrop landed square on his nose. "Or at least have some gaudy gold gates."

"You're not some sex- and blood-crazed stalker. There was me thinking immortality would have taught you not to believe stereotypes," I teased, though my eyebrow was inching closer to my hairline the longer I looked at the unkept house.

Mary rolled her eyes. "A dragon shifter's dwelling depends entirely on what they desire. If they hoard gold, and their desires are wealth, then you'll find them in a lavish mansion. But for those who hoard ancient texts and other magical rarities, they often care less about appearances. If anything, they understand the importance of lying low."

A bat burst from the chimney of the roof, sending a plume of soot into the night sky.

Dylan's eyes widened comically, and he shook his head. "There's keeping a low profile, and then there's living in a creepy house of horrors."

Mary levelled him with the same look she'd give a rambling toddler.

"Let's count ourselves lucky that this dragon isn't the type to lock their place up like Fort Knox." Tom raised an eyebrow, the corners of his lips lifting. "We should have until at least midnight until they are due home. That gives us three hours. We get in, we find that dagger, and we get the hell out."

Dylan paused with his mouth open, no doubt some joke on the tip of his tongue, before snapping his jaw shut and nodding.

I reached out to give Dylan's arm a squeeze as everyone followed Tom towards the dragon's home.

At a first glance, you could write him off as the joker. Since Luke had been taken, I'd noticed that Dylan was actually a mastermind at reading people. He knew when levity was required and exactly what each person needed to lift their spirits. He was an overlooked rock that very much held us together at the toughest of times, and it was no mystery why my mate loved him like a brother. And despite how much he must have been hurting with Luke taken, he put everyone else first.

We fell silent as we drew closer to the dragon's house. The paint on the front door was peeling, red flakes giving way to greying wood. The weathered brass knocker looked as if it might fall off the hinges should it be lifted. Perhaps the dragon had the right idea. His home screamed "Do not bother me" and if he was as into his collections as we were led to believe, it was exactly the vibe he wanted to give off.

Unfortunately for us, we needed to get inside.

Tom hovered his hands over the door. He moved from the edges inwards, never quite letting his fingers touch the surface. He was checking for wards, although without any witch on board, I wasn't sure what our plan was if the dragon booby-trapped his place.

We waited in silence, everyone focusing as we cast our senses out. The only sounds were the wind picking up as rain began to ease off and distant car engines. The smell of damp filled my nose, along with a mustiness that must have been coming from inside the house—I doubted he had many visitors. There was something else, another scent with earthy tones mixed with scorched wood. I sniffed again, trying to pick the scent apart. Not that I knew what dragon smelled like.

My mind wandered back to the times Luke had spent testing me in the Dark Night, the way he had teased me over my answers. Back when we were friends with a bucketful of sexual tension between us. I blinked rapidly, shoving the pang of sadness down.

I knew loss. I knew grief. But missing the other half to your heart was something entirely different.

"All clear." Tom dipped his chin, his voice so low it was only audible to those of us with paranormal ears and any stray cats lurking nearby.

My shoulders dropped an inch knowing we didn't need reinforcements. I'd briefly been in contact with Maya after she was reunited with Gabi back in London. The young witch was desperate to help, but I wouldn't let her. I couldn't. Not even to keep my mate safe.

I shook my head, trying to clear those thoughts away. I had a newfound understanding of how Luke struggled after Alice's disappearance. The nasty self-talk my mind conjured up sounded just like he had spoken about himself, and it made my heart do that thing where it felt like it might implode. The moon winked back into view as a thick cloud passed, reminding me I didn't have time to break.

My curiosity piqued when Mary produced an old key from her jean pocket, but I didn't ask where it came from. Or why I caught the faintest hint of blood on the brass surface.

Just as she placed the key in the worn lock and twisted, the dull thrum of a phone vibrating came from my left.

Craig's lips thinned as he whipped his phone out, a message flashing on the screen. "Our three hours just turned into thirty minutes. Someone tipped the dragon off."

"Wards? Does he have some kind of magical alarm system?" I frowned, glancing back at Mary who was now scowling with the heavy door ajar.

His molten irises darkened. "Nope. Vampires."

I followed Craig's narrowed gaze towards the crumbling chimney, where the bat had bolted from.

Fucking vampire bats.

# CHAPTER 3

I wasn't sure what I was expecting from a dragon-shifter scholar whose speciality was hoarding magical artefacts, but a scaled-down version of the library back in Cambridge wasn't it. Except this time, I didn't have a sphinx to show us where to look, and there was no rhyme or reason to the location of anything.

The moment I stepped into the house, the musty smell of aged paper filled my nostrils. We were met with papers and books piled high to form pillars on either side of the door. But as I moved deeper, the dragon's scent took over my senses. Unlike the stench of tobacco that clung to the walls of a smoker's home, this was a dense scent—a mix of woody smoke and charcoal, like the lingering signs of a bonfire but without the catch in your throat.

Craig flicked on the light, the bulb blinking into existence to highlight more stacks continuing down the hallway as far as my eyes could see. Glass cabinets and heaving bookcases were interspersed between the paper stacks, to the point where it was impossible to see where shelves ended and the overflow began.

"I'm not saying this is like looking for a needle in a haystack..." Dylan's eyes widened, his brow creasing as he scanned the chaos. "But unless this guy has some secret cataloguing system, or the dagger is going to play Marco Polo, thirty minutes might as well be mission impossible."

Josh nodded in agreement, his distaste for the mess written plainly on his face. The guy had no folders on his laptop desktop. This was probably his idea of hell.

"I know they don't teach kids analogue anymore, but thirty minutes isn't that long," Tom hollered from somewhere deeper in the house. "Get looking."

Dylan dropped a random book he had flicked through back on top of the nearest stack, sending dust particles into the air. "Yes, sir."

A low growl from the alpha's direction travelled through the house in response.

I bit back a smile and scanned the packed hallway, inching deeper until I found a doorway obscured by lower piles of what looked like old leather-bound notebooks. "We haven't got much to go on. This guy could have a chest full of daggers." More dust shook off the frame as I nudged the door open to reveal what used to be a living room but had become an overflow area, much like the rest of the house. There were more glass cabinets packed with an assortment of artefacts, including medals and Egyptian vases, and a desk completely covered in books. "Do you think we'd be able to sense the magic?"

Josh shrugged, his long legs stepping over a wall of paperwork with ease. "I think so, but this guy collects rare magical artefacts. Daggers tend to be used in rituals and to kill, so I doubt there's only one infused with magic."

"I hope none of these have eyes." Dylan squinted, nervously eyeing at a book that had jewels along its binding. "In case they rat us out to the dragon."

"Of course. Shouldn't we be worried about the ones with tongues then?" I bit back a grin, sharing a look with Craig as Dylan shuddered in horror at the mere thought. Our story from Cambridge must have given him nightmares.

"I prefer my books without any human attributes or trapped

souls." Dylan scowled, crossing the room to put some distance between him and the bookshelves. "I'm a vibes mood reader, not a vengeful witch. Can we focus on the dagger and not on books that give me the heebie-jeebies, please?"

Josh tapped away on his phone before shoving it in the back pocket of his jeans and clapping his hands together, his bronze brow creasing as he surveyed the chaos with no obvious starting point. "Right, twenty-six minutes and counting. There's no point in worrying about leaving hints we were here. We're already busted thanks to the vampire alarm system."

Everyone in the room could see without the light on, but given we were on a time crunch, I flicked it on anyway. A lone silver candle holder was precariously balanced on the tea-stained pages of an open book lying on the desk. Fire next to a bunch of ancient books made no sense to me, but I guess coughing flames made you more chill about fire hazards.

"Better make it count then." I inhaled deeply, forcing my tense lungs to inflate and my brain to focus on the present. The clock was ticking, not just on the dragon hoarder, but rescuing Luke in time to complete the mating bond. Larissa wanted this dagger, and we needed leverage. I rolled my shoulders and set my sights on a wooden box by the desk in the hopes it was our version of a treasure chest. "Let's find this damn dagger."

I moved on to the desk, giving the books a cursory glance before setting them aside along with the candle holder. Disturbed ash particles danced in the dim light as we set to work. I plonked a stack of books onto the desk to free up the chair and tugged the old chest towards me. Dylan let Josh take the bookcases without argument, opting instead for the dust-clouded glass cabinets. Craig set about digging through a pile of boxes containing old Venetian masks, scrolls, and everything in between. The way we fell into a rhythm together with ease healed something in me, patching up some of the cracks in my heart in Luke's absence.

The air was thick with dirty, clogging my throat as we worked. I prised the lock open on the chest with two extended claws, lifting the lid to reveal a pile of jewellery and sparkling gems. "Damn. Dragons really do hoard."

Josh looked over his shoulder with a chuckle. "Sometimes the stereotypes aren't too far from the truth."

"No shit." I marvelled at a heavy gold necklace, turning it over in my hands, before breaking myself from its spell and shoving the chest to one side. I needed the dagger, not a pirate's loot.

Floorboards creaked above us as Tom and Mary explored upstairs. Craig moved into the kitchen, zipping around with his vampire speed, but something kept me in this first room. I couldn't tell if it was a sixth sense, or if I had no desire to see what other things this dragon had in store.

Sifting through the hoard taught me that I never wanted to house share with a dragon shifter. I'd thought sphinxes were addicted to books, but at least they were orderly. This was chaos. Maybe it would be more tolerable if the dragon preferred to hoard cuddly toys or Taylor Swift merchandise. That I could get on board with.

I could feel distant pulsing coming from different areas of the room. Magic definitely hung in the air. But there was no telling how many artefacts this dragon had in his possession. The pull of magic led me to unlatch a cabinet filled with what looked like a pendant filled with actual blood, followed by a weird spoon-shaped thing, which Josh informed me was used to scoop out *eyeballs,* and finally a creepy ass doll that was going to haunt my sleepless nights for weeks. The thing had no hair, blue eyes that screamed possessed, and was dressed in a black outfit that belonged in a Tim Burton movie.

"When Tom said this guy hoards magical artefacts, I was expecting spell books and crystals. Not shit from a horror movie." I snapped the cabinet door shut, a shiver working its way down my spine. The doll's lifeless eyes tracked my movement as I backed away. "Maybe we're in the wrong room. Maybe this is the whacky, showstopper stuff, when we need to be looking for some kind of armoury."

"Nothing in here. The magic levels are lower too. I guess it makes sense to keep the valuables away from the oven," Craig called out, his footsteps muffled by the amount of stuff crammed into the house. A creative form of soundproofing.

I wiggled a shoebox free from where it was wedged between two books. The contents were practically vibrating with magic. For a moment, I really thought I'd found something. Any embers of hope were quickly doused when I opened the box to reveal a bunch of bones. And according to my werewolf-scenting abilities, these were human remains. Gross. While Dylan feared creepy books, I was the one who squealed when a spider came out of hiding from behind a cobweb-covered book at my eye level.

"Fuck no." I blanched, dropping the box as I leaped back. The bones scattered across the floor, one of them sliding beneath an old wardrobe in the corner.

Dylan popped his head up from behind an empty tank. Perhaps it had once housed a fish, but all that remained now was murky water that distorted his features. "What is it?"

"Nothing. It felt magical, but they were just bones," I grumbled, cringing as I stuffed the bones back into the shoebox as quickly as possible. The small jolt of magic I could feel each time my fingers grazed the cool skeletal surface made my stomach do somersaults. "Ew, this is fucking disgusting."

Something thumped upstairs, followed by Tom yelling down to us. "Everything okay down there?"

"Ten minutes." Josh's voice was grave as he issued the reminder and dropped down beside me to help clean up the human remains that had my skin crawling.

I cursed under my breath, wrinkling my nose as I ducked down on all fours in search of the last bone fragment. The dragon would know we were here, but on the trip into the city, Tom had made a point of hammering home the importance of not taking anything more than the dagger. Dragons were *extremely* protective of their possessions. The dagger we could claim as ours—or blame Larissa for. Some random old bone? Not so much. I pitied whoever it belonged to, but I wasn't adding a pissed off dragon shifter to the list of people who wanted me dead.

Larissa and the prophecy were more than enough heat for this werewolf.

Dust and the deep warmth of oak tickled my nose as I peered under the wardrobe, spotting the bone lying in a patch of dust bunnies. "Gotcha." The bone zapped me with a dose of magic as my fingers closed around it, and I recoiled, smacking my forearm off the furniture's base as I snatched the bone back.

"Careful," Josh warned, shielding my head with his hand as the wardrobe doors popped open from the force of me hitting it.

Magic sizzled in the air, and I looked down to find the tiny nick on my arm healing immediately.

"What the...?" Dylan hopped over a large trunk of goblets and crossed the room to join us, his gaze firmly fixed above my head. "Did you feel that?"

I shrugged, dropping the offending bone back into its box. "Yeah, human remains are creepy."

"Not them." He shook his head, hooking his arms under my armpits and pulling me to my feet so I was facing the wardrobe. "*That.*"

Josh scrambled to his feet beside me, his gasp echoing my own.

The doors to the wardrobe hung open, the edges still emanating with sparks of magic as if they had been spelled shut. Rich burgundy velvet lined the inside of the converted wardrobe, the back modified with shallow shelves evenly spaced, with a gap for the large sword secured vertically in the centre. An array of knives and smaller weapons hung on the inside of the doors. The shelves were stocked full of sealed boxes, blades ranging from more swords to daggers, and even a mace. It wasn't a wardrobe; it was a little armoury.

Craig reappeared beside us in a blur of movement, his mouth popping open to form a small O as he stared at our find.

To the right of the sword was a dagger that fit the one of the descriptions we'd found when researching. There were so many conflicting accounts, but one consistent claim had been that the handle was made from bone. The silver blade glinted, the pale bone of the hilt in stark contrast to the amethyst silk lining the box. Intricate patterns were carved into the handle of the dagger, depicting the moon and other Celtic designs that I didn't recognise. At the base of the box was a small piece of paper, the ink-scrawled words confirming my suspicions.

*Béibhinn's blade.*

Tears sprung to my eyes. After weeks of nothing, we finally had something.

"Incoming!" The boys grabbed an arm each and pulled me down as soot erupted from the fire grate, a cloud of coal covering the room.

My knees hit the ground with a thud, and I cursed before raising my arms and taking cover beside the boys. My eyes stung as I forced them open to find a bat swooping overhead to land by the fireplace.

Craig hissed at the presence of the other vampire. "We need to get out of here now. Time's up."

Tom and Mary appeared in the doorway, their eyes widening at the soot-covered carnage, and then again at the sight of the bat. The hairs on the back of my neck rose as the bat swerved to the far side of the room, a sign that my instincts warned he was about to shift. The building shook as something crashed upstairs. Or landed. Dust showered us, the force rattling bookcases so hard it shook books loose from the shelves. A loud roar that followed confirmed that the dragon was home, and we'd outstayed our welcome.

"Time to go!" Dylan leaped into action, snatching the dagger as the four of us sprinted towards the exit.

The air heated behind us, thick smoke beginning to filter

down the stairs. Another angry shriek from above, followed by the scent of freshly singed wood, was a second warning I didn't need. A horn blared outside. Our signal that Russell had arrived. We raced out the front door and piled into the waiting silver SUV. There was a child seat in the back of the car and sweets hiding in crevices of the seats. It was the weirdest getaway car ever, but as I glanced over my shoulder and came face to face with a whole ass dragon with green eyes and fire streaming from its mouth perched on the roof, I was never so grateful to see the Edinburgh alpha.

"I thought the dragon wasn't home?" Russell hit the accelerator the moment the last door shut.

Tom shook his head, settling into the front passenger seat. "He had a good alarm system. The vampire kind."

We sped down the street, tyres squealing. The dragon beat its wings, ready to follow, but paused when a large crowd marched through an intersection down the road. Protestors waved signs and tricolour flags striped black, white, and green with a red triangle.

Russell made a sharp turn to avoid the march blocking our route, and I gripped the door handle to stay upright. The dragon blasted a fresh torrent of fire from its mouth as we fled, smoke pouring from its nostrils.

Dylan tapped his chin, eyeing the dragon with a mixture of awe and fear. "Is it arson if he burns his own house down?"

The Edinburgh alpha took another turn to bypass a barricaded road, and the dragon disappeared from view once we were a few streets away. We kept as close as possible to the humans protesting through the streets of Edinburgh so it couldn't follow.

"So much for lying low," I muttered, palming my chest as if I could slow my racing heart.

Tom met my gaze in the rearview mirror, his brow furrowed. "He's glamoured, I hope."

"*We* hope, otherwise we'll have some explaining to do."

Russell snorted, flooring the accelerator and clearly enjoying the adrenaline boost.

"At least we got what we came for." Tom smiled from the front seat, and his shoulders relaxed a fraction, as if a small portion of his burdens had been lifted.

Josh whooped behind me, earning a playful glare from Mary, who had squeezed in beside him. Hope was a magical thing, the mood in the packed car lifting despite the flames we left in our wake.

# CHAPTER 4

## EVE

Darkness drenched the acres of land surrounding the Edinburgh pack house. Tall trees marked the boundary of their land, shielding us from prying eyes as we sped down the winding driveway. Russell had generously offered it to us as our base, an old mansion just outside of the city that reminded me of the Crescent house in Kildare, but bigger. It was stunning, like something out of a heritage brochure with its ivy-covered walls and cherry blossoms. The Georgian building had been lovingly restored by the Edinburgh pack. They even rented it out to humans when the pack didn't need the space outside of the full moon.

I had no time or desire to admire its beauty. Someday, I hoped we could come back to visit, when I could actually appreciate everything Scotland had to offer. When the gothic architecture was something I could enjoy and I wasn't breaking and entering, or helping interrogate those on Edmonstone's payroll.

The moment I opened the car door, the scent of pizza made my nose twitch, a telltale sign that Russell's wife, Kelly, had kept Alice company. Their people were kind, and Kelly often checked in and brought us freshly cooked meals. She reminded me so much of Helena, the backbone holding everyone together. My chest constricted. I'd been so used to not having somewhere I belonged growing up that I'd never known how much it hurt to miss it. Not just the place, but the people who made it home.

Everyone piled from the SUV into the house, but I paused in the hallway as a picture on the wall caught my attention. The hallway was full of photos with mismatched frames, a scattering of colour and older black and white photos spanning the length and breadth of the panelling.

Moonlight filtered in through the fanlight window above the front door, reflecting off the glass covering one photo in particular. Half hidden by a lamp, the old photo featured a couple in a park. This one was in colour, but I could tell by the warmth and amount of denim on display that it must have been from the nineties. The young couple looked like they were in their twenties, all smiles as they sat cuddled on a bench. The girl was perched on the guy's lap, his arms wrapped around her and his chin nestled on her shoulder. They were a picture-perfect couple. Both had dark hair, but that wasn't what made my stomach do a flip. It was her eyes.

Despite the aged photo, the woman's bright blue eyes stood out. Identical to mine.

My heart kicked up its pace.

"Penny for your thoughts?" Tom paused beside me, the old floorboards creaking under his weight. He was holding two mugs, one of them extended towards me, his soft gaze filled with gentle understanding.

Tea. The Irish antidote to every problem. A stereotype maybe, but bringing people together and getting something warm in your stomach actually helped. It was a tradition we took very seriously, to the point Helena had stuffed a box of Barry's tea bags into Tom's rucksack before he caught the earliest flight to Edinburgh.

"I..." I opened my mouth and then snapped it shut, afraid that if I started to offload my mind, I might break entirely. And I wasn't sure I could put myself back together again.

"You need to talk, Eve. It's not good to bottle everything up, something Luke didn't learn until he met you."

"I'm not trying to be tough. I'm just trying to... I don't know." My voice faltered, thick with unshed tears.

"Survive." Tom squeezed my hand, the corners of his eyes creasing. "The mate bond is strong. I've been told losing them feels like losing a part of yourself."

"The longer this goes on, the closer it gets to the full moon... I don't want to lose him."

"Even if—and it's not even a possibility because we'll get him back—but *if* you can't complete the bond, you won't lose him. Or us." Tom set the offered mug down on the small console table, nudging the lamp aside so the photo was in full view. "Mating bond or not, you are family."

The certainty behind his words shouldn't have caught me off guard. He'd been steadfast and confident since he arrived. Despite his son being held captive, the only chink in his unshakeable exterior had been a slight tensing of his jaw upon seeing the state Jeremy had returned in. That was it.

He brushed his finger across the glass casing, clearing the thin layer of dust away. "With everything going on, I wanted to give you time to process before bringing it up."

I swallowed hard, but the lump rising in my throat refused to yield.

"Russell told me what Larissa said about your parents."

Tom's words hung in the air between us, drowning out the sounds of chatter coming from the kitchen and my heartbeat pounding in my ears.

I hadn't forgotten what Larissa had told me. After Luke was taken, I'd stuffed it in a box, shoved that box in an airtight container, and then buried it six feet under because it was too much to deal with. And I was too scared to ask the questions for fear the answers would send me over the edge. With Luke gone, losing my mate had consumed my thoughts. Every moment of each day was spent trying to find him. Except late at night, when my nightmares dragged me back to that night in the cemetery.

"Larissa is a lying witch who would say anything to further her own agenda." I shook my head, my voice cracking as I spotted the woman's round belly in the photo. "I can't believe a word she says."

He reached out, his hand a comforting weight as he gave my shoulder a gentle squeeze. "Then believe me. What she said was true."

Larissa had said my parents fled to Scotland. Somehow, I'd ended up here too.

"Luke asked me to help trace your ancestry. I had some suspicions before you both had to leave for London, but I was still waiting on some medical records to be sure. I wish I'd said something sooner. You should have never found out like that." He took a long sip of his tea, as if it would somehow ease the sting of the words that would follow. "Your father was a werewolf named Shane. He fell in love with a human girl called Gráinne, your mother."

Love. *Fuck.* Tears swam in my eyes, blurring my vision as I stared at the photograph.

"Remember I told you Damien killed the original Faolchúnna alpha, Mary's father?" He paused, his thumb swiping back and forth on my shoulder.

I nodded mutely.

"Your parents were young, and Gráinne fell pregnant with you during Damien's claim for the position. Shane came to me for advice because they knew if they were having a baby girl, that you would be a hybrid. They worried you wouldn't be safe if Damien became alpha. So I helped them escape to Scotland with new passports and everything. Russell's pack took them in. It was supposed to be a fresh start, a chance for them to be happy and for you to be safe." Tom's jaw flexed, and he closed his eyes, inhaling deeply before continuing. "I remember when you were born. I have baby photos of you back in Dublin that they sent with postcards. Your parents were so happy, and they loved you so much. They would have wanted you to know that."

Somehow, deep down, I had known it was the truth. Larissa was evil, but she had nothing to gain by spinning a story to hurt me. I'd been an orphan all my life. Her version of events matched with what I was always told; they died in a car crash. My parents being dead wasn't new. But to know that I was robbed of a childhood filled with love and magic, it ripped open old scars I'd fought hard to bury.

His tone shifted, voice becoming strained. "When we got the phone call, it was too late. Russell told us there had been an accident... We knew it wasn't just a crash, that wouldn't have been enough to kill your father. I always suspected it was Damien's act of revenge for me challenging him and forming the Crescent pack." It was rare to catch a slip in Tom's calm exterior, but there was no mistaking the guilt weighing his words. "I thought I did the right thing by sparing Damien. There had been so much death, too much pain. I'll never forgive myself for you losing your family as a result of my choice."

The dam broke, tears spilling down my face as the truth settled and the raw grief ripped through me. Tom wrapped his arm around my shoulders, and I buried my silent sobs in his chest, forgetting he was my alpha. Because he wasn't just my alpha, he was the father of my mate. He was family. There was no doubt in my mind that my parents would have chosen to follow Tom and become Crescents when the packs split. I may have lost them, but I'd found my true family in the end. Or maybe they found me.

Ceramic clinked as he set his cup down, hugging me tightly. "We were told you'd been in the car during the crash. I never thought for one moment you had survived. If we had known, Darren would have scoured every hospital in the entirety of Europe to find you."

"Darren?" I rubbed my nose with my sleeve like a child, but I couldn't stop crying.

A smile ghosted Tom's lips, a mix of sadness and fondness passing over his features as he turned me to face the photo once more. "Your father, Shane, was Darren's little brother."

I blinked rapidly, trying to clear the tears away so I could focus on the image. Darren may have aged, but once Tom pointed it out, I could see the resemblance. The guy's hair in the photo was fluffier, but he had the same features as Darren, right down to the nose. It was the smile that confirmed it. My dad had the same wide grin that I'd grown so used to.

"He's... Darren is my uncle?" Shock rippled through me. The Crescents weren't just my chosen family, they were blood.

Tom nodded, placing his mug down to point at the girl in the photo. "And your mother was Helena's best friend. That's how we met."

I stared at the photo of my mother, my heart warming at the way she cradled her baby bump covered by dungarees and a garish sweater. "Really?"

"Yep. When Shane first told us they were having a baby, Darren was worried, and they had a bit of a wolf moment. Helena had no problem telling them off like they were bold kids. A feisty redheaded girl squaring up to two wolves without any hesitation. How could I not fall for her?" He chuckled, gently lifting the frame off the wall before sliding the photograph out from behind the glass. "She loved Gráinne like a sister and would go to bat for her in an instant. She's going to be so happy when she hears the news, as will Darren."

Fear climbed its way up my spine. "Are you sure?"

I might have been family, but a small part of me worried that I would be a reminder of what they lost.

"We can wait until you're ready to tell them, or I can break the news first. But let me be very clear on one thing, knowing that you are a Crescent, and that the legacy of the ones they loved lives on in you, will bring nothing but happiness." Tom's voice didn't waver as he pressed the photo into my shaking hands, cupping them to make sure I didn't drop it. "You're a Crescent, Eve. You always have been, always will be."

# CHAPTER 5

## LUKE

**D**emon, witch, whatever the hell the creature straddling my waist was, the moment the last word of the prophecy spilled from her lips, something shifted and the stench of ancient power filled the space around us. Magic cracked and sizzled, bright sparks striking through the shadows like forks of lightning. Her smile only widened and became more unhinged as the charged air whipped up into a frenzy, an invisible wind raising the hairs all over my body. A jolt passed through my chest, and not from the slow healing wound she'd dug above my heart. It felt as if someone had grabbed a fistful of the mate bond I shared with Eve and tugged hard, as if they were trying to test it.

My body jerked in response, the silver cuffs sizzling around my wrists.

Her face lit up at my reaction, and the pain intensified as whatever the fuck she was doing seemed to twist or yank the bond further. I couldn't tell if she was testing the strength of my bond with Eve or torturing me like a voodoo doll. "Larissa really needs to respect her elders. As do your kind."

"Stop." I hissed in pain, bile rising in my throat as my body convulsed, both in pain and protest. My temples throbbed, as if I was trying to mentally fight her off and protect a bond that I barely even understood. "Fuck. Stop. Please stop."

I wasn't above begging, and she seemed to like it. The pressure on the bond decreased as she tilted her head to one side, studying me. Her white-misted eyes grew more unnerving when they seemed to lock in on the blood dripping from the wound in my chest. Before I could blink, she leaned in with inhuman speed, her tongue flicking out to catch a droplet before it slipped below my navel. I flinched, and she lifted her head with a smirk that told me her games were only beginning.

She didn't stop there, dragging her tongue along my chest. "Your pleas are almost as sweet as your blood."

My hands balled into fists, the burn of the cuffs a welcome distraction. The witch paused at eye level and pinched my chin between her fingers, her gaze sliding to my mouth. She lowered her face to mine, her blood-stained lips so close I could feel her stale breath. Fear seized me, and I froze.

I could endure torture. But I wouldn't let anyone but my mate touch me like that. I couldn't.

I wrenched my head free from her grip and thrust it forwards, my forehead connecting with her jaw. The sickening crunch of bone hung in the shadows swarming us. I froze, waiting for her to lash out, but the blow never came.

She sank back on her knees, slowly tracing the tip of her forefinger over her lower lip as if savouring the taste of my blood.

I never thought I'd want Larissa back, but they say better the devil you know. Her scent was not that of a vampire. She smelled like death, life, and magic all rolled up into something that felt *wrong*. Whatever this bitch was, she was cut from the same sadistic cloth as Larissa.

"What are you?" I kept my focus trained on her hands, waiting for some form of retaliation or punishment.

Her laugh sent a chill through my bones. "You really are her mate. I never thought this day would come."

"How do you know my mate?" I made a point of not using

Eve's name, though, if this *thing* could literally feel our bond, something told me she already knew.

"So many questions. So little time." Her eyes narrowed, looking up as if she was talking to herself or someone in her head. "I haven't had the pleasure of meeting your mate yet. But now that the prophecy shall come to pass, I'm sure I'll be seeing her very soon if she wants to complete the bond."

A metallic taste filled my mouth as she flexed her grip on the bond once more. "I would rather not complete the bond than risk her life."

She pursed her lips, a single eyebrow arching. "I don't believe that is your choice. A woman will do anything for the man she loves. An unfortunate side effect of the affliction I know all too well."

I gritted my teeth as part of the wound in my chest knitted together, the slowed healing making the process more painful than usual.

"Forgive me if I've lost my manners. It's been... a while since I've had company. Spending too much time tied to this witch has soured my mood." She reached out to brush a hand through her hair, catching it on a blood-crusted mat. Her lips thinned as a low growl rattled in my throat. "You look kind of like him, you know? Not that men were so well groomed back then."

*Back when?* There was a wistful tone to her unhinged ramblings that was completely throwing me.

"I know you're not Larissa. *Who* are you? Did she fuck around with some demon and end up out of her depth?"

She trailed her finger along my chest, smearing the blood still leaking from the healing wound. "Not quite."

My brow furrowed. I was trying to think so hard, but the pain and sleep deprivation were quite literally making my brain hurt. If she wasn't a demon, what else was there? She kept speaking of the past.

"Are you some kind of spirit?" I ground the words out, failing to find the same enjoyment she was playing twenty questions.

But playing along seemed to be less painful than when she'd been digging for my heart or playing with the bond, so I'd bite.

One side of her lips kicked up into a smirk. "Not quite."

She continued drawing on my chest, humming a low melody that I didn't recognise.

There was no such thing as a 'sort of ghost'. They could visit and remain invisible, or if there was a strong pull or unfinished business, they could appear. Poltergeist behaviour was real, but this was another level. The only other time spirits could appear was if summoned. Eve had sworn she was following Kate to the graveyard, and Larissa was a necromancer. They controlled the dead and made them do their bidding. Unless... What could a dead necromancer do from the other side? Did it work both ways?

I gasped as the answer came to me, my eyes widening as she leaned back on her heels and clapped her bloody hands with an enthusiastic squeal that set my teeth on edge.

"A necromancer, just like Larissa." I looked down at my chest to see she had been drawing some kind of runes. Panic surged, and I thrashed, enduring the pain of the silver burning through layers of flesh on my wrists as I struggled to pull the chains loose. But they were still pulled taut above my head, leaving me trapped and at the mercy of whatever deranged soul Larissa had fucked with.

"Relax." The witch pouted like a spoiled little child disappointed by her toy, pointing to the wound on my chest that was now more pink than red and healing quicker. "I was trying to do something nice. A little reward for being so smart. I'm not like the bitch that owns this body. She craves power. All I ever craved was love, and it was my downfall."

Something told me she was swimming in the deep depths of denial. I bit back a retort about the singed skin beneath the shackles that she couldn't be bothered to help. She might claim to be unlike Larissa, but this witch was her own brand of bitch, and I wasn't going to test her boundaries.

"It's a horrible, lonely thing to live your life devoid of love's sweet touch. I was so desperate for someone to truly see me, to be wanted." She sighed, her voice growing sombre as a single scarlet tear slid down her cheek. "You're lucky to have found a mate, the other half to your heart. It's a pity she's destined to die."

Her words dripped with pity that I would never accept, because losing Eve was an outcome I wouldn't allow.

"I don't relish robbing you of happiness. But it must be done. I blame my sister—she had a thing for breaking lovers apart."

My mind was reeling, cartwheeling off a damn cliff as I struggled to keep up. She spoke like she knew it, as if she had *lived* it.

"I am *the* witch." She confirmed my suspicions, the truth from her lips crashing into me with the force of a dragon. The swirling depths of her eyes grew wild. "One of the first, and the maker of your kind."

Memories flashed through my mind of sitting on a fallen tree beside bonfires under the full moon, wrapped in blankets, and nursing a mug of hot chocolate while my father told the pack his favourite stories. And then again after my first run as a wolf, sparks rising from the bonfire into the night sky as he recited the stories of origin. Then I was there with Eve, watching the way her face lit up in the fire's glow as my father spoke of wolves, witches, and vampires. The sisters that created our kind in their fury over a man, over love. Necromancers walked a dangerous line between life and death, but surely it wasn't possible...

*It couldn't be.*

She watched me, a slow smile spreading across her lips as if she could sense my realisation. Could she read minds? Fuck knows what a witch that powerful could do.

"Say it," she purred, dragging her finger up my neck until her nail digging into my skin forced my chin up. "You know who I am."

I swallowed hard, my raw throat struggling to form the words. "Béibhinn."

The storming white depths of her eyes stilled as I spoke her name, her widening smile sent a shudder down my bruised spine.

"The one and only." There was a lightness to her voice, as if a necromancer summoning one of the oldest witches of their kind, one whose off-the-scale temper tantrum resulted in the creation of two new magical creatures, was a funny little joke.

Necromancers were supposed to raise the dead, not allow the dead to inhabit them. To entwine their souls, to share a body, it was unheard of.

"How? Why? You told her how to make the prophecy come true?"

"My, how naïve you useless creatures have become. I create a masterpiece, and she creates glorified golden retrievers." She retracted her hand and with a flick of her wrist, the shadows receded just enough to reveal the moon outside of my cell. "Prophecies are destined to come true; they are fated just as much as your mate bond. But how they manifest and the fates decide to align, that can change. She wanted my help to make sure it worked exactly as she wished. Unfortunately for you, that involves the death of both you and your beloved. But first, you need to complete the bond."

I knew Larissa wanted power, but what was Béibhinn looking for after all these years?

Before I could ask another question, the witch began mumbling to herself. All traces of amusement vanished from her face as looked over her shoulder, her brow furrowing. "No, tell them to go away."

"Who?" My body groaned as I strained my neck to see around her. My hearing picked up footsteps in the distance.

*How did she hear them before me?*

"No!" She leaped to her feet with a speed that I'd associate more with the vampires she created. "That was not the agreement."

The shadows withdrew to the corners of my cell as Béibhinn doubled over, clutching her head as she howled in defiance.

Shadows pulsed and rushed towards the door to cloak it in darkness. I caught the faintest hint of purple bleeding into her irises before the sound of the bolt on the cell door opening stole her attention. She whirled to face the doorway, shadows moving with her as the witch shot across the cell. She caught a man I recognised as one of Larissa's vampires by the throat, turning and driving him back into the wall of my cell with a sickening crack.

The man hissed, his upper lip curling to reveal two fangs. I swear she was about to rip into his throat when the tension left her body and the witch stumbled back. The shadows revealed a second man in a matching lab coat and holding a tray filled with syringes and metal instruments entering the cell to check on his vampire friend, who was still eyeing the witch nervously.

When the witch lifted her head, wild-eyed as she scanned her surroundings, her irises had returned to violet. Larissa was back in control.

Disappointment mingled with relief, my shoulders slumping. Part of me wished I'd gotten more answers, while a wiser part knew that a witch so ancient was too dangerous to fuck with. The way Larissa's gaze roved over her surroundings and the tremble of her hands as she retreated from the vampire told me she was well and truly in over her head.

The one that had been about to become breakfast reached out as Larissa swayed. "Are you—"

"I'm fine," she snapped, slapping his arm away with a trembling hand. "Is everything ready to go?"

"Liar." Fuelled by anger, sleep deprivation, and sheer madness, the thought spilled from my mouth, and I couldn't snatch the word back.

Magic connected with my jaw, the force wrenching my head back, and my teeth clamped down on my tongue. The crunch of bone and familiar warmth of blood gushing down my face warned me that something was broken, and this witch wouldn't heal me. My tongue felt thick, and there was a looseness to my jaw that made my stomach flip.

The vampire cleared his throat, his pupils dilating at the sight of my blood. "Everything is in order." He gestured to the titanium tray his friend was holding, an array of rainbow syringes on display. "We depart tomorrow. Should we prepare the wolf?"

*Depart?* My blood chilled. I didn't know where I was, but the more Larissa moved, the lower the chances of my pack finding me.

I tried to form a smart retort, only for it to come out a garbled moan as pain lanced through the side of my face.

Larissa smirked at her handwork. "Yes, keep him under until we arrive. Will this do anything to his memories?"

"He shouldn't remember a thing." The second man chimed in, prepping one syringe as he approached.

My protests were pitiful and slurred as the bones of my jaw tried to knit back into place, but my magic reserves were too low. I recoiled as the two vampires advanced, but my back pressed against cool stone bricks. There was nowhere to go.

Larissa's throat bobbed as she watched them hold me down, the silver cuffs cutting into my flesh and chains dragging on the floor as I tried to fight them off. I knew it wasn't out of guilt for the blood smeared all over my body, but I caught a glimpse of something in her eyes when the needle pricked my bruised skin. An emotion I didn't think the witch was capable of feeling. But it was there, etched into her pale features. *Fear.*

If the witch who danced with death was scared, we all should be.

# CHAPTER 6

$\mathbf{S}$harp pain struck my chest, as if someone had stabbed a blade through my heart. I shot upright in the bed, my back arching against the sweat-soaked T-shirt clinging to my skin. When the sensation struck again, I cursed, untangling my legs from the duvet and shoving it off the mattress as my temperature soared. Damp strands of hair clung to my brow, and the bed sheets were drenched. Nightmares often plagued my nights, but this was something else.

I swung my legs over the edge of the bed, instantly regretting the movement as my vision swam and a wave of nausea washed over me.

Then it came again, my stomach somersaulting while something tugged at my chest. At the bond.

*Luke.*

I could still feel him. Our bond was my only reassurance that he was alive, but there was no doubt in my mind that he was in pain.

My throat was raw, and I knew I must have been screaming when Alice burst through the door of the room we shared.

"Eve!" Her face paled at the sight of me.

I doubled over and slid off the edge of the bed, my knees

hitting the old hardwood floors with a thud. The next jolt through the bond forced me onto all fours, panting as magic tingled along the length of my spine. The pain urged me to shift, my body thinking I needed to heal. I snatched the damp bedsheets strewn on the floor; my white-knuckled grip unyielding as I resisted the shift, my breaths coming in short pants.

"Pain," I rasped, my head hanging low. "Luke. The bond."

Somehow, Alice knew what to do. I didn't know if it was because she was a Crescent, Luke's family, or simply womanhood, but she dropped to my side and held my shaking body. And when I reached for my chest during the next fresh bite of pain, my nails morphed into claws, as if I could tear my way to whatever was torturing my mate. Alice grabbed me by the wrists and talked me off the ledge through each agonising blow. Tears stung my eyes, every tug on the bond reminding me not only that my mate was in danger, but that our bond could be broken. And we only had until the full moon to complete it.

Her whispered words of reassurance kept me grounded until the pain subsided and the haze lifted. Once my claws retracted, she released my hands and rubbed gentle circles on my back until I stopped seeing double.

She waited until my breathing became less laboured, gently pushing wet hair from my face to dab my forehead with a damp towel. "What happened?"

"The bond." I inhaled a shallow breath, leaning into her touch as I fought to slow my thundering heart. "The bond. Someone was hurting Luke, but it was like they were doing it using the bond."

"That's not possible." Alice rose from my side to rummage through the chest of drawers.

She'd gone into the city with Craig to do a speed shop to pick up basics for everyone shortly after we arrived at the Edinburgh pack house. I'd no interest in shopping at the best of times, but I was grateful for her knowing what everyone would want. It wasn't just my mate being held captive; she was missing her big brother. The more Alice had come out of her shell since being home, the more the similarities she shared with her mother showed. Just like Helena, she was always looking out for everyone.

Alice turned back to me with a cosy burgundy knitted jumper and comfy leggings in her arms and dropped them on the bed. "The bond is sacred. It's fate. A witch like Larissa wouldn't possess the kind of magic that could influence something as ancient as a mating bond."

I rubbed my chest with the heel of my palm, my mood softening at the sight of the fluffy socks she had also picked out. "Who knows what Larissa is capable of? I don't think she has any sort of moral compass. Her heart is an endless pit of hatred."

"I wonder who hurt her," she mused, beginning to strip the sweaty pillowcase.

"What do you mean?" I made to stop her, but she swatted my hand away and pointed to the pile of fresh clothes.

She shrugged. "To be consumed with so much hatred, something had to be the trigger. I find it hard to believe people are born evil."

Was that true? Were we all just a product of everything we endured? But then would everyone who had a bad childhood or difficult upbringing be cruel? And those who had experienced indescribable loss would become lost to the pain from then on, fuelled by revenge? That didn't sound right. I'd found people with the biggest hearts full of love and kindness often had the darkest starts in life. It was a choice, a strength to be forged in fire and rise with both the yearning and capacity for love. To want better. To choose to give yourself to love despite the pain.

"I think we all have a choice. We can either give into the pain, or we can open our hearts for a better future. I don't know much of Larissa's past, but I don't see a shred of humanity left in her."

Alice tilted her head, steely defiance flashing in her eyes as her tone soured. "Oh, I wasn't excusing her behaviour. I'll never forgive her or anyone involved in the kidnappings. It's fucked up."

"Sorry, I didn't mean—"

"It's okay, I've come to terms with a lot." She sighed, visibly forcing some tension from her shoulders. "I'm still not completely over everything that happened, but I am grateful that beyond blood tests and scans, I got off lightly. I don't know if it's because they were afraid of what Dad would do if he found me, or if Ryan had some sort of conscience buried deep under his daddy issues, but I am grateful that I didn't suffer as much as others did."

I thought back to the newspaper clippings, and the murders we had linked to the Faolchúnna pack and Larissa. Then to the way Luke had spoken about Alice before I found her, when he thought his sister was dead. I remembered how she had looked the night we rescued her, how frail she had been, how scared and quiet she remained until she found her spark again. The all too familiar feeling of anger rose, mingled with fear. Alice had said before that she never encountered Larissa during her time there. I wasn't sure the witch would spare Luke in the same way.

"I've a lot of feelings still. Anger, resentment, guilt for the pain it caused my family, gratitude that it wasn't worse." She paused, considering her words carefully before she continued. "But I also pity them. That witch deserves whatever karma comes her way. At the same time, I think it must be so sad and lonely to spend your life motivated by revenge, in search of power when it's an empty prize."

"It wasn't your fault," I whispered, reaching out to squeeze her hand.

A faint smile curved her lips. "I know. Just like Luke getting taken isn't yours."

Her hand was smaller than mine, but her words landed like the blow of a heavyweight's fist to my gut. And she knew, she knew exactly what she was doing thanks to being a gold-fucking-star student in her therapy sessions.

"I heard she was cast out by her family for abusing her necromancer abilities from a young age," She stripped the sweat-soaked duvet cover off the bed. "Her father remarried after her mother died, and apparently she was passed over to be next in line in favour of her younger sister."

I wiped my tear-stained cheeks, gathering up the soft bundle of clothes like it was a set of armour. "I lost both of my parents. It's never driven me to kidnap or torture anyone. And this sounds all too like the jealous sister in that story Tom told under the full moon. Do witch sisters always end up wanting to kill each other?"

"No, some are normal, the Royals are... the Royals." She gathered the sheets into one pile and tossed the dirty linen into a wash basket in the corner, motioning to the ensuite door. "Go clean up, gather yourself, and I'll be waiting with some caffeine and cake that Kelly left us downstairs."

As much as the idea of soaking in the fancy clawfoot bath was tempting, I knew the noisy Georgian plumbing of the old building would wake anyone sleeping nearby. "I'm okay. I'll follow you down."

She arched an eyebrow at the first part of my response, knowing full well that none of us were okay, but she didn't push it. "Five minutes and I'm sending a search party."

I mustered up a pathetic attempt at a smile, waiting until she slipped out the door before letting my shoulders sag. I was far from okay.

But I had to be.

Alice hovered outside the room, something I'd have guessed even without my supercharged werewolf hearing. I rolled my shoulders, counting to ten before hauling myself to the bathroom. Once the tap was running, Alice's footsteps slowly faded down the hallway. The fancy bath was calling to me; I wanted to lie in it and be transported back to the eighteenth century. But I couldn't, because magic had its limitations—and the old plumbing was loud.

So, I cleaned up with a washcloth and grabbed the stack of comfy clothes Alice had picked out. My gaze snagged on my reflection in the mirror as I tugged the T-shirt over my head. I paused, that familiar sense of grief and unease settling over me as I stared at the crescent-shaped scar between my shoulder blades barely visible in the dim light. The mark that made me the sacrificial lamb and put everyone who loved me in danger.

A chair scraped the floors downstairs; my warning that five minutes was up, and I'd spent most of it dissociating.

There were people waiting for me, people who cared. As much as I wanted to crawl back under the covers and hide away from the world, we needed to find Luke. And I wanted that too, more than anything.

I finished getting dressed and tiptoed out of the room. Moonlight flooded the landing as I forced myself to put one foot in front of the other. I flipped the moon off, cursing her and her damned countdown as I descended the creaking stairs just in time to hear the kettle click off.

"Morning, sleepyhead," Dylan's chipper voice greeted me from beyond the living room door, unnaturally peppy for this hour of the night.

I nudged the door open, rubbing my eyes and squinting as I stepped into the room. Josh was stationed at the head of a large dining table, working away furiously with two laptops in front of him. Dylan sat to his right, spinning the dagger between his fingers while he flicked through a stack of papers. The rest of the table was littered with old books and texts, coupled with newspaper clippings and various printouts. We'd stopped short of a corkboard with red threads joining the dots, despite Dylan's joke about turning into it a dartboard for our enemies.

*Why was the big light on? What kind of heathen kept that on during an all-nighter?*

"Alice has the kettle on, but you look like you need something stronger." Josh lifted his head from his laptop, his bloodshot eyes matching my own.

I glanced out the large sash windows, but there wasn't the slightest hint of light penetrating the inky sky.

"Whiskey?" Dylan offered, raising the half-empty glass in front of him. The sadness creasing the corners of his eyes told me he was missing his drinking buddy.

Alice wouldn't have told them what happened upstairs, but I'd been screaming, and there was no mistaking the worry they were all failing horribly to mask.

"I'd rather not see my dinner again. Someone was fucking with the bond and it hurt—a lot—but I'm fine. I promise." My lips twitched as I tried to force a smile, tension hugging my shoulders like the coils of a snake. I tore my gaze away from the constellations sparkling outside, crossing the room to drop into the dining table seat opposite Dylan. "Nothing coffee can't fix."

"If Mary catches you caffeinating before dawn again, she'll confiscate the coffee machine." Josh snorted, his taps on the keyboard growing harsher by the second.

"She's one to talk." Alice stepped through the double doors leading to the kitchen, steam wafting from the spout of the teapot in her hand. "I had to cut her off the other day."

The image conjured in my mind of Luke's little sister ordering Mary, the woman we'd come to know as pretty kick-ass, was one I was sorely disappointed to have missed. I bit back a laugh to avoid waking those still upstairs. "I wish I could have seen that."

She shoved a pile of notepads out of the way to reveal a set of mugs that were on rotation, grinning as she sat beside Dylan. "It's even funnier when it's Tom telling her off. They squabble like siblings. I kind of wish she'd joined the Crescents all those years ago, and I think Dad is happy he can finally have some of his old friends around."

"I swear, if this doesn't work, I'm going into early retirement." Josh slapped the keyboard, glaring at the screen as he shoved the laptop away.

Alice arched an eyebrow, nudging one of the freshly poured mugs towards him.

The silver blade of the dagger glinted as Dylan missed a move, and it clattered onto the table. "I don't think you can retire before you've finished uni, man."

I chewed my lower lip to fight back the smile brewing. "He has a point. Plus, you're trying to crack something they've kept hidden for years, and Trinity doesn't teach Magic Encryption 101."

"Cass removed those for me, and Maya talked me through the rest," he grumbled, the words 'Murder Juice' written across the steaming mug now in his hands all too fitting. "What if there's nothing on here in the end? All I've gotten is a few emails and business stuff. Yeah, I'm sure they're running some of it through the business, but proving that isn't gonna be easy. We have Gabi and Alice, but it's their word against some of the biggest alphas."

Alice propped her elbows on the table, dipping a biscuit into her tea like the sweet treat might soften the truth. "Plus, with the vamps and witches they have on their side... Who's gonna believe us?"

"There's enough evidence once you start pulling on the threads. We just need something to make them sit up and listen. Something to force Edmonstone into a corner." I cupped my hands around the warmth of the mug she set in front of me. "If we can at least get the UK packs turning on him, it's somewhere to start."

Josh leaned back in his chair to stretch, ruffling his hair with a sigh. His fade was quickly growing out, his natural curls beginning to take over. "And Larissa?"

"Oh, the witch who wants to murder me and my mate to bring to pass some shady prophecy?" I shrugged, the bone deep tiredness I felt adding a bitter sarcasm to my tone. "Well, that's just not happening. She can't complete the spell without the dagger."

"And she's too late to the party on that one." Dylan flipped the dagger so that the handle landed in his palm, grinning like a bold toddler as he poked Josh's biceps with the tip of the blade.

"Asshole." Josh smacked his friend's hand aside, rushing to dab the single drop of tea from the laptop keyboard where his wrist would rest. "Put that away."

Dylan snickered, his amusement faltering as he caught Alice staring wide-eyed beside him. "What?"

Her face paled, her mouth hanging open.

"Alice?" I frowned, glancing between the two guys who matched both my bewilderment. "What's wrong?"

"Give me the dagger." Her voice shook as much as her hand, motioning for him to pass it over. "Now"

Tension snaked its way around my shoulders as I watched Dylan pass the dagger he'd been playing with.

The mood in the room soured, and in charged silence, we watched Alice turn the dagger over in her hand. She pursed her lips, sliding her thumb along the carved bone of the hilt and then along the knife's edge.

Before I could move, she had the tip of the dagger pressed against her hand and blood pooled in her palm as the blade bit into her skin.

"No!" A chorus of protests erupted, and we all leaped to our feet, Josh nearly sending the laptop flying in the process.

Dylan was nearest, springing into action and grabbing her by the wrist. His grip forced her fingers to flex, the bloody dagger clattering as it hit the wooden floor at Alice's feet.

"What the hell are you doing?" he demanded, turning her hand over to examine the wound.

Josh and I were beside them in an instant. Just in time to see that the cut had already knitted itself back together and the bleeding had stopped.

"No... No, no, no." Alice wrenched her hand free. She crouched down to snatch the dagger off the ground, tears brimming in her eyes as she held it out. "Please, this can't be happening."

"Alice, what the fuck is going on?" Josh snatched the dagger, tossing it onto the table where it landed with a dull clink.

"It's not silver. The blade isn't silver." Alice shook her head, squeezing her eyes shut as if she could will it to be false.

Dylan picked the dagger up, piercing his thumb gently with the blade. He didn't flinch, instead his shoulders sagged. "She's right. Silver wouldn't heal so fast."

My heartbeat rang in my ears. No.

My phone buzzed on the table, and Maya's name flashed up on the screen. I scrambled to answer the call before the vibrations could wake the whole house, my mood brightening at the sight of the witch's name.

Alice paced the room as I flicked the phone on speaker and set it down in the middle of the table.

Noise hummed on the line, muffled voices rising in the background. I glanced around the table, the furrowed brows of my friends mirroring my own.

"Maya?"

The unintelligible voices grew louder, angrier, before Maya's voice finally answered.

"Edmonstone is calling a meeting with all the packs. You need to get back to London. Now."

# CHAPTER 7

## EVE

A deep, gnawing sense of unease settled in my bones as I stepped out onto the pavement. There wasn't a single shred of my being that harboured an ounce of desire to return to London. This city was where I'd really fallen for Luke, where he'd confessed his love for me, and where our mate bond had come to life. But having my mate ripped away tarnished those memories, and facing them cut like a knife.

My throat tightened at the sight of the winter sun dancing off the glass exterior of the London alpha's office. The flashy building towered above us, imposing—just like its owner. My stomach revolted at the memory of him getting too close and personal with me during our last meeting. But then I remembered Luke ready to bring down the place to get to me, and the smallest hint of a smile ghosted my lips.

Alice stepped beside me, the sombre understanding in her eyes speaking volumes as she linked her arm with mine. We'd gone from having one piece needed to stop the prophecy to nothing at all. Larissa had Luke, and for all we knew, she could have the dagger too.

Tom strode ahead while Dylan, Craig, and Josh flanked us.

the latter glued to his phone as he monitored updates on his latest attempt to hack the flash drive.

The rest of our group spilled from the fancy armoured minivan, many of them Edinburgh wolves who had joined us as a show of support for their alpha. Russell wanted to make a point with our arrival. Edmonstone had summoned all alphas of the English packs, along with those in Scotland and Wales, and the Edinburgh alpha was pissed he was left off the list. Thanks to a tip off from someone close to Edmonstone, but loyal to Gabi's parents, we knew when and where they were meeting. Already some other wolves had turned up, stopping to chat in the foyer outside. There was no hiding this time, no sneaking in. The Irish may not have been on the list, but we were sure as hell crashing the party.

"Eve!" The tingle of magic reached my senses just as a familiar figure cut through the crowd, her long braids nearly taking a werewolf's eye out as she shoved past.

The moment she stepped into my space, I could sense the spell surrounding her. One look at the nearest security camera tracking her every movement told me it was likely a sound bubble, as did her smirk when she gave the camera a one-fingered salute. Thanks to the glass exterior, we also had a full view of the receptionists spying on us. But we weren't hiding this time.

I opened my arms just in time for the witch to barrel into me, the warmth of Maya's magical signature enveloping me like a warm hug. "I'm so glad you got here safely."

"I never got the chance to thank you," she whispered, her voice thick as she hugged me tighter.

Behind Maya, a young woman similar in age hung back. Her cheeks had more colour than that night in the graveyard, her black hair shiny and healthy rather than matted and soaked.

"There's no need to thank me, I'm just glad she's safe."

Maya's eyes were glassy as she released me from her embrace and stepped back. "But Luke—"

I took her hands in mine and shook my head. "Luke will be fine."

My words held more conviction than I felt, but it had to be true. There was no other option.

She nodded with a sympathetic smile, giving my hands a reassuring squeeze before motioning for Gabi to join us.

Alice threaded her arm through mine, silent as her narrowed eyes scanned our surroundings. Tom was talking to werewolves I didn't recognise, with Mary by his side. Hopefully, her presence would help us prove the Faolchúnna pack couldn't be trusted, and that Edmonstone was in bed with them. Russell and his younger brother, Callum, were both in deep conversation with other wolves. The Edinburgh alpha's bellowing laugh was always distinctive, but I got the feeling he was amping it up to draw attention.

More werewolves arrived by the minute. Some greeted Tom with varying degrees of enthusiasm before filtering into the lobby, others stopped to chat, and a few ignored his presence entirely. Any time their gaze slid my way, Tom's demeanour stiffened. I didn't need to read emotions to know that many packs didn't like hybrids. It wasn't news to me. Given the Faolchúnna pack's stance and Edmonstone's involvement in the kidnappings, it didn't take a genius to know Alice and I going to be a hit with everyone.

"Like clockwork," Josh muttered, staring at the building across the road.

I followed his gaze to find a raven sitting on top of the building opposite. Its head swivelled, locking unblinking eyes on us.

Craig's lip curled enough to flash his fangs at the bird. "That didn't take long."

"So much for not tracking us," I murmured, swallowing as I remembered the first raven the London alpha had sent. The way it had literally killed itself to deliver the message.

Gabi excused herself from a conversation, navigating through the throng of werewolves to join us. She was dressed in a pair of jeans, a black wool coat, and a ruby knitted sweater that made her complexion glow, disguising her gaunt cheeks. Her haunted gaze met mine as she approached, a sign more work was still to be done for her to be free of whatever Larissa and the wolves had put her through, much like Alice. But she was safe, and that's all that mattered.

Despite the twinge in my heart knowing Luke wasn't, it didn't detract from the pride that swelled knowing he was part of the reason she was rescued.

"Hey, it's good to see you again." I smiled, unsure whether I should hold out my hand or act on my impulse and pull the girl into a hug. I settled on a friendly nod, as if my pack and I hadn't trashed a graveyard and taken on a psychotic witch to free her.

Her smile was tight and uncertain, but it reached her eyes. "Maya is right. Thank you for saving me that night."

"It's fine." I repeated the same lie I'd been telling myself and everyone around me since.

Images of lightning and Luke giving himself up to Larissa in my place hurtled through my mind's eye. Around us the noise of the city rose as commuters left their offices and the street grew busier, thousands of sounds and smells to distract me. Except one scent in particular caught my attention. Another hybrid.

"No, it's not." The correction caught me off guard as a man stopped behind Gabi, his hand resting on her shoulder. He was at least a foot taller, but the family resemblance was unmistakable. And he was a hybrid, most likely the reason they had chosen his daughter for their warped experiments. "I'm Ezra, Gabi's father, and I will never forget the risks you took to save our daughter. What you did showed bravery and courage, and a selflessness that is often lost in the world these days." While she was the spitting image of her mother, Gabi shared her father's eyes. Dark brown, filled with compassion and kindness. His were brimming with love for his daughter. "My wife and I will forever be in your debt for returning Gabi to us."

I didn't miss the pang of guilt that punctuated his words. Maya had told me a vampire had been sent to threaten the family when they refused blood money from Edmonstone, Gabi's parents had fought them off. Despite Ezra's soft tone, there was no doubt that he would walk through the fiery pits of hell and back and again for her.

I nodded, the wave of emotion triggered by the sincerity of his words, a siren's wail robbing my voice.

"He's right." Gabi shook her head, pulling her coat tighter around her as a gust of wind whipped through the street. "You saved my life. And I know what that cost. I'll never forget it."

Of course, she would have sensed it. Werewolf mate bonds were a form of magic. My chest tightened.

"It's lovely to meet you," Alice said, breaking the silence. Her arm was still linked with mine, supporting me both emotionally and physically by making sure I stayed upright when their gratitude threatened to bowl me over.

Thankfully, Tom chose that moment to join us, walking over with his phone to his ear and the rest of our group in tow. He said a quick goodbye before greeting Ezra with a smack on the back and a wide grin. He motioned to the queue of werewolves heading inside, one still in deep conversation with Gabi's mother. "We better get inside. Wouldn't want to leave dear Henry waiting."

Russell snorted, his distaste for the London alpha written all over his face.

It felt good to be finally taking on Edmonstone. Dylan had challenged Tom one night about our lack of action, but our alpha's response had been firm: *There is no merit in taking action out of fear, acting on impulse often worsens the situation. When we take action, it will be with purpose.*

Valeria said goodbye to her friend before joining our little group, greeting her husband with a kiss. She offered me a smile and some words of thanks, making my eyes threaten to leak once more.

Our group had hatched a plan during the eight-hour drive. A number of wolves weren't buying Edmonstone's story that the kidnapping had been caused by rogue wolves working with Larissa. The London alpha was notorious for utilising rogues—wolves who had been cast out by other packs—to do his dirty work in exchange for being able to stay in the city without repercussions. It was time for Alice and Gabi to tell their stories.

We couldn't guarantee everyone would listen or believe us, but Ezra and his family were well respected in the supernatural community, as was Tom. All we needed to do was cast enough doubt to get people asking questions, and their lies would unravel. Tom thought it might force Edmonstone to betray Larissa and reveal Luke's location to save face. I wasn't so sure. But one thing was for certain: I would walk in there and back their claims, because any woman brave enough to speak her truth deserved to do so with an army of support behind her.

The security cameras dotted around the building's exterior swivelled towards us, dead-eyed and ever watchful. I could only imagine the vein popping in Edmonstone's forehead at not being able to hear us.

"Are we all sure about this?" Tom aimed his question at the couple, before turning to Gabi with a softer expression. "Especially you, Gabi. I know how hard this is. I don't want to put you through it if you don't feel ready. And it's okay if you don't, we can find another way. Josh is close to cracking the flash drive."

Hope unfurled its feathers like a phoenix rising at his words, fanning the flames of the fire burning in me. I was more than ready to take Edmonstone on. Last time I walked out of there with my mate hand in hand, this time I wasn't leaving without answers.

Maya had linked her arm with Gabi's, much like Alice had with me. She gave her friend a sympathetic pat on the arm, but her hard glare towards the skyscraper in front of us was at odds with the warmth of her actions. "We won't judge you if the answer is no."

I was nervous about involving Maya. She had no links to the werewolf packs, but Ezra had proudly announced that she was family during our call and planning session. I knew all too well that you don't leave family behind, and that was the end of the matter.

Gabi fidgeted with the hem of her sleeves, but her jaw was set as she stared up at the sun beginning its descent behind the looming office block of the London alpha. I didn't know the girl well, but I couldn't hide my admiration at her resilience.

"You don't owe us anything," I added, watching her closely for the slightest of tells that she wasn't fully confident in her decision. "I don't want you to do this unless it's one hundred percent what you want."

She shook her head and rolled her shoulders, unwinding her arm from Maya's to grab her friend's hand. With fingers intertwined, she stared down the door with the same steely determination. "I'm sure."

Tom clapped Ezra on the back, his shoulders seeming to almost grow wider and his form grew more imposing as he stepped towards the building and led the way. "Let the fun begin."

The raven's beady eyes tracked us until we reached the revolving doors. I glanced back as the bird kicked off with a heavy beat of its wings, soaring into the sky with a shrill departing call that felt like an omen.

# CHAPTER 8

## LUKE

Someone was inside my head, pounding my brain with a sledgehammer. Either that or I was dying. I was dying and my brain was about to explode from the pressure building there. My eyes were sluggish to adjust to the dark, and I clutched my head as warmth spread down the back of my neck, my hair damp and crusted with something.

I rolled onto my side and groaned, every fibre of my body protesting at the movement. I hurt all over, as if someone had injected me with acid and it was corroding my veins. My stomach lurched and the scent of vomit filled my nostrils. The stickiness at the back of my head wasn't blood, it was puke.

With shaky arms, I crouched on all fours over a patch of watery vomit that was mostly bile thanks to Larissa's starvation tactics. Pain radiated from my ribs as I retched, vision swimming. Lifting my head was a struggle, but I found my gaze snagging on claw marks gouged in the metal wall.

I threw my senses out, body shuddering as I fought to hear beyond what must have been soundproof walls. All I could make out was the distant roar of the wind, but then I noticed salt in the air, followed by a sour scent that made the hairs on the back of my neck stand on end.

I spun to find Ryan sitting at the opposite end of the rectangular room, his dead-eyed stare fixed on me. My stomach somersaulted at the sudden movement, but I forced the lump in my throat down. I must have looked pitiful crouched in the poorly fitted sweatpants, covered in vomit, but the wolf in me would never cower to that bastard.

"What the fuck are you doing here?" I growled, my scorched throat begging for water.

His eye roll was accompanied by his signature moody scowl. "Babysitting."

I recognised the tiredness in my bones and pain lancing through my body: nightshade. It made me feel like I'd been hit by a bus and thrown off a cliff for good measure; my magic sapped of its energy. They must have given me another one of their nightshade concoctions that they were trialling. Then again, maybe I should have been grateful to be alive. Nightshade was supposed to be lethal to werewolves; she needed me alive.

Ryan sat in the middle of a row of three seats that looked like those on an aeroplane, with straps that bolted across the middle. Metal wrapped the entire room, no windows or doors in sight. I struggled to my feet, legs shaking as I gripped the wall to drag myself upright.

"Careful," he warned, his bored tone lacking an ounce of concern. "As much as I'd love to rip your heart out, I was asked to keep you alive."

"Her heart."

He cocked his head to one side, the movement stilted. "Excuse me."

"*Her* heart. Eve is my mate." Facing him, I lifted my chin. "My heart is hers."

He crossed the room in seconds, my hands shooting up in defence just in time to get my fingers under his hand before it closed around my throat. He hoisted me off my feet, the wall rattling as he slammed me against it. "I should have killed you that night in the park."

My muscles were crying out in pain, but the defiant roar of my wolf side was fighting through the nightshade. "You had no chance of killing me that night, or ever," I spat, my split lip stinging as I smirked and dug my half-formed claws into the fleshy inside of his wrist. "I know my dad regrets not killing yours, though."

His irises flashed silver. "Was losing one parent not enough? I don't think you know what a real alpha looks like."

"And I don't think you know what love looks like, but this isn't a fucking therapy session." I slammed my head forwards, enjoying the satisfying sound of his nose cracking. He dropped me, rushing to cover his nose while blood gushed down his chin. I bolted to the opposite side of the room, my chest heaving from the effort. "I know Eve's one in a million, but you really need to get over it."

"You stole her." He stopped pinching his nose as the wound healed, his shirt splattered with his blood.

"You can't steal people. Though I can see why you'd struggle with that concept." I shook my head, feeling behind me for any sign of an exit or hidden door as I skirted around the wall. "Eve was never yours. She chose me long before she knew about the mate bond."

The bond flexed as if it was listening, warmth blooming through my chest.

"You're lucky Larissa told me to spare you." Ryan tried to make it sound like it was a request, not an order, but his gaunt cheeks caught my attention. "I suppose I should be grateful you woke before they're due to move us. Now I don't have to strap you in like a sleeping toddler." He plucked a pair of silver handcuffs off the seats, the chain joining the cuffs clinking as he dangled them in the air. He kept a black leather glove between his skin and the metal, a cruel sneer stretching across his face. "It's much more fun doing it while you're awake."

His sleeve slid up enough to show a glimpse of red, angry skin on his forearms. Then I noticed the creases in his normally pristine suit, and that it was grease slicking his short curls back, not hair gel.

I laughed, the hoarse sound ripping my raw throat. "You're more delusional than I thought, if you believe you're here as a guard dog. You're just as much her captive as I am."

Rage contorted his sharp features, then he lunged. Pain lanced through my body when he slammed me back into the metal wall again, and I could have sworn the room rocked. I groaned, my magic reserves scraping the barrel as I dug my claws into his chest and shoved.

He pulled me down with him, and I threw my weight back so that he landed beneath me. We hit the ground with a loud bang, my knees burning from the impact. I straddled his hips, and now it was my hand wrapped around his throat while I pinned his arms above his head with the other.

"What's wrong? Bitten off more than you can chew?" My body trembled with the effort to keep him down. But even weakened, tortured, the anger I held for the man who had put my mate through hell fuelled me. "What did you to piss her off? Because being locked in here with me is your punishment, and for once, I'm on board with the witch's plans."

A deep growl rattled in his throat as Ryan tried to draw his knee up, but I clamped my thighs around his to pin his legs down.

"Looks like she played with you, too. But even after getting a taste of your own poison, you can't see it."

Ryan tore a hand free, snapping one handcuff around my wrist. My hiss echoed his when the glove he was using for protection slipped before he could lock the cuff into place, exposing his skin to the silver.

"Bastard." I clamped my hand over his, but the pain was worth the look of horror etched into Ryan's features. He howled as the silver seared our skin. "No father who cared about their kid would let the witch near you. You're just a pawn in his games."

"You're wrong," Ryan roared, thrashing beneath me as the metal scorched his skin.

"You know..." I inhaled deeply, enduring the pain, and slammed his hands back against the ground, keeping him pinned. Welts were forming on my hands to match his. "I would pity you, but you're an irredeemable scumbag. *You* stole my sister. *You* hurt Eve. You made her hate herself, hate the wolf side of her. You stole so many moments away from her. You made her fear something she should have loved, and I will spend every day of my life making sure she knows how beautiful, strong, and incredible she is. I will show her how to embrace her wolf side because you don't get to take that away from her."

The briefest glimpse of regret broke through the fear in his eyes, but it vanished the moment a loud bang came from the other end of the room.

Metal groaned, and the far wall swung open a crack. Salt air rushed through the gap, and my head snapped up. I was distracted long enough for Ryan to throw me off him, the metal handcuffs crashing to the ground.

"Is everything under control here?" A blonde-haired vampire poked her head through the gap, red speckles appearing in her golden eyes at the sight of our blood. I recognised her as one of Larissa's henchwomen.

Ryan winced, dusting off his now ripped trousers. He straightened, rolling his shoulders back and resuming his stuck-up asshole act. "Of course."

"Doesn't look like it." The vamp ran her tongue over a set of sharp fangs. "The humans can hear the banging and are getting suspicious. Get shit under control. We depart in ten."

"Tell Larissa I need to see her." A low growl rumbled in Ryan's chest as he approached the vamp, wiping blood from his chin. "Now."

"I'm not delivering that message. I like my head intact. She's already gone ahead anyway." The vamp grinned, the wind whipping at her hair.

The sound of machinery and tyres reached my ears, along with waves crashing against stone. We weren't in a room; we were in some kind of storage crate by the sea. A port.

"Where are you taking us?" I asked, mentally calculating if I had enough strength left to get past the vampire. But her scent was mingled with two others, one a Fae, and I could hear voices behind her.

Ryan turned to me, his icy tone dripping with the promise of revenge. "Back home, where I can make sure you pay. And when Eve comes to save you, I'll make sure you never see her again."

"If Larissa gets her hands on Eve, neither of us will see her again. She doesn't care about your stupid werewolf experiments," I snapped, advancing on Ryan. "She plans to complete the prophecy."

"I know," he sneered, his icy tone just like his father's. "You'll be gone, and I'll be heir to one of the most powerful packs in the world."

"You don't know the full truth."

Someone yelled outside.

"We've been compromised," said the vampire before she sped into the shipping container, form blurring.

Strong arms wrapped around me from behind, dragging me backwards, and I spotted the corners of Ryan's lips lifting.

"No, Larissa told me all about the prophecy." His arrogance was suffocating as he cocked his head to one side. "You will die, Eve will survive, and everything will be as it should."

There was a flurry of activity behind us, the temperature inside the crate rocketing as Fae magic sizzled in the air. I struggled against the arms binding me, my exhausted muscles straining, and magic licked my skin as it wound around my wrists.

I locked eyes with the pathetic excuse for a wolf in front of me, hoping that his misguided obsession with Eve would make him hear the truth in my words. "Why would I lie? Larissa wants to sacrifice Eve."

"No, she doesn't."

"You're a fucking idiot. Open your eyes! Just because you want to believe something, it doesn't make it's true." I gritted my teeth as the magic pulled my arms behind me, a sick pop sounding from my left shoulder. "Eve must die to complete the prophecy."

Ryan's eyes widened, and fiery pain exploded from between my shoulder blades. I roared, my legs buckling as I was forced to my knees. At the same time, the bond tying me to Eve went taut and my heart skipped a beat. Something deep within told me to fight, to clutch onto consciousness as the nightshade threatened to drag me under. As always, it was her voice that echoed in my mind.

*Luke.*

# CHAPTER 9

## EVE

We'd been escorted in the back entrance like a dirty secret during my last visit. This time, we waltzed straight through the front door. Tom and the Edinburgh werewolves led the way, closely followed by Ezra, Valeria, and Mary. Gabi's parents cast furtive glances back at their daughter as she walked alongside Maya. Alice and I were the last to enter the building, flanked by Luke's closest friends. Craig took up the rear, red bleeding into his molten irises.

The reception area was just as lavish as the areas I remembered, with polished black granite floors and fancy sculptures that screamed money. A large reception desk lined one wall, and the fresh scent of sea salt tickled my senses as I zeroed in on the staff. Edmonstone's choice of a mixture of sirens and Fae to work the front desk was disturbing yet unsurprising. Not because there was anything wrong with sirens, but given his leadership and tendencies, there was no way the choice wasn't for a darker purpose.

Dylan rolled his eyes with a low whistle. "Talk about making a statement."

I'd expected the packs to have been familiar with the place, but apparently the London alpha never called a group meeting on his own turf. So this was definitely a message, a purposeful show of power.

Luke had threatened to trash his office last time. I had no problem following through on that promise.

A blood-red carpet directed guests towards an expansive staircase where it split in two directions and converged onto a wide balcony level, forming the first-floor foyer which overlooked the impressive reception below. Large, abstract art pieces lined the interior walls, illuminated by sunlight that filtered through the glass exterior of the floors above, flooding the place with natural light that bounced off the glossy surfaces. Instead of the modern chrome office aesthetic, the London alpha had opted for a lavish gold, from the intricately carved banisters somehow spelled not to crush the glass balustrade to the chandeliers floating in the air above the foyer. Any human clientele would have searched for the invisible wires holding them in place, but I could sense the magic. Everything about the place was a show of opulence, and it made my skin crawl.

I craned my neck to see past the chandeliers and towards the maze of stairs and balconies leading to the upper executive floors. "His office is on the top floor."

Before Tom could make a beeline for the elevator, a receptionist glided into his path, stopping him in his tracks.

"Can I help you, sir? I don't believe your name is on the list." His customer service smile on display, even while almost toe-to-toe with an alpha.

"I don't believe you asked my name." Tom refused to take a step back, his response clipped. Mary bristled beside him.

"My apologies, sir." The siren's too bright smile didn't falter despite his tone, his voice eerily melodic. "What is your name?"

"James Roberts."

He canted his head, eyes narrowing. "Mr. Roberts has already arrived."

"Well, you must tighten up your security in that case, because

I am Mr. Roberts, and I have somewhere to be," Tom lied, sidestepping the siren and motioning for us to follow.

The siren's hand snapped out to grab his arm, but his fingers closed around air as Tom dodged with ease.

A low growl rattled in Tom's chest as he turned on the siren, his eyes flashing silver in warning. "Like I said, we have somewhere to be. You wouldn't want to leave Mr. Edmonstone waiting, would you? He's expecting us." He turned on his heel and proceeded towards the elevator bank.

Russell swanned past with his signature swagger, flashing the disgruntled receptionist a wide grin. "I'm Russell Stewart, by the way. Alpha of the Edinburgh werewolf pack. I think you forgot my invite." He winked, earning an eye roll from Mary, and they strode after Tom.

Gabi's eyes widened and Maya smirked as we all filed behind my alpha. The young witch was going to be a handful, and I wasn't mad about it. With witches like Larissa on the loose, we needed more with good morals.

The siren knew we weren't invited and smelled one too many witches, but he let us pass. A different staff member at reception pushed what looked like a panic button, but we weren't sneaking in. We wanted the London alpha to know we were coming. I wanted someone else to feel their time was running out.

"You're a disgrace to our kind." Craig glowered at the vampire, following us towards the elevator.

"This place is ridiculous," Mary muttered, her eyes widening at the black chaise lining the back of the elevator, of which Callum took full advantage.

He sat with his legs spread wide, making himself comfortable while leaving only standing room for the rest of our group, and staring down another siren who approached as the door slid closed. He stopped short of waving them off.

I hit the gaudy gold button for the penthouse and turned to Mary. "Have you met Henry before?"

"He visits Damien regularly, but I always steer clear." Mary shook her head, her upper lip curling in distaste. "He was always insufferable, even as a teenager. Unfortunately, he grew into his ego and not out of it."

Ezra snorted, earning an elbow from his wife who looked like she was walking the line between holding back a laugh and losing her nerve. He draped his arm around Valeria's shoulder, pressing a kiss to the top of her head. I could feel her magic subside as she relaxed into his touch. Her powers smelled like summer and fresh blooms. I wasn't sure if the scent of magic told me anything about someone's heart, but her magic was light and airy compared to the caustic burn of Larissa's.

This time, the floors didn't drag by. The doors opened to reveal the penthouse level, the foyer empty but for the same moody personal assistant to the London alpha. Her eyes narrowed at the sight of me. The picture Luke's temper had smashed was still missing off her wall, and I'd no doubt that if I checked under the stone bench surrounding their stupid water feature, his nail marks would still be there. There was nothing relaxing or inviting about the space, no matter how hard they tried.

"I don't believe you gentlemen have invites." She stood, the hardness of her expression mirroring the stone sculpture nearby as she adjusted her pencil skirt. Her lips pressed into a thin line at the sight of hybrids, witches, and vampires storming the office. "Mr. Edmonstone is currently occupied, but I'm certain he'd be pleased to speak with you if you're willing to wait *patiently* until he's available."

Callum's lips peeled back, but Russell placed a hand on his younger brother's arm in warning. Mary stood alongside Tom like a guard dog, her arms folded as she leered at the receptionist. Ezra and Valeria flanked the two young girls. Ezra was a member of one of the English packs, but he wasn't an alpha and therefore didn't make the cut.

The foyer was empty. Even Edmonstone's office seemed unoccupied. But beyond his office and those of his sons, lay another room with the same frosted glass door as the rest and shadows moving behind it. Werewolf-grade soundproofing wasn't enough to mask the many scents leading to that doorway. I could sense the magic from a distance, no doubt some sort of magical lock, so we couldn't just barge in. Craig's form became a blur as he raced over to check the rooms before reappearing by my side with a nod of confirmation.

"That won't be necessary." Tom's lips spread into a wide, cold smile. He strode up to the receptionist and planted his hands on the desk, and his voice dropped low. "Mr. Edmonstone has been watching us since we arrived. I suspect he'd prefer if I walked in calmly rather than risk causing a scene, don't you?"

She flashed her teeth but took a step back when a low growl brewed in Tom's chest. "He instructed me to keep you waiting outside, where you belong."

A small part of me pitied her. Edmonstone never played fair. Who knew if she even wanted to work this closely for him? Was she a part of his power-hungry followers, or was she tethered to him by blackmail?

"I'm sure he told you to give us the runaround, but unfortunately for dear Henry, he's not the playmaker this time." Tom shoved the desk forwards, the muscles of his shoulders and back flexing under the thin layer of his T-shirt. Unlike the witches, we skipped the outerwear and were running hot today, especially when facing off against another pack. And Tom's alpha side was showing tenfold today. He picked up an ugly glass paperweight with a figure of a wolf, gaudy gold swirls, and 'Edmonstone' written on the surface, twirling it in his hands. "And I'm rapidly running out of patience."

Alice chewed her lip, muffling a small laugh as she watched her father. Amusement danced in her eyes, but also pride. I wondered what it was like to grow up with parents who would fight for you like this.

He flung the paperweight at the wall, the glass shattering on impact and falling to the floor like hail. The werewolf receptionist flinched, her lips twisting into a scowl. I noticed that Tom chose an item on her desk that wasn't personal, because even in alpha mode, he was kind. Unfortunately, she didn't seem to appreciate his kindness. Either that or I was right, and she *was* on the power-hungry Edmonstone-obsessed team.

I hadn't noticed her pressing any buttons, but the lift pinged and two hulking bodyguards stepped onto the floor. Russell and Callum immediately closed the distance behind me and Alice, the corded muscle of their necks flexing as they faced the werewolf security duo.

"I'm not going to play the villain here. If Edmonstone thinks I'll trash the entire place to make a point, he's wrong. Thank you for agreeing." Tom's tone cooled, and he didn't show a hint of amusement at the receptionist's baffled expression. He nodded curtly in Russell's direction. "It's been a pleasure."

Russell and Callum sprang into action, taking one burly security wolf each. Even outside of the full moon, their strength far outweighed that of the London alpha's lackeys, and they overpowered them with ease. The receptionist backed up against the wall as she watched the two security guards be neutralised. Her eyes flashed silver, but she made no effort to step in and spare them.

Callum tackled his target like a rugby player, his shoulder connecting with the man's exposed torso below the ribs. They hit the ground just as Russell grappled with his opponent, catching him in a headlock and hurtling him into the nearest wall. The security guy's head hit the wall with a crack, and he slumped to the floor, unconscious. Meanwhile, Callum straddled his guard, who now had a blooming black eye and looked close to passing out too.

"Which one?" Callum grinned, revealing bloody teeth.

Ezra's eyes were wide, but Valeria's sparkled with amusement and a smile played on her lips. Maya's reaction was similar, though Gabi's satisfaction seemed subdued by nerves as she glanced towards the doorway.

"Was that necessary?" Mary heaved an agitated sigh, motioning to the two Scots who appeared buoyed by the chance to take out some frustration.

Craig shrugged, flashing me a wide grin. "Well, I enjoyed the show."

"You act like we didn't grow up together sometimes," Tom chuckled, pointing to the one Callum had given a shiner. "He'll do."

Russell released the werewolf he was holding by the collar, stepping over the man's unconscious body as it slumped onto the marble floor that was now spattered red. His younger brother got to his feet and grabbed fistfuls of his security guard's shirt, yanking the man upright. The guard swayed, his eye purple and swollen, held in place by a gleeful Callum who marched the werewolf towards the door and motioned with his head for us to follow.

"You should have been in that meeting, you know," I added as we walked past the receptionist, who looked like she was rethinking her role. "You would have been there if your alpha wasn't an asshole."

Her lips thinned, revealing hints of canines. I flashed mine in response, my nails morphing into claws as I waved. She could scent I was a hybrid, and I would have loved to put her in her place, but we had more pressing matters. I resisted the urge to flip her the bird and focused instead on Tom, who placed the semi-lucid werewolf's hand on the door handle and pushed down while Callum propped him up.

Magic sizzled in recognition, and the door clicked open. Russell braced himself alongside Tom and helped his brother shove the security guard through the doorway. We watched as the door swung open, and the battered bouncer pitched forwards, collapsing in a dazed heap. As he fell, Edmonstone came into view. He was standing at the head of a rectangular table in an expansive boardroom, taking up the bulk of the room and addressing the wolves gathered as if he was some kind of politician. Given the lies and manipulation he spewed, he fit the bill.

"What is the meaning of this?" Edmonstone boomed, the buttons of his slim fitted, slate-grey suit straining as he puffed his chest out.

The giant boardroom table must have seated nearly forty pack representatives, all of whom were staring at the bloodied man lying prone on the floor, staining the pristine cream carpet that I was sure Edmonstone regretted choosing at that moment.

Faces gathered round the table reflected an array of emotions, ranging from outrage to curiosity as their collective gaze landed on us. As expected, a few noses wrinkled in distaste at the sight of us hybrids.

Tom stepped forwards, his casual outfit of a T-shirt and jeans a subtle jab of disrespect. "Hello, Henry. I could claim you forgot my invitation, but I'm not in the mood for your lies. And unfortunately for you, we're on a bit of a time crunch."

Murmurs broke out, questioning the meaning of our arrival.

Edmonstone's face was like thunder, and his eyes flashed silver. "This is a private pack meeting for those in the UK. I don't want to get into politics, but I believe Ireland gets quite upset when included under that umbrella. And I would *hate* to cause offence."

*Motherfucker.*

Alice's throat rattled with a growl of warning beside me. Werewolf or human, we were *Irish*, and the London alpha poking fun at an age-old wound was asking for trouble. Especially when he was connected to one of our own being taken.

"Petty, but not unsurprising." Mary shot Edmonstone a scorching glare.

Tom rolled his shoulders with an over-exaggerated sigh. "Whatever happened to treating other packs with respect? Or has your ego grown so out of control that you think you are above the rules of etiquette?" His voice filled the room, every head turning towards him as his powers seemed to swell. Alphas felt different, and while they couldn't perform coercion like vampires, his words commanded attention. "But you don't obey the rules, do you, Henry? No. You think you're *untouchable*. That's a mistake."

Russell joined Tom's side, running a bloodied hand through his hair that gave him red highlights to match his brother's natural hair colour. "You also excluded the Edinburgh pack from your invite. Is that to be taken as an act of aggression?"

Edmonstone's jaw ticked, but the low growl that had been building in his throat died out as Tom stepped out of the way to reveal Gabi and her parents. His smile grew wider while Edmonstone paled. A chorus of gasps echoed, and Gabi's name rose in the room as a whisper.

"What? Your precious security system couldn't see through the glamour?" Ezra spoke up, his hand resting protectively on his daughter's shoulder. The London alpha's eyes practically bulged out of his head. "You thought threatening us would work when hush money failed?"

Maya's face lit up, her lips quirking into a smug smile.

"You called a meeting without the parents of the girl who was kidnapped by *your* associates? That's more than suspicious—it's a coverup," Tom challenged, each word doused with loathing as he motioned to the young witch who was staring down the London alpha with unwavering determination, her parents and Maya standing in support. "She was rescued from Larissa by *my* pack, working alongside the Edinburgh wolves, and you dare to exclude us from this meeting so you can weave your lies?"

"These claims are outrageous," Edmonstone hissed, spittle flying from his mouth as his mask slipped.

Tom's eyes flashed silver, his magic surging. "You're pathetic. Leader of the London packs, 'protector', yet you work with Larissa, Damien, and hell only knows who else in pursuit of power. Your gaudy little empire isn't enough to satisfy you."

The room exploded in an uproar; someone howled for security while others demanded answers.

Ezra guided Gabi into the room towards Tom, but then he motioned for Alice. Her lower lip shook as she looked to me for support. I gave her side a squeeze before nudging her forwards. Tom had pulled her aside before we left Edinburgh, asking if she would speak up to back Gabi. One kidnapping could be written off. Two was a pattern that was harder to ignore. Pride swelled in my chest as I watched the girl I'd found all those months ago on the Faolchúnna pack lands step up to the plate, ready to speak her truth. The bond in my heart twisted, as if Luke was there in spirit for his little sister.

"It's time for the truth." Tom's voice was thick with conviction, and he took the two girl's hands with a gentleness that Edmonstone could never dream of. A true leader. He turned them to face the room full of werewolf representatives, giving them the floor. "Every werewolf, witch, or otherwise here today deserves to know the truth about what has happened. The balance between our species is in danger, and your stories deserve to be heard."

# CHAPTER 10

O f course, when a woman tries to speak her truth, people rarely listen with open ears. The same was true for a cohort of the pack representatives Edmonstone had gathered in the boardroom that evening. The moment Tom gave the floor to Gabi and Alice, a wave of protests broke out. The London alpha launched himself at Tom, but my alpha caught him by the shoulders and ran him backwards. Edmonstone's back hit the wall, his lips curling in an ugly snarl. Magic surged as Maya and Valeria moved in unison to create a barrier to hold the London alpha in place. His expression was priceless, the vein in his forehead throbbing and angry as he struggled against the invisible force that pinned him.

"You can't do this," the London alpha spat, unable to so much as jerk his head to signal for his supporters to jump us. Not that any of them looked willing.

"Careful, Henry." Tom cocked his head to one side, the smirk playing on his lips the image of how Luke looked when he one-upped someone. It was the perfect mix of taunting and smug, two expressions I wasn't used to seeing on him. "Don't lose your head."

Our group had taken up a protective stance on either side of

Alice and Gabi. I imagined this was what staring down the barrel of a gun felt like as I faced off with a room full of wolves, many of whom would possibly skin me alive given the chance. Their hatred was palpable, but there was a hunger for truth among the sea of faces.

A loud growl of warning ripped from Tom's throat, and he turned to address the room once more, command ringing in his words. "Edmonstone, along with select members of his pack, has been working alongside the Faolchúnna pack to perform experiments in order to strengthen the werewolf bloodline. They have banded together in an effort to eradicate hybrids and make werewolves the '*superior species*'. Both women who stand before you today were taken and held against their will, subjected to their tests." Distaste dripped from every word as Tom stared down the parties present. "Edmonstone gathered you here today to spin a false story about rogue wolves. When he's really working with other players, including affluent vampire covens and the disgraced witch, Larissa, to perform tests on hybrids and other supernaturals in pursuit of power."

Whispers that erupted were quickly silenced by a blanket of power emanating from Maya.

"Anyone who does not wish to hear their truth, please leave now," Tom ordered, motioning to the exit. Blood flecked the frosted glass of the door, the security guard starfished on the ground proof that his threat had weight. "I won't tolerate another interruption."

A handful of men rose to their feet, their judgemental glares quickly becoming glued to the floor as they hightailed it past Edmonstone and out of the room. The London alpha spewed threats at Tom, but Maya quickly used a sound bubble to mute his vitriol. Valeria nudged the unconscious werewolf out of the way with her foot, leaving streaks of blood in his wake, and slammed the door shut.

Tom spread his hands, gesturing for the audience to sit. I was surprised to see everyone's ass hit their chair immediately. An

Irish alpha commanding this many foreign packs was unheard of. But Tom had a strong reputation, and Luke's mother was a member of one of the London packs. I recognised her old alpha from pictures Luke had shown me. He and his wife watched Tom intently, concern creasing his features.

Alice spoke up first.

"The Faolchúnna pack held me captive for five years." She didn't stutter, pausing to let her truth hang in the air. It was smart for Alice to go first; no one present was loyal to Damien. She surveyed the room, not shying away from eye contact as she waited for the murmurs to die down. "I was sixteen when I was taken, groomed by the Faolchúnna alpha's son, Ryan."

Several gasps rang out at his name, followed by some "surely nots" and degrading comments about his father's character that I had to agree with.

"I went out one night to meet Ryan for what I thought was a date in a park on the outskirts of Dublin city. I knew he was from a rival pack, so I snuck out because I was worried my family wouldn't approve," Alice explained, leaving out the bit about her having a huge fight with Luke just before she was kidnapped. "They were right to worry. The moment I walked into the clearing where we agreed to meet, I was stabbed in the back with a blade coated in nightshade. I remember the feeling of my magic slipping away and the pain that brought me to my knees. I could smell my flesh burning from the silver blade. There was another blow to my head, and then everything went dark." Alice wound her hands behind her back, glancing over at her father, who nodded in encouragement. She set her shoulders, taking a drawn-out breath before continuing. "I came to alone, trapped in a windowless room with a locked door. Nothing but a bed, a narrow room to one side with a toilet and sink with a sliding door, and a tray of cold porridge on a small nightstand. Every piece of furniture was nailed down. The bathroom had no mirror. Which is for the best, because I don't know what I would have done if I had to look myself in the eye as the days ticked by."

Gabi's throat bobbed as Alice recounted her story. Luke's sister moved to talk about the experiments, the blood draws, the way Damien would oversee most of them, and the rare occasions she was allowed to see daylight. My blood boiled when she spoke of the punishments she endured for misbehaving. I focused on her words, doing my best to push down the urges of my wolf side that wanted to rip everyone involved apart.

Tom watched his daughter with pride, but the fingers of his clasped hands flexed. There was a pain behind his mask of confidence, and the same familiar guilt Luke struggled to shake. She had told us the stories before, but I doubted it hurt any less as a parent each time. We all stood and listened while two of the witches kept the London alpha silent.

"I was taken because I'm a hybrid, and Damien wants to use our powers to improve the strength of *'pure'* werewolf bloodlines." Her lips twisted in disgust and several werewolf representatives hung their heads. "He wants to eradicate hybrids altogether. Larissa is facilitating his research, along with Lars."

Someone cursed under their breath.

"Yes, *that* Lars. He's just as sick as his reputation. We intercepted one of their events in Dublin, where they were exhibiting some of their *'specimens'*. I'm sure you heard about the fire." She turned to Edmonstone and motioned for Maya to drop the spell muting him. "That was the last time I saw Mr. Edmonstone. But the first time I met him was when he came to witness an experiment on me. I'll never forget his smirk as they injected me with nightshade to determine the lethal dosage for hybrids."

"That's an outright lie!" A stout man with a moustache that reminded me of a walrus jumped to his feet, his face redder than the mahogany table he banged in the process. "Henry has been nothing but supportive of the hybrids in my pack. My daughter is one."

"Then you should thank the stars that he didn't choose to

use her as a pincushion." Alice didn't miss a beat, her words cutting like ice.

Edmonstone cut in, his voice cool but a pitch higher than normal because of the magic Maya was constricting around his throat like a noose. "You have no proof of this."

"Actually, we have CCTV footage of you entering the hotel lobby that night in Dublin." Tom's silver eyes were filled with the promise of painful revenge. "Do you have a projector in here? I'm sure I can get the footage up on the big screen if you want to play spot the alpha."

My eyes widened, and I looked around to find that Josh had left the room. I'd been too caught up watching Alice to notice.

*Had they really done it? Had Josh broken into the drive?*

Russell grinned as Callum rooted around for a remote for one of the giant TVs mounted on the wall.

Tom's smile grew when he caught my gaze, and he nodded in answer to my silent question.

Tears stung my eyes, and my knees threatened to buckle, my heart hammering so fast I thought it might burst. We had it. Finally, something was going right. We had proof and hopefully something on Luke's location.

Alice stepped back with a small incline of her head, handing the floor over to Gabi.

"I was held by my captives for around two years," she began, her gaze cast downwards, and her shoulders hunched. Despite the tremor in her voice, she spoke steadily as she began her story. "I was coming home from a night out with college friends in the early hours. It couldn't have been past one. We took the Tube to Baker Street and then split up. I took the same route to my room every night. I guess they knew that. I was fine on the Tube, but by the time I got near the Boating Lake, I started feeling woozy. I knew I was going to puke, so I ran to the bushes and that's when they jumped me."

One of the witches must have unleashed their powers on

Edmonstone, because something snapped, and he howled in pain.

Gabi jumped, glancing over her shoulder at the women restraining him. She rolled her shoulders and took a deep breath before continuing, eyes downcast once again. "I didn't sense them coming. No magic, no scent."

"If you didn't see your attackers, how can you dare to blame Edmonstone when he exhausted every resource possible to find you?" a sour-faced man in an outdated pin-striped suit interrupted.

"But he *did* find me." Gabi's head snapped up to meet the cold man's gaze, her nostrils flaring. "They took me to one of their facilities, and Mr. Edmonstone was one of the first people to pay me a visit. So I suggest you shut your mouth unless you want me to rush to the part where I explain how your son accompanied him."

The brunette beside him gasped, her hand flying to her mouth while the man I presumed was her husband turned a damning shade of puce. He shrank back in his chair as if it might save him from the anger now brewing on her pretty face. I zeroed in on the woman, and an equal mix of disgust and amusement washed over me. A hybrid. How could a man be married to a hybrid while harbouring such senseless hatred towards her kind?

Something Kate had once said when we watched a married couple argue in a restaurant jumped to mind. *Lies give men the illusion of power. They get off on the control. It's easier to manipulate someone you resent, and cowards love to imagine they're a white knight.* Seeing her words in motion made me sick, but his wife seemed less like a damsel in distress and more like a dragon ready to take him out for her children.

A phone rang out, the dull buzz drawing my attention to the top of the room.

Edmonstone's tongue flicked out to catch a drop of blood from his lower lip, and he smirked. "Right on time. You should get that." He locked eyes with me, flashing a bloody grin as he nodded towards his pant pocket where the annoying melody rang from. "It's for you."

Maya raised her hand, and with her lips pressed together in a thin line, she used her magic to tug the phone from his pocket. The name flashing on the screen became clear as the device levitated towards me. Larissa.

I snatched the phone. Dread wrapped its talons around my spine, dragging its claws down my back.

"Hello?" I forced the word out, knocking the phone straight to loudspeaker mode.

Something howled in the background, but the bond between me and Luke stayed quiet.

"Oh hello, darling. I heard you have Henry all tied up," Larissa drawled, raising her voice as something crashed and the sound of wind picked up on the line. "A girl after my own heart. I've been playing with your better half too—the poor man is exhausted."

My fingernails morphed into claws, a low growl building in my throat. The hunger in her voice was unmistakable. The thought of her touching him, playing with him, *hurting* him, made the red mist descend. It took all my self-control not to crush the phone to dust.

"Give him back, Larissa," I hissed, my claws piercing the aluminium casing of the phone. "It's me you want."

"All in good time. Tell Henry I said thanks for the distraction. He's been a very good boy, and he'll get his reward all in good time."

The London alpha scowled and tugged against his restraints, his face heating at her words.

"You played us." My tone hardened as Maya tightened the magic bindings, the pain contorting Edmonstone's features doing nothing to ease the anger building inside me.

"That's right, I needed to make sure you wouldn't get in the way," Larissa cooed, her smugness only fanning the flames of my temper. "I'm taking Luke back to Ireland, though my staff got a little trigger-happy with the nightshade. Hopefully he pulls through. Then we can really start to play some games."

She killed the call, and my stomach plummeted.

Tom strode across the room, his arm wound back. Mary followed, the corners of her lips lifting as Tom's fist connected with Edmonstone's nose, the rival alpha's head cracking against the wall with the force. "That's for Alice."

The door burst open, and Josh sprinted inside with his laptop in hand. "I have Luke's location! They're in Southampton. According to emails to his PA, they're moving hybrids from mainland Europe back to Ireland through the UK."

"That's two hours away," Russell said, tossing the keys to Dylan. "Go. There's a chance you could get there before they leave."

Josh nodded, already tugging me towards the door with Alice and Dylan. "If we floor it, we stand a chance."

Fuck werewolf powers, I'd have given anything to be able to teleport in that moment.

I paused as we rushed towards the door to look back at Gabi and Maya who were still surrounded by the other werewolf packs. I couldn't tell by their faces if they believed us, but in that moment, all that mattered and my only heart's calling was to find Luke.

"Go get your mate," Maya urged as Gabi's parents joined them, followed by Russell and his pack. "We've got this."

Mary nodded, joining the group. "Go, I'll hold down the fort here."

"Thank you," I whispered, tears sticking in my throat as I sprinted out the door.

Craig ran beside me, his fingers lacing with mine in a silent promise. I met Tom's gaze, and nothing but dogged determination shone in his silver irises as he led the way.

The last time I'd spoken to Larissa, the witch had stolen my mate. No way in hell was I letting her take him again.

# CHAPTER 11

EVE

**D**arkness cloaked us as we crept down the road lining the harbour in the van, my heartbeat ramping up with every second. I knew we couldn't go in all guns blazing without raising suspicion, but my hand hovered over the door handle, every fibre of my being screaming to follow the tug on the bond as we grew nearer.

"He's here." My voice was a whisper as waves crashed in the background.

Stacks of shipping crates obscured our view of the sea, but I could taste the salt in the air. Josh had sweet-talked the security guarding Southampton Port to let us in, along with planting our names and car registration in their cleared vehicle records on our way there. Thankfully, it had worked, and Dylan's suggestion of driving straight through the barriers wasn't needed.

A mix of emotions washed over me, fear and hope mingling together until they were indistinguishable. There was an overriding sense of desperation, knowing this was possibly our only chance to save Luke before the next full moon. I'd always scoffed at the concept of mates in TV shows, wondering why someone would ever want their fate chosen. But even without magic binding us, I'd have chosen Luke in every lifetime.

Knowing that choice might be ripped away from us made the part of me that always longed to belong threaten to snap entirely.

I didn't know how ports worked, but I expected them to close at night. Two of the ships docked were completely dark, but as we rounded a corner towards the pier, a third came into view. The lights were on, and a crane lifted a slowly spinning shipping crate, which stood strong despite the winds ripping through the harbour. People ran back and forth from the ship, some carrying boxes and others driving forklifts.

Dylan parked as close as he could without us being seen, pulling up behind a parked truck with a long trailer and killing the engine. My heart flipped, adrenaline coursing through my veins as I scanned the harbour, knowing my other half was almost within reach.

Tom undid his seatbelt, gracefully climbing through the gap between the front seats to join the rest of us who were seated along the sides of the van. "We have one chance to get Luke out of here. Let's make it count." He dropped straight into alpha mode, crouching at the centre of the small space. "Josh and Craig, you're with Eve. She stands the best chance of finding Luke. Watch her back and look out for each other. Alice and Dylan are with me. We'll run interference and keep them distracted."

We all murmured in agreement, but Alice barely inclined her head, eyes watering.

"It's not because I don't trust your abilities, sweetheart." Tom's expression softened, and he reached out to squeeze her hand. "But I won't be able to focus on finding Luke if I don't have eyes on you."

Alice turned to me, her voice thick with unshed tears. "Get my brother back, please."

Her request robbed me of words, bringing tears of my own springing up. My heart twisted, the bond practically throbbing with energy, and I nodded.

"If anyone runs into Larissa, do not engage. I am not coming home without a single one of you," Tom ordered. "That includes you, Craig," he added, turning to my best friend. "Eve is one of our own. That makes you family too."

My heart swelled until I thought it might burst. I'd never felt such a sense of belonging. There was a strength to it, but also a fragility knowing that we could lose my mate if I didn't find him in time.

"Anyone who knows how to use one, kit up," Josh ripped a box off the wall of the minivan, popping it open to reveal three guns. He motioned to the firearms, grabbing one for himself and popping the magazine in with practised ease. "The bullets are coated in silver. Claws are great, but we need to keep our distance as much as possible. I've counted some Fae and vamps too, so keep your wits about you."

Dylan climbed in the back and grabbed the second pistol. It was Alice who surprised me when she reached for the third. Though, of course Luke's little sister was trained in firearms. I'd no doubt he would eventually train me in everything possible when he got the chance.

"Ready?" Tom's fingernails morphed into claws as we gathered by the rear doors, lined up in our two assigned groups.

Craig crouched beside me as Josh shoved a second magazine in the back of his cargo pants. "Let's go get your fella back." He grinned, throwing his voice so it sounded like something his nan would say.

My smile was brittle, but I forced myself to face forward as Tom opened the doors. The moment my foot hit the ground, golden eyes locked on us.

"I think they were warned about us." Silver ringed Dylan's irises as he stood beside his alpha.

"Not us." I shook my head, fear and adrenaline rising to a crescendo. "Me."

The trailer rattled beside us, the screech of claws against metal piercing my ears. I leaped back when I spotted a figure crouched above us. Craig was glued to my side as we stared at the man rising to his feet, his eyes matching the colour of the moon and mouth twisting in a nasty snarl.

"Go. Find my son," Tom ordered, every inch the alpha as he placed himself between us and the werewolf. "We'll deal with this."

The werewolf lunged at Dylan, but he dropped and rolled causing the werewolf to overshoot his target and crash into a crate behind Dylan. The noise drew the attention of others loading the ship. A set of vampires dropped what they were carrying, heading straight towards us. That was our signal to move.

Josh took my hand and pulled Craig and I away just as Tom launched into action. We weaved through the trucks parked nearby, and I caught a brief glimpse of Alice through a gap, pride swelling at her smirk when she dug a single claw into her wrist. The scent of her blood bloomed in the air, and more shouts echoed as the vampires zeroed in on her, more of them abandoning their loading duties.

They were warned about a hybrid. I doubt they were told there'd be two.

We jogged in the opposite direction, Craig splitting off for a moment to lure away a stray vamp before rejoining us. The sea air burned my lungs as we ran, skirting around trailers and peeking in the back doors of trucks, only to find them all empty. Josh climbed into one to examine a large wooden crate but shook his head after he dropped back down beside us. We raced across the harbour, hiding behind cargo and machinery as we moved under the shadows.

"Can you sense him?" Craig whispered.

"No, but I can feel him." I pressed my palm to my chest, wishing I could grasp the bond and just pull myself to him. It didn't work that way, but his presence was stronger. He was close.

I tried to pick his scent out, but not a single werewolf smelled like him, and the sea salt had a cleansing effect that degraded how long any scents lingered.

Josh ran a hand along the nearest truck, pressing his ear

against it as he whispered for Luke, while Craig picked up a metal pipe off the ground and started trying to pry the back doors open.

A gunshot rang out in the distance, and I flinched, ducking to join Craig. The doors groaned in protest before giving way, swinging open to reveal an empty cage in the corner and padded walls smeared in blood.

Craig's eyes turned crimson, and I inhaled sharply. It was vampire blood.

"Keep going. He has to be here." The words caught in my throat, but we moved to the next truck. "At least we know we're in the right area."

"We don't have time to open every single one." Josh jogged over, his brow creased. "We need another way."

I closed my eyes, trying to feel him through the bond. *Luke?*

My shoulders sagged when there was no answer, hope withering. Our mind link hadn't worked since he was taken. At first, I thought it was only because of the distance. But now I wondered if the witch had done something to break it entirely.

We skidded to a stop as the ship's horn blared, the sound rattling in my chest. The three of us crouched behind a stack of pallets, watching as those still ferrying cargo picked up their pace. We were running out of time.

"I don't think he's in the trucks." Craig's throat bobbed as he peeked around the edge of the pallets, his face paling as he pointed towards the crane. "I think he's in one of those."

Shipping containers were lined up alongside the ship ready to be loaded, some wooden and others metal.

"They couldn't..." My panic rose as I quickly lost count of the number of containers. Fear clawed its way up my throat as I watched the crane hoist one into the air.

"They could, and they would." Josh laid a heavy hand on my shoulder. "Animals are transported in them."

I focused on the metal crates, my stomach lurching at the

thought of Luke being treated like a caged animal. "They don't have air holes. Even werewolves need air."

"Magic," Craig said, his voice dripping with disgust. "Not that it makes it any better."

"Them being spelled would explain why you can't hear him, even though we're close." Josh scanned the area, his nails morphing into claws.

With the floodlights lighting the harbour near the ship, there was no way we could cross without being seen, but we had no other option.

"If you see him, tell us. Do not go rogue. Luke will kill me if anything happens to you." Josh pulled the gun from his back pocket, glancing around the edge of the pallet before looking back at me. "On three." The muscles of his bronzed biceps flexed, the skin around his shoulders seeming to almost ripple as his magic kicked in as much as it could outside of the full moon. "One."

Craig flashed his fangs, his cold glare fixed on the vampires pulling a wooden crate onto the ship. "Ready."

"Two."

Josh aimed his gun at a werewolf driving a forklift towards the ship, one eye closed as he focused his aim. I held my breath as he pulled the trigger back. "Three."

The moment the silver bullet hit its target, chaos erupted. Those still loading dropped what they were holding, all heads turning towards the forklift where the werewolf slumped lifelessly as he sped towards the base of the crane.

We didn't waste a moment sprinting out of our hiding place and keeping to the edges of the clearing on our race across the harbour. I kept a tight rein on my wolf side, but let my nails extend to form claws, fingertips tingling.

Fae, vampires, sirens, and even a demon sprang into action, and they hollered for help. A wailing howl pierced through the commotion and echoed into the night sky. It wasn't one of pain; it was a summons.

Craig crashed into a vampire who sped into our path, a guttural growl ripping from my friend's throat as he tore into the vampire's. I tore my gaze away from the spurting blood, sidestepping a siren who rushed towards me with their triangular teeth bared.

The forklift hit the base of the crash with a deafening crash. Metal groaned, the mast swaying as it fell off balance.

"Over here!" Josh yelled, grabbing Craig by the shirt and hauling him sharply to the right.

We leaped over a stack of tarped pallets to hide behind one of the containers as the crane came crashing down. I covered my head, shielding myself from the exploding debris. Chunks of cement flew into the air, and the ground trembled beneath our feet, cracks radiating from where the container it carried landed.

The container rolled onto its side, the metal exterior buckling, and one corner embedded in the harbour.

I clung to the bond, bile rising in my throat as keening wails of pain came from the steel box. The doors burst open, but it wasn't Luke who emerged. Human figures climbed out the rubble, their shoulders hunched and their movements disjointed. One of their heads turned in our direction to reveal a face that was half-human, half-skeleton.

Craig cursed, his molten eyes turning ruby red. "I know I'm a vampire, but some things really should stay dead."

"Couldn't agree more." I recoiled as my eyes met empty eye sockets. It shrieked, nothing but a black gaping hole where its mouth should be.

We weaved between the rows of containers, our path towards the ship now cleared.

I could hear the pack fighting in the distance, the sound of claws ripping through flesh and metal screeching ringing in my ears. My heart was warring between the desire to find my mate and the urge to protect my pack.

Shadows moved out of the corner of my eye, and I froze, stopping so quickly Josh bumped into the back of me.

"There." I rushed forwards, pointing towards a steel crate at the edge of the harbour by the back of the ship. "He's there."

It wasn't just shadows. There were wolves. Their shadow-cloaked bodies nearly blended in with the night, but as I neared, I could smell the scent of death and make out their skeletal forms. Three wolves paced in slow circles around the steel crate.

The bond binding me to my mate hummed in confirmation. He was there. He had to be. Larissa only cared about the prophecy, and Luke was part of the key to that.

"I can feel him."

One of the shadow hounds' heads snapped up as we approached, glowing silver eyes locking on me. But I was looking past it to where the shipping container door stood ajar. Where a man stood, battered and bruised, but still standing. Fighting. My heart leaping at the sight of him.

Craig and Josh were on my tail as I ran towards the wolves, the magic of my wolf side begging to be set free.

Luke was struggling against a man and woman I didn't recognise, flurries of movement barely visible as they came in and out of view through the opening.

Craig's arm shot out to grab me around the waist, hauling me back when a mass of shadows leaped into our path.

I looked up to see a shadowy wolf-shaped figure blocking our path, the wind causing decayed flesh hanging from its ribcage sway like the most morbid wind chime. A fourth zombie wolf.

Looking beyond the shadows licking along its back like flames, I watched in horror as the vampire slammed something silver into my mate's back.

His roar of pain was my summons.

*Luke.*

Something deep inside me snapped as I watched them bring the man I loved to his knees, our bond alight as my instincts took over. It wasn't just rage; it was a carnal need for vengeance.

# CHAPTER 12

**M**y paws met the ground, claws scraping the pavement as I transitioned into my wolf form. Magic washed over me, every inch of my body thrumming with energy. The shadow wolf threw its head back and howled to the skies.

I could smell the nightshade from a distance and felt it making the bond tying our hearts together weaken. While it didn't allow me to feel his pain, one look at Luke poured gasoline on the fire burning in me.

He was hurt. Bruised, but not broken.

I leaned back on my haunches, my howl not an answering call, but a promise.

I'd break them.

Craig had jumped away the moment my shift took hold, but he was by my side now, one hand resting on the fur behind my neck. Josh stepped up on my left, his moonlight eyes hard with determination.

I lunged at the hound in front of me, my claws scraping against bone. Their jaw snapped towards me, loose skin flying with spittle as they reared up on their hind legs. I ignored the sting of their shadows and snapped at their throat, struggling to find a grip as they thrashed. I couldn't sink my teeth into flesh, scraping bone while theirs grazed one of my legs.

Through the gaps in their ribs, I saw two more of the undead wolves break away from their positions guarding. Craig and Josh were on it, trusting me to handle myself as they took a wolf each.

I let my centre of weight shift back, throwing the hound off balance and sending us falling backwards. I tucked my legs as my back hit the ground, punching my hind legs through its exposed chest. My paws connected with their spine.

Shadows whipped from its outline as the wolf was sent flying. It hit the top edge of the nearest container with a sickening crunch, falling to the ground with a thud. Its bony frame shuddered as it rose to its feet once more, the one-side of its remaining lip peeling back in a snarl.

I leaped to my feet, my head low to the ground as I stalked forwards. The wolf showed no signs of pain, but one bone in its right hind leg had snapped and was now hanging from the femur by a thin sinew of decaying muscle.

Beside me, Josh flung his zombie wolf to the ground. He planted his foot on the hound's exposed spine and pointed his pistol at the wolf's chest. I flinched as the trigger clicked, the silver bullet vanishing into a mass of shadow as it connected where the wolf's heart should have been.

Craig's opponent howled, a mourning keel as shadows swirled around Josh's feet. He jumped back just as the shadows coalesced in the hound's chest where the bullet had vanished. Its glowing eyes dimmed, the shadows flaring out from its body before vanishing completely. The wolf sagged, bones clattering to the ground as the magic possessing it left its body.

The hound I'd wounded surged forwards, kicking off its remaining hind leg and barrelling into my side. We skidded back together, my claws cutting into the cement. We were a clash of bones of flesh as I fought to get a grip on them. My claws scraped bone, and shadows lacerated my tongue as I clamped my jaw around their scapula.

The scent of rotting flesh filled my nostrils, and I spat a chunk of grey skin onto the ground, diving to the side to escape their snapping jaws. We collided again, my paw slipping against a rib when it snapped. Their claws dug into my chest as they pinned me down.

Their teeth grazed my throat, and I struggled to find purchase to throw them off.

*Eve.*

I looked at the shadowy mass of wolf towering over me, instinct taking over. Shadows burned as I locked my teeth around two of the ribs and bit down with force. They splintered in my mouth, slicing my tongue. Then the hound clamped its jaw around my throat.

Pain radiated from my throat as I pitched my head forward once more, their teeth tearing through my skin as I strained against them. The shadows were blinding as I shoved my muzzle through the gap in its ribs and opened my mouth, sinking my teeth into where its heart should be.

My jaw closed around something, and I bit down, pulling back with force as I tore a clump of shadows from its ribcage. The pressure on my throat eased, and the wolf fell, collapsing into a mound of broken bones on the ground beside me.

I spat out whatever was in my mouth, watching in disgust as the shadows retreated into the bones and vanished completely. I didn't have the time to wonder who the wolf might have been before Larissa raised it from the dead, because the call of my mate throbbed with each beat of my heart.

Craig finished off his wolf with a flourish, and we moved towards the container. The door had been slammed shut, the same blonde vampire who had stabbed Luke standing outside with her feet planted wide. She was scowling, as if we had upset her perfectly curated plans. The wind gusted, and her golden eyes dilated when the scent of my blood reached her.

A man with short black hair and ice-blue eyes stood beside her, the tips of his fingertips covered in frost. I could sense the magic in him, except his signature screamed Fae. He smelled like fresh winter snow, but the deadness behind his eyes soured it. The last remaining zombie wolf stood before them, dropping its head low with a growl.

"Have you come to join your mate?" The vampire's brittle smile was caustic. She ran her hand through the wolf's shadowy fur as if it was a cute little pet. "In the cage where you belong?"

The Fae chuckled, and I bared my teeth. Any thoughts I'd had about sparing them withered and died. As did my patience.

I launched myself at her, my paws pounding the ground. She fled like a coward, speeding away in a blur. But I tracked her through the maze of containers, my throat raw as it pumped air into my lungs. A gunshot followed by an inhuman shriek told me Josh had the last shadow wolf under control.

I spun, my jaw catching her wrist as the vampire tried to slice her talons through my side. I yanked, teeth ripping into her skin as she tumbled to the floor with a shriek.

I was on her in an instant, my claws slicing into her shoulders as I pinned her there face down. Blood smeared her arms, and her fangs glinted in the dim light as she twisted her head. Vampire bites were lethal to werewolves, but this one had tasted her last drop of blood forever. Fear sparked in her eyes when I drew my head back, but I didn't hesitate. I struck with precision, driving my canines through the muscle of her neck until my teeth hit bone. I locked my jaw and twisted until I heard a loud crack.

The vampire's body went limp beneath me, her sour blood coating my tongue. I dropped her, blood and spittle coating her back as I shook myself off before sprinting back towards the sound of the others fighting. Back towards my mate.

Craig was already wrestling with the ice-coated container door while Dylan finished off the Fae, frost crusting the ground around them.

I watched Craig pry the door open, metal groaning and bolts snapping as he tore the door clean off with his strength.

My breath caught in my throat as I found Luke on his knees

and forearms in the centre of the container. His bare back was covered in a criss-cross of cuts and angry welts all down his spine. A loose pair of tracksuit bottoms hung on his waist, covered in a mix of blood and vomit. Behind him, Ryan lay slumped unconscious in the corner, his head lolling to one side.

Luke's entire body shook with effort as he lifted his head. I shifted back the moment his hazel eyes met mine, my wolf form melting away.

"Luke." His name fell from my lips, voice cracking as I took in the outline of his ribs where deep purple bruises covered large patches of his skin.

Silver speckled his irises like stars, relief washing over his handsome features as I dropped to my knees in front of him.

"Eve," he rasped, a tear slipping down his cheek. He groaned as he tried to push up onto all fours.

"I'm here," I whispered, gently helping him to sit up on his knees. He did his best to hide his flinch when I touched one of the wounds on his back. I tasted bile at the back of my throat. "Careful, Love."

Luke rested his forehead against mine, his hooded eyes straining to stay open as if he was afraid I might disappear.

"I'm here, you're safe." I cupped his face, wiping away tears on his blood-smeared face with my thumb as my own began to fall. "I've got you."

And I did. I would always come for him. Luke had saved me in so many ways, now it was my turn to save him.

I brushed my lips against his, the bond between us humming at the feeling of being back in my mate's arms. He reached a shaking hand up to clasp the back of my head, his fingers threading through my hair, and he kissed me deeply, his movements slow and deliberate, as if he wanted to remind himself that this was real. We ignored the chaos outside, the sound of fighting in the distance. For one moment, it was just us and the world faded into the background. He was my home; I was home.

"I'm never leaving you again." He paused, his throat bobbing as his gaze searched mine. "I thought you wouldn't find me in time."

I shook my head, gently nudging the tip of his nose with mine. "I wasn't going to let that happen."

His laugh was a rough bark that quickly descended into a cough. He winced at the movement. "You're starting to sound like me."

A scream of agony echoed from outside, followed by a dull thud. Josh joined us moments later, covered in blood. The way his face crumpled at the sight of Luke made my heart crack.

"He's okay," I said, more to reassure myself than anyone else. "He's going to be okay."

"I'm sorry." Luke wiped his mouth with the back of his hand, which did nothing but smear blood and dirt around. "I'm disgusting."

My brow shot up. "Luke, you could be covered in fish guts, and I still wouldn't care. You're safe. That's all that matters."

Some colour worked its way into his pale cheeks as he glanced over at the vomit-splattered area of the container floor. My heart twisted at the sight of his embarrassment. He had nothing to apologise for.

Craig moved behind us, nudging Ryan's leg with his foot. Then kicking when my ex didn't move in response. "He's out cold."

Blood crusted Ryan's chin, a small amount still draining from a needle wound on his hand. The skin of his right wrist was pink and raised, but nothing compared to the blistering burns all over my mate's forearms.

"What's he doing here?"

Luke took a deep, shaky breath. "He said he was supervising me, but it looked more like he was being punished for something."

"He let us get away after the car crash..." I frowned, watching as Craig pulled up Ryan's sleeve to reveal a fresh needle mark that hadn't healed. Luke and Ryan both stank of nightshade. "Has he turned on Larissa?"

"No. He's delusional. I tried to tell him Larissa was punishing him, but he wasn't listening to me. He knows about the prophecy." Luke's voice was hoarse, but his tone was certain. He linked his fingers with mine, his raw knuckles cracked and bloody. "I tried to explain that Larissa wants Eve dead, that it's part of the prophecy, but he wouldn't listen. He'd follow his father off a cliff. There's no talking him round."

The ground beneath us shook, the metal frame of the container creaking as a loud bang came from outside.

"We need to get out of here before the witch decides to show up." Josh crouched beside Luke and hesitantly rested a gentle hand on his friend's shoulder. "Do you think you can move?"

"There's no need. I have him."

Tom stepped into the container, brushing himself off as if he'd just gone for a run.

A myriad of expressions flitted across Luke's face, his throat bobbing as his father approached us. His shoulders dropped when Alice strode into view, the beaming smile splitting her face matching her father's at the sight of Luke in my arms. Dylan brought up the rear, his T-shirt hanging on by a thread.

Joy, something my heart had been robbed of for weeks, swelled inside me as I sat back to let Alice fling her arms around her brother. He grunted but nuzzled into her hair and squeezed his little sister in an embrace that conveyed more than words ever could. Dylan ruffled Luke's hair gently, all of us exhaling in unison as the weight of the past few weeks fell away. We weren't out of the woods. There was still a prophecy hanging over our heads, but we had won this one.

Tom let Alice have her moment before stepping in. He crouched to pull his son into a hug, eyelids closing over glassy blue eyes.

Alice reached out to take my hand, squeezing tightly as Luke buried his head in his father's chest like a child.

"Let's go home."

# CHAPTER 13

## LUKE

**W**e had a few hours to kill until the next flight home. Our personal assistant at Château Minuit guided us to the gym facilities to clean up and remove the nightshade from my system. Feeling more like myself, I was done showing restraint after watching Eve in a towel. While I was relieved to see my family again, there was only one thing on my mind once we were alone.

The moment the doors of the elevator clicked shut behind Eve, my mouth was on hers. Her lips parted for me, and her breath hitched as I ran my nails down the curve of her back and under the oversized hoodie before leaving the gym. A low growl rumbled in my throat as my fingers squeezed into the bare skin of her ass.

"Naughty." I nipped her lower lip, growling in approval at her lack of underwear.

I'd dreamed about her every single night, of kissing her, touching her. Her kiss was a feverish confirmation that she needed this just as badly, her frame pressing mine against the elevator wall as she gripped my hips.

The cool elevator wall stung the healing wounds on my back, but all I focused on was the feel of her full lips against mine.

"Luke." Her whisper was lost in our kiss. I pulled her tighter against me, letting my hands drift lower. "We can't here."

The elevator pinged.

Adrenaline pulsed through my veins, my tired muscles straining as I hoisted her into my arms. She wrapped her legs around my waist, her squeak and the flush of her cheek only driving me on as I kissed my way down the column of her throat.

"What, Love?" I murmured against her skin. I stepped out of the corridor and walked us towards the penthouse Lawrence had set up for us. "Are you afraid someone will see?"

The hotel corridor was empty save for flames flickering in sconces.

"Your family is in the building," she teased, entwining her fingers behind my neck and letting her head fall back as my lips brushed lower.

"They're on another floor. The place is *very* soundproofed, but if you want me to stop," I murmured, dropping my hand to pinch one of her hardened nipples through the hoodie that I was ready to shred, "just say the word." The moan that slipped from her lips was music to my ears; the way her body arched into my touch only spurred me on. I cupped her breast before tugging the neckline down to graze the tip of my canines over her collarbone. "What was that? Do you want me to stop... or to claim that tight pussy of yours?"

Whatever she saw in my eyes made her thighs tighten around me and a pink hue crept down her neck as she moaned her plea. "Please."

"Please what?" I smirked, biting into her soft skin. Blood rushed to my cock while I carried her to the door and pinned her against it, the wooden frame rattling. I slid my hand down to drag my thumb along the curve of her inner thigh. "Use your words."

Her hips bucked in my grip, heels digging in just below my ass. She glared at me with lust-hooded eyes, pursing her lips.

I dipped my hand between her legs, the drag of my finger down her centre loosening her sinful lips.

"Please, Luke," she panted, her nails biting into the back of my neck as she squirmed. "I need you. I need you now."

She whined when I removed my hand, but the sound was swallowed as I locked my lips with hers. With one arm locked around her, I flung the door open, and we were already on the floor by the time it slammed shut.

The bed beckoned from across the room, but I dropped to my bruised knees, ignoring the bite of pain as I lowered her gently onto the fur rug.

She stared up at me with those bright blue eyes I often lost myself in. Her lips parted; the hoodie hiked up so that the swell of her breasts was visible. My hungry gaze travelled lower, to the sight of her spread legs baring her pussy to me. I couldn't believe such a beautiful creature wanted to call herself mine.

Her smile faltered as she propped herself up on her elbows, tracing her fingers over the angry, raised skin where my heart beat only for her. "Oh God…"

I swallowed, placing my hand on hers. "What have I told you about saying other names in the bedroom?"

Eve wasn't buying my humour, swatting my hand away as she leaned up to press a gentle kiss over my heart. The heart that was hers. "I'm so sorry."

"There's nothing to apologise for. I'm safe now." I cupped the back of her head, pressing my lips to her temple, and then the bridge of her nose above the dusting of freckles I loved so much.

Tears glistened in her eyes as she looked up at me. "She didn't… did she?"

I shook my head, lacing my fingers with hers and pressing her hand above my heart as the bond stirred. "No, she didn't touch me like that. She tortured me and treated me like a dog, but she didn't go there."

Eve nodded, but her eyes narrowed.

"I promise. She's never had these lips." I kissed her gently, slowly exploring her mouth with my tongue. "My heart, my body, it's all yours. I will tell you everything that happened, but right now, I want to—I *need* to—make love to my mate."

She ran her hands over the healing wounds on my chest, leaning up to pepper light kisses over them. She sat up, shifting me onto my back. The path of her mouth changed direction, and she trailed her tongue down the centre of my abs.

"Eve…" I arched an eyebrow, my cock twitching as her fingers gripped the edge of my waistband.

She shushed me and tugged my sweatpants down, her pupils dilating when my hard cock sprung free. She closed her hand around my hard length, her touch sending electricity jolting down my spine. "Let me look after you." Her voice was a seductive purr as that decadent tongue of hers flicked out to catch a drop of pre-cum beading on the tip. "Please."

The fiery sunrise over the sprawling skyline of London was the most incredible backdrop for this beautiful woman on all fours, lowering her head to take my cock in her mouth. She dropped lower, back curving and sending her ass in the air as she wrapped her lips around me.

My balls tightened, and I tangled my hands in her hair. "Oh fuck."

Despite often escaping to my dreams while imprisoned by Larissa, the nightshade kept me too exhausted to ever get off. I wasn't going to last.

Eve hummed her approval, sending vibrations through me that had me struggling not to push her head down. She pulled back just enough to swipe her tongue across the slit at the top of my dick. "Stop holding back," she ordered, smirking before lowering her voice. "Take me, all of me."

With that, she closed her lips around my cock and sucked hard, and my hips lifted to meet her wicked tongue. The deeper she took me, the more she unravelled my remaining resolve. I fisted her hair as I snapped, slamming my hips up until the head of my cock hit the back of her throat.

She gagged, the muscles of her throat tightening around me

in the most addictive way. I relaxed my hand enough for her to pull back if she wanted, but she kept her head down with a possessive growl that made me want to claim her.

I tightened my grip, eyes rolling into the back of my head as I moved her head up and down. The pressure in my balls was building as she deep-throated me, the way her back arched and her eyes watered only spurred me on. I watched in awe, wanting to memorise every inch of her stunning body as she gave herself to me.

Her lust-filled gaze was heavy lidded as I slammed my cock into the back of her throat one more time before pulling out. I didn't give her a chance to recover, flipping us so she was spread out on the carpet beneath me as the head of my cock nudged her slick entrance.

"I love you so fucking much." I swiped my thumb across her lower lip to catch the drool running down her chin, trailing my lips along her jaw. "I've missed every part of you. Your smile. Your laugh. Your body." My voice dropped low as I pressed against her drenched pussy. Weeks of built-up desire and yearning were begging to be unleashed. "Every night, I dreamt of you."

"I love you too."

Eve cupped my jaw and leaned up to press her lips to mine. Her kiss was deep and filled with longing, her tongue stoking the fire burning deep within me. I trailed my hands down her sides before digging my nails into her hips and pressing my cock into her tight pussy. My body caged hers against the plush rug beneath us as I slowly filled her up inch by inch. The sensation of her body stretching for me was something I'd never get tired of. Her head fell back as she gasped and broke our kiss, chest heaving.

I didn't let her catch her breath. The cry of pleasure she released when I drew my hips back and thrust into her called to my wolf side, the bond thrumming within my chest. Her moans of ecstasy echoed mine as we moved together, and I claimed her with deep strokes, a new day dawning behind us.

# CHAPTER 14

## EVE

H ome wasn't just a place; it was our people. That was never clearer than when the terminal doors at Dublin Airport opened to reveal Max standing in arrivals, clutching a sign that said 'Welcome Home'.

My heart was a puddle as his little face lit up at the sight of Luke. Max sped across the floor to greet his brother, almost knocking an old lady over as he weaved through the crowd.

Luke crouched down slowly, but he no longer flinched in pain thanks to Lawrence's staff patching him up and helping drain the nightshade faster. He opened his arms just in time as Max flung himself at his brother.

Max squealed and kicked his feet when Luke lifted him off the ground, then he wrapped his legs around his big brother's middle, clinging like a little koala.

"Hello, buddy," Luke said, nuzzling the top of Max's head.

My ovaries were going to burst. Max being at the airport wasn't part of the plan, but with Darius' security lurking, I could see why Helena caved to his demands. They deserved this moment, all of them.

I hung back as Tom and Alice rushed straight over to Helena, who pulled them both into a tight hug. Josh's family was there too. Beth quickly beckoned Dylan to join them, but he hesitated and glanced back at me.

"You good?"

I nodded, and Luke wrapped an arm around my waist while Max regaled him with a rambling lowdown of events.

"I'm good," I promised, reaching out to give Dylan's hand a squeeze.

He nodded, bounding over to Josh's family with an energy to rival Max. Dylan had confided in me about his mam during one of our late nights in Edinburgh; his mother passed away shortly after he was born, and he lost his father to grief. Tom took him in without question.

"You missed my game," Max huffed, smacking Luke over the head with his little scrapbook. The sign welcoming us home had a small drawing in the corner that could be described as a football goal at a stretch. "I goaled."

"You *scored*," Luke corrected him gently, his laughter a tonic. He released my waist and took the weapon off Max to examine his sign properly. "Well done, dude."

Max turned his attention to me, almost taking my eye out as he leaned over in Luke's arms to plant a wet kiss on my face that landed closer to my eyebrow than my cheek. "Eve! You were gone so long."

"I was." I couldn't stop the smile curving my lips, turning my head to kiss his brow in return. "I promise, we'll never be gone that long again."

Luke and I shared a weighted look. We were still exiled and in danger, but we had no intention of letting Larissa and the Faolchúnna pack win. We couldn't. That was a future that could never come to pass.

Alice skipped over to join us, leaving her parents in their own bubble. The way Tom looked at Helena as she cupped his face, tears glistening in their eyes, was the kind of love they spoke of in fairytales. I wanted to stay in this moment so badly, one where we were all safe and happy.

"There's someone here for you," Alice said, motioning to the crowd waiting behind the arrivals barrier that nearly every Crescent wolf had completely ignored.

All but one.

"What?" I swallowed the lump rising in my throat.

Darren stood back with his hands in his pockets, shifting his weight from side to side. His muscular frame strained at the shoulders where his shirt was too tight. I don't think I'd ever seen Darren in a proper shirt. Paula and his daughters must have stayed at home because he stood alone.

The moment his head lifted and his blue eyes met mine, identical to my father's from the photo, I knew in my bones that it was true. I was his niece.

I'd asked Tom to tell Darren before we landed, but everything was so rushed I wasn't sure if he'd found the time. The alpha was one of his oldest friends, so it made sense for Tom to break the news. That's the lie I told myself, when the truth was I couldn't face the rejection if Darren decided he didn't want to claim me as family.

That fear dissolved as Darren started towards me.

He smiled, not his usual playful grin, but a softer expression filled with genuine warmth—and love.

Luke's lips brushed the shell of my ear as he leaned in and whispered, "Go say hello, Love. He's been waiting a long time to meet you."

I felt Luke nudge me into motion, and there were no jokes or witty remarks when Darren threw his arms around me. He squeezed me tightly, something healing and shattering in my heart all at once.

"I can't believe it's you," he whispered, clutching the back of my head when I began to sob into his chest.

Raw emotion poured out of me as we hugged for the longest time, ignoring the next wave of travellers who rushed past. I could see Luke watching with a smile over my uncle's shoulder; my mate never once taking his eyes off me despite the crowds.

Darren pulled back, holding me at arm's length as he looked me over like a dad would to check that their kid was okay. "I didn't believe Tom when he said it," he said, his voice cracking as his gaze searched my face. "We did everything to save you—to save Shane and Gráinne too. When I got the call..."

I sniffed, rubbing my damp cheek. "It's okay. I'm okay."

"We checked all the hospitals just in case you survived." His shoulders sagged, and he hung his head, guilt flickering across his face. "If I thought for one second that you were out there, I'd never have stopped looking."

"You couldn't have known, but I'm here now," I whispered, pulling him back into a tight hug. Grief twisted like a knife in my gut at the thought of the childhood I could have had, the memories I was robbed of. I'd seen Darren with one of his little girls; he treated Niamh like a princess.

"You're right. I just... I wish things could have been different." His stubble tickled as he nestled his chin on the top of my head, the tension slowly melting from his body. "If you ever get bitten by a vampire and swan off to London again, I'm going to be on the first plane after you."

"I wouldn't expect anything less."

We stood there, grinning with wet cheeks, in the middle of the airport terminal, two souls meeting for the first time all over again.

"Come on." He broke our embrace and took my hand. The others were already heading towards the exit with their bags in tow. "We need to get you home before a different type of welcome party arrives. But first, we have one stop to make on the way."

DARREN DROVE us to a forest halfway between Luke's house and the pack property in Kildare. He sped down a long winding drive lined by dense woodland that led to a large car park, gravel crunching beneath the tyres as he parked up beside a grass verge.

I stepped out of the car, pulling my coat tighter around me as the winter wind billowed, and empty branches swayed on the tall trees that bordered the green space. The scent of pine filled my senses, reminding me of Luke.

"This way," Darren said, starting down a small path that veered off towards a walled area to the side of the car park.

He'd cracked jokes in the car, telling me everything from what his kids—my cousins—had gotten up to lately, to how Tom had officiated his wedding. But now that we had arrived, there was a sombreness to his tone.

A set of black iron gates creaked as he nudged them open, a small patch of paint flaking where an open padlock hung from a chain.

I followed him through, my gaze scanning the ruins attached to the gate. The stone wall looked like it was the remains of the castle boundary, and less than half a building remained, any trace of the roof or parapet long gone. Leafless vines of ivy climbed what was once the interior, moss and dense shrubbery covering the rubble around the base. Nature had claimed the castle ruins a long time ago.

We continued, rounding a corner where the path split in two. A dirt path lined by the tall forest continued straight ahead, following the outside of the castle wall. The other path gave way to gravel and a grassy area cordoned off by a modern cement wall.

My head snapped up at the sound of a familiar giggle, body going rigid when I glimpsed a figure threading through the trees. Long blue hair flowed behind them as they ran deeper into the thicket of trees. My heart thundered. I stepped towards the tree line, splintering a twig under my foot. Birds in the nearest tree scattered in a flurry of movement.

"Eve?"

I looked to where Darren had paused, concern creasing his brow. When I glanced back at the forest, she was gone.

*She's not here.* I told myself, cursing Larissa for reopening that scar.

"Everything okay?" Darren wore the same expression Luke did when he was afraid I was about to snap under the weight of everything.

"Coming." I shook my head and broke into a jog to catch up with him. "Sorry, I thought I saw something."

"There are plenty of runners and dog walkers around this part of the trails."

After rolling my shoulders to shake off the feeling of being watched, I noticed a turret of an old, gothic-style church peeked over a thick hedge. Unlike the castle that had fallen to the elements, the church was well kept. There was a lawn at the front with benches and flower beds empty save for some winter-hardened shrubs. Off to the side, gravestones peeked from the unruly grass. A lump formed in my throat.

*Why are we here?*

Darren noticed I'd stopped again and reached for my hand. His palm was clammy against mine. "Trust me."

I swallowed hard but followed as he pushed through the gate, and we set off down the side of the church. There was a notice on the chapel door detailing the time of the next sermon, and golden plaques with dedications were nailed to the benches we walked past. It was so quiet, the only noises that of the forest. Branches rustled in the wind, birds called to one another, small mammals scurried in the dense undergrowth among the ruins, and in the distance, a small stream gurgled. It was full of life, yet so peaceful.

The graveyard was covered in tall grass that came to above my knees in parts, the stone exterior of an old structure overgrown with weeds. There were no neat rows, only worn paths where the grass had been trampled. A mixture of gravestones and raised stone slabs in varying stages of erosion were dotted throughout.

I could have sworn I caught a shadow disappearing between two ivy-covered trees, their branches entwining to form a natural arch draped in vines.

My gaze snagged on a moss-mottled gravestone. Dirt caked under my fingernails as I scraped it clean. 'April 13th, 1806'. Tension gripped my shoulders, my stomach doing a little flip at the sight of Kate's birthday. Not the right year, but I felt like I was seeing little signs of her everywhere.

Darren nodded, his steps careful, making sure not to step on any broken headstones or ones that had almost become part of the earth again. "This place is old. When the Crescent pack formed and we made our home in Kildare, we didn't have anywhere to bury our dead. There is a small chapel near the pack house now, but not back then."

My throat squeezed, doing a poor job at letting oxygen into my lungs. "Back then?"

"Back when your parents passed away." Darren steered me towards a set of graves at the base of the graveyard, the stones here far less weathered. "I thought about burying them on pack lands, but it felt wrong because Shane had never joined. They left before the packs split, and although I know he would have followed Tom, it's not a choice that should ever be made for a wolf."

I nodded, my mouth drying up when he stopped by a grave with granite headstones and a bunch of fresh carnations at the base, as if someone had visited recently.

"Burying my brother with our parents wasn't an option after leaving the Faolchúnna pack, so I brought them here." Darren's voice cracked as he kneeled to right the flowers that must have blown over in the wind. The pink carnations stood out against the scattering of snowdrops growing up around the bottom of the gravestone. "I used to walk around the lake here if I needed a break back when we were still setting things up. I actually met Paula here, of all places. She was out jogging, and I nearly sent her flying because I was off in my own world." His laugh was brittle, and he plucked a single carnation from the bouquet and held it out to me, his hand shaking. "So, I took them here—somewhere that brought me peace and happiness—in the hope that it would bring them some too."

I accepted the flower, meeting his gaze with gratitude and damp cheeks. Heart hammering, I took one final step to face the gravestone. The white granite glistened in the winter sunshine, displaying the names engraved along with the dates of their passing in beautiful calligraphy.

*Shane Donohoe.*

*A loving husband, son, and brother.*

*Gráinne Donohoe.*

*A loving wife, daughter, and best friend.*

There was a finality about seeing their names on the grave, like it finally laid to rest the many unanswered questions that had haunted my nights. I'd always wondered why no family ever came for me, why I was left to navigate life alone. But I'd found my place in the world. Discovering my fated home included my true family all along was a bonus.

Beneath their names was another inscription:

*And their beloved daughter Eve.*

*May they run free for eternity and the full moon guide them always.*

"They got married." I crouched down beside Darren, tracing my fingers over their engraved names. The corners of my lips lifted despite the tears streaming down my cheeks. "In Scotland?"

"Yep, they eloped in the Scottish Highlands before you were born. I gave him hell for eloping. He promised he'd come back here with you when it was safe, and we could celebrate then." Sadness stirred in his eyes as he shrugged his coat off, laying it out at the bottom of the grave. His knees clicked as he sat and motioned for me to join him. "I still have photos he sent back at the pack house. We can go through them after the full moon if you'd like?"

I spun the stem of the carnation between my finger and thumb, blowing a kiss onto its petals before placing it down among the snowdrops. "I'd really like that."

Darren's smile brightened when I joined him. He looped his arm around my shoulders, pulling me into his side. "Your parents were mad about each other. I was so scared when Shane told me your mam was pregnant, but they were so damn happy there was no talking sense into them."

"Love makes people do crazy things," I murmured, letting my head fall to rest on his arm.

He chuckled, giving my shoulder a squeeze. "It sure does, but it also gives life to some of the best surprises. Like you."

My cheeks flushed, emotion robbing my voice.

"They loved you, Eve. So fucking much. I'm so grateful that Luke brought you back into our lives."

"Me too."

A tidal wave of emotions washed over me—everything from sorrow that I'd never know my parents to joy at getting to know my uncle and his family better. The future was bright, if I squinted to drown out the darkness threatening us.

"You've grown into a fine young woman who leads with her heart. Loyal, brave, and kind." Darren pressed a gentle kiss to the top of my head. "They would have been so proud of you."

I promised myself I would fight tooth and nail to stop this prophecy from coming true. Not just for my mate, but I had a family to make new memories with. My parents had fled their pack and died to keep me safe. I couldn't let that be for nothing.

A silent tear slid down my cheek. He noticed, slipping into dad-mode as he pressed a tissue from his pocket into my hand and pulled me closer. I soaked his shirt again as I cried, but he didn't bat an eye, gently stroking my back as he told me stories about my mam and dad. They were gone, but a piece of them lived on through us.

We sat for a long time in comfortable silence as the birds chirped around us, mourning the people we had lost and the time that was stolen from us.

# CHAPTER 15

## LUKE

"I t's good to see you back, trouble."

A single fang peeked out as Jonas grinned, leaping over the counter of the Dark Night bar in one smooth movement. His image blurred as he shot across the room and appeared in front of us. Eve squealed as he picked her up in a hug, spinning her around at vamp superspeed.

Eve didn't appreciate my laughter when he set her down. She whirled on me, her face a pale shade of green. "Where's the alphahole attitude when I need it?" She swayed as she prodded my chest with a sharp nail. "Hmm?"

I stuffed my hands in my pockets to hide my clenched fists, shrugging with a smirk. "Jonas is a friend. I trust him."

My long-time friend looked between us, gold swirling in the molten depths of his eyes as they narrowed. "Something is different."

I caught Eve's finger before she could poke me again, pulling her into me. Her dramatic eye roll as I stole a quick kiss stirred a desire in me to make her look to the heavens for an entirely different reason. I nipped her lower lip, and the way her cheeks flushed the most delicious shade of pink told me she was thinking

Jonas cleared his throat.

Noise filtering from the kitchen caught our attention, and we turned to see Darius enter the room with a box of liquor, double doors swinging shut behind him. His usual stoic expression softened at the sight of us, a wide grin spreading across his face. "Oh. Congratulations, guys."

"Congratulations? On what?" Jonas' brow practically arched into his perfect hairline as the realisation hit, his eyes widening comically. "Oh. *Oh.*"

"What?" Eve turned to Jonas, and we stepped apart as the rest of the gang filtered into the Dark Night.

"They're mates!" Dylan skipped inside, his voice a pitchy melody while he danced around us like some sort of demented jester. "Bound by the fates, destined for one another. It's truueee lurrrve, baby."

I clipped Dylan around the ear, failing to fight back my smile. The sun had only set, darkness blanketing the city outside the large bay window of the nightclub. The paranormal haunt hadn't switched to night mode yet, the upper floor still smelling of coffee beans as vampires sipped their first caffeine shot of the morning. Dylan, however, was apparently off to an early start.

"He hit one of the tequila bottles we got at the duty-free," Alice explained, perching on a leather stool beside the bar. "And by hit, I mean he downed it on his own because none of us wanted to pre-drink."

Jonas shook his head. "You guys have a tab here. Why's he in such a rush to get the party started?"

"We're here to get Darius to check the dagger, not to drink." I sighed, snatching a glass out of the way as Dylan wobbled onto a stool and flopped his elbows onto the bar.

"He's 'celebrating' us getting the two lovebirds back on Irish soil," Josh quipped, choosing the seat farthest away from Dylan before unpacking his laptop.

"Nope, he's upset because his ex was here when he dropped by earlier." Craig wandered behind the bar to fill up a glass of water, sliding it across the counter towards Dylan. "She has a new boyfriend."

"Rub it in, why don't you?" He scowled, nursing the water like it was a glass of whiskey.

Ah, the infamous vampire that had broken our poor golden retriever's heart.

"It's for the best. Dating a vamp is all fun and games until someone gets bitten." I clapped him on the shoulder, nodding for Jonas to keep the water coming. "It sucks though, mate."

A small titter of laughter came from Alice's direction.

"Mates." Dylan's sigh was wistful as he stared into the bottom of his water glass as if he might read it like tea leaves. "That sounds nice."

Josh snickered at my unintentional pun, but it was Eve who climbed onto the barstool beside Dylan. She looped her arm around him, struggling to reach across the span of his muscular shoulders. "You'll find the right person someday."

He nodded solemnly, downing another gulp of water. I noticed the glass fizzing, and my worry dissipated slightly. Craig must have popped something in there to speed him along on the train to sobering up. The vamp learned quickly.

I knew it broke Eve to know her friend was a vampire, but it did make it far easier to have him be a part of her life. Being born into the world was different to being turned; some people never fully adjusted. But Craig had taken to his new life with ease, and sometimes I found myself wondering if some humans were destined to become vampires.

"Congrats." Jonas glided past, squeezing my arm with a warm smile, motioning for a young witch busing tables to cast a privacy spell. "I couldn't be happier for you," he said, planting a kiss on Eve's cheek. "Both of you."

"Thanks." I rubbed the back of my neck, feeling the bond kick in a little as Dylan rested his head atop Eve's. I stepped behind her, relishing the way she instinctively leaned back against me as I slid my arms around her waist. "What have we missed since we left?"

"Shouldn't we be asking you that?" Darius cocked his head, glasses clinking against the shelf as he set about preparing everyone their usual drink. "According to Lawrence, you guys left quite a mark on London."

I rolled my eyes. "If Lawrence told you everything, then there's nothing for us to tell."

"We didn't do anything to the hotel." Eve shrugged, nestling back against me. "And the crane wasn't our fault. One of their own took it down."

"Grave robbing was Larissa," Dylan piped up, his cheeks looking far less flushed.

"Same with the car crash." The corners of my lips twitched as everyone named off the many crazy things that had happened since we were exiled. Yet, here we were. We gave him the expanded version, explaining how they'd held my uncle captive, Edmonstone's involvement, rescuing Gabi, and then the most important piece. The prophecy.

Jonas' golden eyes twinkled as he slid me a glass of liquid to match. "So much for keeping a low profile."

"Not my forte." I took a long sip, relishing the burn in my throat. "Are you sure we're safe here?" I asked, tension drawing my shoulder blades together as two centaurs crested the stairs, their hooves clipping the ground. "We're still exiled, technically. I presume the Royals have been notified of what went on in London, and I imagine Edmonstone blamed us for that too."

"The Dark Night is my property, my land, and my territory." Darius's eyes blazed, darkening to a russet amber. The muscles of his biceps flexing beneath his flawlessly tailored suit as he motioned at the thin layer of magic cloaking us. While he lacked magic, he was plentiful in his connections. "So, they can fuck off."

Alice giggled, sharing a look with Alec. The young vampire

lurked in the background, switching the pastry counter to a fancy display of different Fae spirits. With his jet-black hair and pale skin, he looked like every boy band poster she used to have pinned to her wall. The blush tinging her pale cheeks made me wonder if my sister had a crush. I made a mental note to 'talk' to him later.

"So, Eve is the key to the prophecy?" Jonas handed his partner a glass of blood, with something added so the viscous liquid shimmered under the light cast by the chandelier hanging above us. "A direct descendent of Cadhla?"

Eve nodded, and my grip on her waist tightened as she twisted in my arms and lifted her hair to show them the crescent-shaped scar on her upper back.

"*C'est dur à croire.*" Darius reached out as if to touch it but immediately retracted his hand with a grin when he caught my eye. "Even at my age, the story of our creation always felt like a legend. Mythical. I never once thought it could be broken. Many have tried and failed over the years to find a cure."

Craig drummed his fingers against the bar, staring out the window behind us at the setting sun. Our overcast weather and long nights most of the year were part of the reason Darius and Jonas moved to Ireland—that and the French Revolution.

"Something happened when I was with Larissa," I said, pausing as every head turned in my direction. My dad's words stuck in my head. While I'd spoken to Eve about my time with Larissa, delving into it with the others opened me up to a vulnerability that made me squirm. Eve rested her hand over mine on her waist and squeezed. "She wasn't always herself."

I waited for someone to crack a joke, for the "Is she ever?" but it never came. Even Dylan, whose eyes seemed brighter, watched me patiently.

"I mean, she was always a little bit psychotic and talked a lot of nonsense," I continued, interlinking my fingers with Eve's to keep myself grounded. "But one night, her powers changed. The room was filled with shadows—magic I don't think she normally possesses, like those undead hounds—but these flooded the cell, and the tendrils moved like they were under her command. She was able to touch the magic bonding us somehow. That's when I knew it wasn't Larissa anymore."

Eve's grip on my hand tightened, her voice barely a whisper. "That night before we rescued you. I felt it."

"She started talking some really weird shit. When she recited the prophecy, the magic that she used was something ancient—like what we felt in the library. She was talking about love, rambling on and on about betrayal, until I realised who she was. I don't know how or what kind of magic Larissa is playing with, but she was possessed by Béibhinn."

"Is that even possible?" Alice asked as gasps echoed throughout our group, covering her chest with her hand.

"I don't know, but it didn't seem like it was the first time it had happened to her."

Darius knocked back a long swig of his drink, his lips stained ruby when he set the glass down. "With a witch that powerful? It's possible. The dagger holds the magic of both sisters, two incredibly powerful witches. If Larissa fulfils the prophecy to harness its powers, it will grant her the closest thing to immortality, along with access to all the elements."

I can understand wanting to claim the power imbued in the curse by bringing about the prophecy, but I don't know what the spirit of Béibhinn has to gain."

One signal from Darius and the entire upper floor of the Dark Night emptied. Not a single person dared argue with him or resist, though some vampires did grumble on their way downstairs.

Darius waited until the area was empty before spreading his hands on the bar. His collection of gold, antique rings on his fingers glinted under the candlelight cast by the chandelier above us. "Show me the dagger."

Alice slid the navy box from her bag, her mouth downturned as she lifted the dagger from the amethyst lining and laid it down on the bar.

"Interesting," Darius murmured, stroking his long fingers across the intricate carvings on the dagger's bone hilt. He plucked it off the countertop, and ran the blade along his finger so lightly it didn't so much as dent his skin. "It's imbued with a very old magic. You mentioned in a text that it was labelled as being Béibhinn's blade?"

"Yes, but it's not silver." Josh pulled up a tonne of scanned book pages from the research we'd slaved over. "There were conflicting descriptions of the blade's appearance, but the blade was always silver. That's why werewolves are susceptible to it."

Darius motioned for Eve to hold out her hand. His eyes met mine with a knowing smile when I clamped my hand over hers and held out my own instead.

He pricked the top of my finger with the blade, ruby bleeding into his swirling eyes as a single droplet formed. I didn't so much as flinch, and the moment he withdrew the dagger, the wound healed.

"I've been around enough silver the past few weeks to know what the burn feels like," I said. Eve stiffened, and I gave her a reassuring squeeze. "The dagger is fake."

"Why would the dragon shifter collect a fake? Surely he would have known?" Alice frowned, her eyes narrowing towards the blade as Darius placed it back into its box.

"The dagger is spelled to feel like an ancient magical artefact. Perhaps it even is one, just not the one you seek." Darius sighed, his brow creasing.

"So, we're back to square one."

"Not square one," Eve corrected me, her head falling back against my chest. "We got you back."

"I wasn't supposed to be gone in the first place." I stroked her side with my thumb as I rested both hands on her hips. Ever since I'd returned home, I needed to have one hand on her at all times.

At first, I thought it was the bond. But as I watched her sleep one night, I realised it was fear.

"Do you have any of the research with you?" Darius placed the lid on the dagger's box and handed it back over to my sister.

Josh opened his laptop, and his fingers flew across the keys. "We only have a handful of photos from the books Eve and Luke found in Cambridge, and a bunch of pages we scanned from other old texts and grimoires we could get our hands on."

Darius pressed a gentle kiss to Jonas' cheek before joining Josh's side. The two began scrolling through pages of research while the rest of us discussed the prophecy.

Josh smashed the space bar on his laptop, muttering a curse.

"They've locked me out of the systems the flash drive gave me access to. Except for mobile phone logs, they're still tapped." Josh hammered his fist against the bar, and Jonas snapped up his glass, already pouring another. "I pulled as many files as I could yesterday. But all we know is that they've moved most of the people held captive to Lars' property. Except that's like Fort Knox; we can't just swan in there."

"We have a contact in his coven who had confirmed that Larissa is staying there." Jonas glanced around to make sure the silencing spell was still in place, despite the DJ warming up the sound system downstairs. "Lars rarely leaves his territory, but he was seen visiting the Faolchúnna pack the day after yous landed."

"That's not a coincidence," Dylan muttered, seeming much more like himself.

"No, it's not. He was planning to cancel his annual gala to celebrate Imbolc in favour of scheduling an emergency meeting of benefactors to put a contingency plan in place."

Alice scowled. "Why would he celebrate Imbolc? It's literally a celebration of life."

"From what I've heard, he twisted it to mean something else for his coven. It's just another name for a fucked up sacrificial ritual," Craig explained, his upper lip curling in disgust.

"Any captives remaining in Ireland are apparently under his

care." Jonas raised his voice as the music in the club beneath us kicked off for the evening. "What happened in London did not go unnoticed. The Royals will definitely send someone to look into this, so he can't cancel the ball without raising suspicions."

"Stop," Darius ordered, his finger hovering so close to the screen I saw Josh's eye twitch. "Go back for a second."

"This?" Josh clicked a few keys, his eyebrow arching.

"I've seen that dagger before." Darius nudged a reluctant Josh's hand out of the way, pinching his fingers to zoom on the trackpad before turning the screen to face the rest of us. "I think this is it."

The image was a screenshot of a faded drawing from one of the books Jeremy had sent us from his research on the prophecy. It was a dagger similar to the one they had stolen from the dragon, but the blade was longer, with a pattern of Celtic knots carved into the silver. The handle was labelled as bone, but this one was covered in runes and carved to form a trinity knot at the pommel.

"Where have you seen it?" Jonas leaned across the bar to get a better look at the screen. His eyes widened when Josh enlarged another drawing of the dagger, this one in faded colour. "Lars. That night we rescued Craig, I saw him pulling the dagger from a vampire's chest."

Darius nodded. "He's not a dragon hoarder, but he has quite the collection of riches—and collateral. I'm not sure how he got his hands on it if it was supposed to be protected by the werewolf packs. If Larissa was grilling Luke about the dagger's location, Lars either doesn't know the importance of the dagger, or he's hiding it from her as leverage."

"I hope it's not the latter"

"Even if it is, it's only a matter of time before she figures it out. With Béibhinn possessing her, she might be able to lead Larissa straight to it."

"Mary was headed back to Cambridge anyway. If she could check the text containing the prophecy for any trace of the dagger… Alice suggested, slipping off her seat to go take a closer look at the laptop and snap a picture to send on. "We need to know for sure."

"If it is, how the hell do we get into Lars' place without losing half of us to vampire venom?"

"Lucky for you, Lars must invite us to any official events out of respect for other covens." Jonas grinned as Darius rejoined his side. "We normally turn down the invite unless we have a tip to rescue one of the young vampires from his coven, but we can make an exception. If you can get yourselves there, we can get you in."

I didn't like the idea of returning to the disgusting vampire's sordid lair, but I'd do it if it meant finding the weapon Larissa planned to kill my mate with.

Eve took a deep breath, her shoulders tensing. "Is there any way to talk to spirits on the other side if you're not a necromancer?"

"A medium could. Why?"

"Kate led me to the graveyard in Edinburgh that night. Maybe she knows something."

Something in her voice told me she was hiding something.

"Eve." I dropped my voice and threaded my fingers through her hair, tilting her head up to look at me. "Have you seen Kate since?"

Her throat bobbed, cheeks colouring. "I'm not sure. I think I might have seen her at the graveyard with Darren, though she's not buried in either of those places."

"No, but maybe she's tethered to you," Josh said, twirling his empty glass. "I've heard of it happening before to a witch I had a thing with. Her brother haunted her for a while. It was quite the mood killer."

"Eve has a witch bloodline," Jonas added while readying a much needed second round of drinks as the bass beat kicked in downstairs with the DJ's practice set.

"I can see if she has a contact." Josh pulled his phone out, his brow creased.

"No need." Darius snatched something sparkly off the top shelf, setting it down on the bar with a sigh. "I know the best one in town."

I wasn't sure I wanted to see our future, but I guess we were going to see a psychic.

# CHAPTER 16

## EVE

I don't know what I was expecting when Darius gave us his contact, but meeting at a barrister's office wasn't one of them. She was practising out of an old building in the city centre, large sash windows giving us the perfect view of the canal as we waited. The human receptionist that welcomed us inside tapped away at her keyboard.

"Are we sure this is the right place?" I asked, eyeing the plush cream carpet that was miraculously stainless—the only hint of magic at play.

The door across from us creaked open, a sky-high stiletto stepping into view. I looked up, my mouth dropping open as a stunning woman in a hot pink suit stepped out of the room, shiny brown curls tumbling down to her waist while shorter layers framed her face. I stood with Luke, captivated by the depth of her bright blue eyes, accentuated by her bronze eyeshadow. She looked like a supermodel ready to take on a catwalk, not a boring court. All she was missing was a wind machine.

"You're in the right place." Her lips pulled back to reveal a dazzling smile as she held out her hand to me first. "I'm Leanne."

"I'm Eve." I shook her hand, tilting my head to examine the

nail art on her pink nails. Delicately painted runes shimmered in the light. "Nice to meet you."

Luke arched an eyebrow at her firm handshake, nodding in respect. "Luke Whelan."

"It's a pleasure. I called Darius the moment his name popped into my head."

"You knew we were coming?" I asked, following as she ushered us inside her office.

"Only once you realised you needed me." Her smile brightened, and her long curls bounced with every click of her stilettos. "Sit, we have much to talk about."

Her office was large by the city's standards, the furniture a mix of grey velvets and rich wood. The outer wall had either been removed or spelled to give her an unobstructed view of the city. Given it was an exterior wall and the telltale tingle of magic, it must have been the latter.

"What were you expecting, a crone?" She looked between us, her lips twitching. Her appearance was bubbly, but her tone brooked no argument. "I'm not a witch. I'm a psychic, so something has to pay the bills. Sorry to disappoint."

"No, that's not it at all. The last psychic we met was... Well, she was creepy as hell," I said, the image of the old woman in London resurfacing as I rushed to apologise. "I'm sorry if we offended you, I really wasn't sure what to expect. She was an old lady with white eyes, and she felt different. Old. Like her magic itself was old?"

Leanne's magical signature wasn't as strong as a witch's. Besides the faint hint of lilac, I could barely get a read on her at all.

She canted her head to one side, gaze fixing on something beyond me. "Sometimes the deities get involved. Interesting. I like the hair."

"The... what?" I sank into one of the soft, velvet cushioned seats in front of her desk, my eyes widening as the small pieces of dirt on the carpet from my boots disappeared.

"Gods and goddesses." She shrugged, and I found myself wondering if I'd ever feel like I'd found a foothold in the paranormal world for longer than a week.

"We didn't mean to cause offence," Luke said, taking the seat next to me.

"It's not your fault," she exhaled, glaring at her computer monitor as a notification pinged. "I spent most of the morning in court with an insufferable ass of a werewolf, so I'm a tad prickly."

"Wait." I sniffed, catching the barest hint of a scent that made bats flutter in my stomach. "Ryan?"

"Let me see," she murmured, tapping her lower lip with the top of her pen as she scrolled through something. "Ah, yes. Ryan McKenna. Do you know him?" Before I could answer, she glanced over my shoulder and burst out laughing, her lips curving into a perfect smirk. "I get it now. Don't worry, he lost the case. He still had a black eye that seemed sluggish to heal. Is that anything to do with you?"

Luke scratched the back of his head, doing a pitiful job at hiding his own smirk. "Maybe."

Looking around at the plethora of awards and achievements hung on her walls when she couldn't be older than in her mid-thirties, I'd no doubt she wiped the floor with him. She didn't look like the type of woman to tolerate bullshit, in or out of the courts.

"Wait, are you talking to someone?"

"Yes, isn't Kate the reason you're here?"

I turned my head so fast a muscle in the back of my neck spasmed, but the space behind me was empty. I thought I would feel her.

"Kate?" My voice wavered, and I swallowed the lump rising in my throat.

"Yes, she's here. Just not as corporeal as in Edinburgh. Not in the same way Larissa—is that right, yes?" She paused, staring past me once more before nodding. "Not the same way necromancers can. I'm a clairvoyant medium; I can communicate with the dead if they are receptive and still on this side of the veil." Her piercing blue eyes landed on Luke, her expression growing sombre. "And I can see the future."

Anxiety knotted in my chest.

"Can she hear us? Why is she still here?" Luke shuffled his chair closer, resting his hand on my thigh.

"That magic she was brought back with is not something I've ever come across in my work," Leanne said, her brows drawing together. "It's an old magic, a method of necromancy that was banned. Kate's soul was placed in a body it didn't belong to and glamoured to appear as she once was. It was temporary. The body chosen deteriorated, and now her soul is left wandering the planes of our world. So, it tethered itself to the nearest familiar thing."

Luke squeezed my leg. His thumb brushed back and forth, concern creasing his forehead as he watched me. "Someone she loved."

I thought back to the amount of magic Larissa must have unleashed that night in the graveyard. That's when her spell on Kate must have broken.

"Kate says she couldn't fight Larissa's command. It's important to her that you know she would never do anything to hurt you."

"I know," I whispered, struggling to keep the tears building in my eyes at bay. "Does she blame me for her death?"

Luke's hand stilled.

"No." Leanne's voice was certain, her expression softening as she paused. "Kate loved you like a sister. She says you're not to blame for what others do, especially when it's an act of revenge for you simply surviving."

I nodded mutely, chewing my lower lip and attempting to keep my shit together. I kept searching for her, trying to feel her, desperately wishing I could just hug my best friend one last time.

"Is there anything we can do to help Kate pass over to the

other side?" Luke looked ready to snatch one of the tissues off the desk at any moment.

"No, she's worried about Eve. She won't cross until the danger has passed and she knows everyone she cares about is safe." Leanne shook her head, her lips quirking. "And that includes you too, Luke. She said to pass on her congratulations over the mate bond. She's glad Eve found her person, someone who loves her as much as she deserves."

I didn't doubt her psychic abilities, but hearing that was a confirmation I never expected. And closure that I never thought I'd receive.

"Thank you," I murmured, taking Luke's hand in mine as I searched the room for my friend. "Can you tell her that I miss her? I love and miss her so damn much."

"Kate knows, and she loves you too. She can hear you whenever you're in places where the veil is lower, for example at burial grounds. She's been watching you and Craig. She wants him to get his happily ever after too but said he needs to switch up the hair colour. Blue washes him out." Leanne laughed, spinning her pen between her fingers as if it was just a normal four-way conversation. "Is Kate the only reason for your visit, or was there something else?"

I looked at Luke, uncertain. My main concern had been finding out if Kate was still here and how to help her find peace.

"The witch Kate mentioned, she's coming after Eve to break a spell." Luke chose his words carefully. She might be Darius' contact, but we couldn't be sure who to trust. "The seer who spoke to Eve before said she was marked, as if her future was predetermined. Can you see if there's a way to stop it?"

Leanne shot him a knowing look, as if Kate and her psychic abilities were filling in some gaps. "I can try, but if she truly is marked, then her future may not be visible to me." She placed her pen down and leaned over her desk, holding her hand out with the palm facing up. "Give me your hand."

I wasn't sure if I wanted to know that future. What if she said

I was destined to die? My mortality was something I hadn't come to terms with yet.

I scooted forwards, dragging the legs of my chair along the carpet, and placed my hand in hers. "It's okay if you can't."

The light outside the window seemed to dim while she unfurled my fingers. Energy jolted from her fingertips as she traced the lines of my palm, much like the old crone had. I studied her face, trying to catch the slightest hint of an answer.

"Nope, she's shrouded." Leanne released my hand and sat back, her nose scrunching. "I'm sorry, I wish I could tell you more. Kate mentioned a prophecy. If that's the case, her future isn't written in stone."

"So we have a chance?" Luke asked, his expression brightening.

"The threads of fate are always changing. Even when I see a future, it's never completely guaranteed." She stared out the window. "You can take the call outside if you like."

Luke's puzzled expression turned to surprise when his phone vibrated and The Imperial March blared—his special ringtone for his dad.

"Sure, sorry about this." He gave my leg a pat before stepping outside, the door clicking closed behind him.

When I turned back to Leanne, she rubbed a perfectly shaped brow with a sigh, concern etched into her features.

"I'm not sure how to tell you this," she admitted, clasping her hands and placing them on the desk.

"You saw something about me, didn't you?"

"Not you, your mate."

My stomach dipped, the familiar sense of dread stirring there. Luke's voice drifted from outside, but I couldn't make out his words. "What did you see?"

"There is death surrounding you—both of you. I can only see glimpses through Luke's side because of his link to you. Death doesn't always mean literal death; it can be a rebirth, the end of an era," she rushed to explain, though her sombre expression did nothing to ease my worries. "A rooftop, a betrayal, and death. I know, very Shakespeare, but it's all I got before your bond kicked in and blocked the message."

My mind was spinning, anxiety spiralling as I tried to put together a puzzle without all the pieces.

Leanne reached across the desk to take my hand, a surge of magic passing between us. Her eyes glazed over, the blue of her irises growing hazy as her voice deepened. I tried to snatch my hand back, but her grip tightened like a vice. "Time is running out, Eve. Trust your instincts and always remember who you are. Hold on to the bond you share with your mate and your pack. That's the key." She released my hand, shaking her head as if she was snapping out of a daydream. "Sorry, I didn't mean to let whatever that was through. I try to avoid channelling, but sometimes the spirits are insistent."

Luke popped his head around the door, arching an eyebrow as I snatched my hand back. "Mary confirmed it's the dagger. She's going to come back after the full moon."

That gave us five days. Five days until we had to face another threat. The last thing I wanted to hear after being told I had death following me around.

I tried to convince myself that Leanne was sensing the prophecy. But the way her gaze lingered on Luke made fear lick down my spine. I'd come so close to losing him, I wasn't doing that again. I couldn't.

Luke waited by the door as I got to my feet. This time, when Leanne offered her hand, her eyes were back to their bright blue. "I'm sorry about that. Please remember that your fate isn't sealed. She wants you to fight until the very end."

Something told me she wasn't talking about Kate.

# CHAPTER 17

### LUKE

I raced down the stairs, narrowly avoiding a slip when my foot snagged on one of Max's many toy cars on the last step. The Kildare pack house was huge, and yet he still managed to make a mess.

"Max, you almost lost Bertie." I shook my head, something that would have once set off my temper now making me smile instead.

Yes, stepping on my little brother's toys was annoying. But the hurt lasted for a second, and there was a time when I wondered if I'd ever see him again. It was a small price to pay to see his dimpled cheeks as he sprinted past holding a book that looked suspiciously like the one Niamh, who currently chased him, was reading that morning.

"I saw that." I chuckled, rushing to shove on my trainers as Max's high-pitched giggle echoed down the hall.

Eve had sent me for a nap while she went for a walk with Alice, but I couldn't sit still with my excitement. Tonight was the first run of the full moon cycle; the night we would complete the bond that tied us as mates for life. Did I like that every damn pack member would know we fucked tonight? No, it made the protective nature of my wolf side rage. But we decided together that we didn't want to deprive the pack a night of the full moon just because we needed to complete the bond. Plus, with everyone around, we were safer.

"Luke, can you come here for a minute?" My dad's voice drifted through the sliding doors that led outside.

I had wanted to set up a surprise for Eve later, but there was an alpha-edge to his voice, along with over two decades of experience, that told me I wouldn't win that argument.

The sun was beginning to lower in the distance as I stepped out into the garden. Dad sat alone on one of the large wooden logs around the unlit fire, eyes focused on the forest and expression pensive.

I frowned. Worry was something my dad rarely let show, no matter how bad things got. The tension rolling off his body set me on edge.

"Everything okay?" I shoved my hands in the pocket of my hoodie and walked over, anxiety settling between my shoulders.

Ever since we set foot back in Ireland, I was waiting for something to happen. We were still exiled. Ryan's pack and Lars were on the move. We'd exposed their plans, and it was only a matter of time before they came for revenge, or Larissa sought Eve out.

"As okay as it could be." His smile didn't reach his eyes. "We haven't had a chance to talk much since you got back."

I stopped beside him where the grass gave way to dirt and ashes, scuffing a rock with the toe of my trainer. "We've talked loads?"

"I mean properly, Luke." Tom shook his head and patted the spot beside him on the couch, his sigh heavy when I didn't take the offer. "We've spoken about the Faolchúnna pack and the prophecy. We've made plans, and you talk about Eve freely, but we haven't spoken about your future," he paused, finally drawing his attention away from the trees to fix me with the same fatherly look that made me feel like he could see through any mask I tried to wear, "or the past."

"We can't complete the mating bond until the full moon." I squirmed under his gaze, trying to divert where the conversation was headed. "The past is in the past. We need to focus on the future and taking down Larissa."

"Only a fool ignores the past, for it shapes our future." The muscle in his jaw ticked, and his lips pursed into a thin line. "I saw you, Luke. We all did. The welts on your back, the cuts and bruises, the pain in your eyes. You can't go back to normal and pretend that it didn't happen."

"I'm fine now."

"Fine is a fallacy. You were kidnapped and tortured; that leaves a mark. One that not even werewolf healing can erase." His blue eyes were paler than I remembered, and new wrinkles had etched their mark onto his face. "You were the one who advocated for Alice to go to therapy. What makes your experience any different?"

"I chose to go. I knew what I was agreeing to when I asked Larissa to take me over Eve."

"Knowing what you're willing to sacrifice for your mate and living the aftermath are two different things."

I shook my head, memories of Larissa ripping my chest open with her magic flashing through my mind. "I'd do it again."

"I know. I'd do the same for my family," he said, tilting his head to one side. "There's no shame in acknowledging it. You know that, right?"

"Acknowledging what?"

"Hurting. Showing pain. Admitting that a traumatic event left a scar." He ran a hand through his hair before curling forwards, resting elbows on knees. The sadness seeping into his words caught me off guard. "Being an alpha is an amazing privilege, but it's a heavy cross to bear."

*Oh, here we go.* I bristled, ready for him to tell me that my escape to London and sacrificing myself was more proof that I wasn't good enough to be alpha. That I needed to grow up.

"To lead the pack, you must embrace your whole self. The

good and the bad, the past and the future. You can't lead with your truth if you lie to yourself. During my time as alpha, I've made many mistakes. Those regrets stay with me, but I don't hide from them. I speak to my wife, my friends. I confide in those around me to share the load." His eyes shone with concern, and I realised the tension in his body wasn't worry for our pack or our impending plans to infiltrate the ancient vampire's coven. He was worried about me. "You've come so far. Your strength and bravery were never in question, but you learned to open up. That is the key to finding the balance between being a strong alpha and a fair one."

I sat on the log beside him, swallowing hard as more memories surfaced. My blood. The stench of her suffocating magic. The pain.

"She hurt you. There is no shame in letting others see your pain for them to help you heal from it." He reached out to pat my leg, and the setting sun highlighted the dark circles under his eyes.

*Looks like I'm not the only one who isn't sleeping.*

I was almost fully healed from Larissa's torture, but replenishing my magic required sleep—something that didn't come easily. My dreams were plagued with nightmares of losing Eve at the witch's hands.

"I'm not saying this to pressure you. Take your time, but know that Eve and your friends will always be there to listen when you need it."

"And you?" The corners of my lips lifted slightly.

"Please try to get some rest," he said, glancing over his shoulder as a crash came from the house. Through the windows, we saw a string of kids bounding out the kitchen doors, their laughter ringing. The leader clutched a bag of cookies in his hands. A strange expression flitted across my dad's face. "It won't be long before Damien and the witch retaliate, along with Lars. Many of the vampires working with Edmonstone were from his coven."

I hoped that I could sleep easier once we completed the bond, but something told me it would just add to my fear of losing my mate—something I'd never accept. "I'll try."

"I'm still looking into the prophecy. There must be more to it... Every spell has a counterbalance."

"I hope so."

He fell silent, his focus drifting to the tapestry of pinks and red the sunset had painted the sky above us—nature promising us the perfect weather to celebrate the full moon.

"Dad?"

"Yes?"

"I'm sorry for how I handled things after Alice was taken. I know I didn't make things easy on you." I wrung my hands, afraid to look up from the ashes. "I was so angry, and I took it out on you."

"You were young, Son."

"I was eighteen." I cringed as I thought back to that version of myself. I was stupid and arrogant and thoughtless. Everything an alpha shouldn't be.

"You were both still children, despite how desperate you were to become adults."

He clapped his hand on my knee, and there was nothing but love in his eyes when I finally felt brave enough to meet his gaze.

"Does the power of becoming an alpha make you this wise, or have you just listened to too many podcasts?"

That earned me an elbow to the ribs. I wheezed and Dad laughed, the worry leaving his features briefly.

"No, you learn from your mistakes. It's easy to sound wise when I've lived longer than you. It's only with age that we realise how we should have cherished our childhoods instead of wishing the time away."

"I see that now. Back then, I just wanted to prove myself."

In truth, I still did.

"You never needed to prove yourself to me, you always had my love. I'll accept your apology if it makes you feel better, but despite your teenage outbursts, I never doubted you. I know everyone says that about their kids, but I knew you were destined for great things." Sincerity shone in his eyes as he pointed to the forest ahead of us. "This was always going to be yours to protect someday. When the time comes, I know in my heart that you'll be a worthy alpha, Luke."

His words caught me off guard, quieting the doubting voices in my mind for a moment. I leaned in, bumping my shoulder with his as we watched the sun lower behind the trees. "I love you too, Dad."

THE FULL MOON shone above us, the magic ingrained in my body swelling in response to her call. Stars twinkled behind wisps of cloud, any heat from the winter's sun long gone thanks to the clear skies. My breath misted in front of me as I stepped beside my dad, my excitement quickly turning to anxious energy. He'd completed his usual speech thanking everyone for joining and wishing us a happy Imbolc, but all eyes were still on our alpha— and now me.

"Tonight, you run with me," he said, the full moon boost to his strength making me stumble forward as he clapped me on the back.

We were gathered in the same forest clearing as always, the same place I had shifted before my first pack run. And for some reason, I felt like I was about to go through another rite of passage.

I glanced over my shoulder at Eve. She was standing between Darren and Paula, talking animatedly with a beaming smile about something Niamh had said to her earlier.

"You can fall back with Eve later." He followed my gaze, a knowing smile tugging at his lips. "It's time you learned the ropes and people see that you've stepped up to your duties."

Duties. He never forced it on me. One of our earliest conversations when I started joining in the pack runs was him telling me that it was a choice. That I didn't have to lead if I didn't want to. I was a teenage boy, *of course* I wanted to be alpha. But Alice being taken changed me, and that responsibility became something I feared.

Looking at Eve, that responsibility no longer scared me because it wasn't a choice. I wanted to protect those I loved, I always had. That's why losing Alice had shaken me up so much.

I had a lot of things to thank my mate for, but helping me see a different side of myself—a side that was worthy to follow in my father's footsteps someday—was near the top of the list.

"Ah, young love." Dad chuckled, shaking his head as he looked between us. "I'm really glad you found her. Even if I did tell you to stay away from Ryan's pack, I guess Eve being your mate meant that was never going to happen."

"Honestly, I don't think I'd have listened whether it was fate pulling us together or not."

Eve caught my eye, her cheeks dimpling as she smiled and inclined her head. *Stop stalling. Go lead with your dad, Mister Alpha.*

I rolled my eyes and turned back to my dad, the corners of my lips twitching. "Okay, I'm ready. But I still don't get what I'm doing. I've run with the pack a zillion times."

He shrugged. "You've never led."

"Only the alpha can lead."

"According to who? I don't see the moon saying anything, so unless she wants to come down here and tell me otherwise, I want my son to lead this run alongside me." My dad's silver eyes shone with pride, his head raised high as he made sure every single werewolf gathered heard. He unbuckled his belt, the sound of the metal hitting the ground triggering everyone else to strip down too. "I'm sure your mate will be fine with her family while you lead for a bit. She has you for a lifetime."

I swallowed the growl building in my throat as I caught Eve undressing from the corner of my eye. Hours. Just hours left and we could complete the bond.

"Okay, I'm in." I kicked off my shorts aside, keeping my focus straight ahead at the well-worn path through the trees. The bond in my chest thrummed with anticipation.

My dad shifted first, the air around him shimmering as his body morphed into that of a wolf. His shift triggered my own, and the kiss of the moon unleashed my magic. I dropped to all fours as the change washed over me, my limbs tingling and a burn travelling along my spine. My paws hit the ground, claws sinking into the loamy earth.

I was a younger version of him, my creamy coat holding more honey tones than his greying fur. I had grown taller than Dad in recent years, but the rippling muscles of his back were one of the many signs that he was the alpha and could still hand me my ass. Last time there was snow in Ireland, I'd tried to wrestle him, and he'd whooped my ass so badly I got frostbite.

He dropped his head, butting my muzzle with his nose. His moonlight-silver eyes crinkled as he turned towards the forest, and I fell into step beside him.

Dirt and small clumps of grass flew into the air as the alpha kicked off his haunches and sprinted off into the dense forest. I sprinted after him, the ground beneath us shaking.

*Go ahead for a bit, Son.*

I turned my head to find my dad's luminous eyes fixed on me. My brow furrowed. But it wasn't a request, it was an order from my alpha.

It felt wrong, but I slowly inched ahead until it was me leading the pack, exhilaration zapping down my spine.

I'd run with my pack before, but he was right. Leading the pack was different. There was nothing in front of us but wide open space, nature allowing us to run freely while the moon watched over us. There was no one to race, no changing your path to avoid someone cutting across or making room for anyone. It was just you and the night, and the chorus of thunderous paws behind you.

Tendrils of light fog rolled through the forest, veiling the undergrowth as our paws pounded the forest floor. My dad's howl echoed in the night, sending bats fleeing from their beds and birds into a chirping frenzy. I looked back to see him tossing his head back as he howled a second time, this time the pack joining in unison. Eve had joined him, my mate's blue eyes practically glowing against her dark coat.

And when I opened my mouth, a loud howl ripped from my own throat, it felt like the moon answered.

# CHAPTER 18

## EVE

**T**he celebrations had begun to die down by the time Luke and I managed to sneak away. He'd asked Dylan and Josh to help us get away early, but they'd been having too much fun. Despite my eagerness to complete the bond, I think Luke felt bad tearing me away from my first proper run with my family.

Waiting all night was driving me crazy.

"Are we nearly there?" I was practically bouncing on the balls of my feet as I followed him through the forest.

He grinned, mischief sparkling in his eyes. "Almost."

We'd shifted to run most of the distance, but he'd asked me to transition back into our human forms for the last stretch. The suspense was killing me.

The pack's laughter and conversations had long faded into the distance as we trekked deep into the forest.

"Remind me again what was wrong with your room?"

"There's no way in hell I'm completing the mate bond in a house full of family and friends," Luke said, the look of dismay on his face comical as he held up his index finger. "One, because it feels like a momentous occasion that warranted something nicer than a room down the hall from my parents." He held up a second finger, and my mind was automatically in the gutter.

"Two, neither of us are great at volume control. I do my best to control the possessive side of the bond, but I didn't want to be plotting about tearing someone's eyes out while making love to you."

I licked my lips, grateful he was walking ahead because my self-control was slipping by the second.

A narrow stream gurgled where the dirt path ended, a grassy hill dotted with trees that grew at a slant to catch the sun.

Luke crossed first, his feet sliding on the mossy stepping stones that peaked above the shallow water. "Careful," he warned, holding his hand out to help me tiptoe across with far less grace. "Don't want you to get wet."

"I feel like you're about two seconds away from a dirty pun that's going to ruin the mood," I muttered, rolling my eyes towards the starry sky.

The hill was steep; the fog-dampened grass slick against my hands as we climbed to the top. Luke paused at the top, waiting for me to reach his side. He'd promised to bring me somewhere special, and he did not disappoint.

My mouth hung open as I took in the view of a small lake soaked in moonlight. Dense forest surrounded the lake on all sides, its grass-covered banks speckled with snowdrops.

"They're wildflowers." Luke's hand traced slow circles on the small of my back. "Different ones bloom throughout the seasons."

I could only imagine how beautiful the surroundings looked painted in different colours as the seasons transitioned. The moon hung low in the sky, casting a soft glow across the water's misty surface.

"It's..." I turned in a slow circle, struggling to find the words. I wanted to frame the moment forever. "It's beautiful. I don't have a better word for it."

"I found the spot when I first shifted. Since then, it's always been my secret haven." Luke stepped behind me, brushing his lips over the crescent-shaped scar between my shoulder blades. His hand slid from my waist as he gestured to a blanket laid out on the grass, complete with a picnic basket, a bottle of champagne and chocolates sticking out of the top. He'd really thought of everything. He led me down the bank and helped me over the large boulders at the base. My feet met the soft threads of the blanket, and any lingering tension in my shoulders unwound as the moon basked us in her light. "Now it's yours too."

"Thank you for sharing this with me." I interlaced my fingers with his, a soft giggle slipping from my lips as he pulled my body flush against his. "And for making tonight so perfect."

It was perfect. *He* was perfect. But when he leaned down to kiss me, I found myself pulling back.

"What's wrong?"

Worry creased his brow, and my stomach sank. Something had played on my mind ever since we rescued him, and we needed to talk about it. It felt like he had a mask on sometimes, and I didn't want anything tainting tonight for us.

"I know it's not the right time. It's probably the worst time," I began, my words stringing together in a nervous ramble. I studied the ground for a long, torturous moment before finally looking up at him, those hazel eyes of his forcing the truth out of me. "I need to know what happened with Larissa."

"I told you. She didn't do *that* to me."

"I believe you." I cupped his jaw, brushing my thumb across his cheek. "But she did hurt you. You told me I could tell you anything. If I'm supposed to be your mate, and this is you and me forever, I need you to get what happened off your chest. You deserve to enter our future without the past weighing on you."

"I'm fine—"

"No." I refused to let him complete the lie. "Be honest with yourself. You deserve to complete this bond knowing that I love you—every part of you—no matter what you've been through."

How many times had Luke made me look deeper at myself? To peel open the layers that hurt to uncover the truth? He was the reason I didn't blame myself for Kate's death, the reason I'd learned my worth. I was using his tactics against him, but he needed to acknowledge what happened.

"You did this for me. I'm going into this knowing that you love me unconditionally, the light parts right down to the darker thoughts that haunt me in the night. You deserve the same."

Luke's throat bobbed, his loaded gaze searching my face for a long moment. He took my hand, wordlessly pulling me down onto the blanket with him. I sat across his lap, wrapping one arm around his waist while our joined hands rested on his chest. I could hear his heart hammering beneath my palm as he held me, silently staring out at the still lake.

He cleared his throat, pressing a tender kiss to the top of my head before he began. "Larissa didn't touch me sexually, but there was always the threat of it hanging over me." He ground the first words out, but his story quickly spilled from his lips as if it had been waiting to be set free. "She treated me worse than a dog. I was barely fed, pumped full of nightshade and whatever else they decided to test on me. I spent half the time unconscious, and honestly, those were the better parts because at least I could visit you in my dreams."

I held his gaze as he recounted his time spent with Larissa, confiding everything including how she'd left him bleeding out after her sessions and the way she would torture him for information until he blacked out.

Each piece of the truth landed like a blow to my core, but it wasn't just anger that bloomed inside me. It was sadness knowing what Luke had endured to keep me safe.

"She played with me like I was some kind of toy, a punchbag to take out her frustrations on." Luke twirled a strand of my hair around his finger before brushing it behind my ear. "She was angry and relentless. I wasn't what she wanted... She needed you. But she also needed us to complete the mating bond for the prophecy to work properly. So, I knew my life was safe. I just didn't know how far she'd go to hurt us."

I waited until he finished speaking, then squeezed his hand as

I pressed a gentle kiss to his chest where the scars had since healed. "I'll kill her for what she did to you."

His exhale was shaky, but his shoulders lifted as he stared down at me with nothing but love shining in his eyes, silver swirling in their hazel depths. "What did I do to deserve you?" he asked, the moon hanging low but silent above us as he brushed my lips over the tip of my nose. I wanted to stay here in his arms for eternity, where we were safe, and he looked at me like I hung the stars in the sky. "I love you."

The bond in my chest throbbed as I traced my fingers along his jawline, tilting his head down towards mine. "I love you too."

Magic sparked like electricity between us as he captured my lips with his. He kissed me slowly, and I relished the taste of his lips against mine. His tongue parted my lips, a low growl rumbling in his throat as he unlaced our fingers to knot his hand in my hair and deepen the kiss.

My stomach flipped, heat rushing to my core as his tightened fist tilted my head back. His tongue danced with mine, his hard cock pressing into my hip a promise of what was to come.

Luke's kiss grew hungry, bruising, and his hand shifted lower. He rolled my pebbled nipples between finger and thumb, his hum of approval as my body arched in response only stoking the fires of need burning within me.

I was breathless by the time he broke away, lips trailing lightly down my throat. His touch blazed in his wake, his firm hands gripping my waist as he lifted me like I was nothing and spun me to face him completely. My knees hit the blanket, the length of him brushing against the heat pooling between my legs as he held me there straddling him. My eyelids fluttered shut when he teased my breasts with his wicked tongue.

"Luke," I breathed and placed my hands on his broad shoulders, digging my nails in with a hiss as he tugged my sensitive nipple between his teeth. "I need you."

He swiped his tongue across my sensitive flesh once more with a sinful look in his eyes before slowly lowering me to the ground. He looked like some kind of god as he crawled over me bathed in moonlight, his muscles flexing and coiled with tension. He nudged my legs open with a knee, his touch featherlight as his hands moved over my breasts, goosebumps raising in the wake of his touch. He drew his fingers along my arms before gripping my wrists with one hand.

I swallowed, my hips writhing restlessly as heat built between my legs.

"Patience," he warned, his voice dropping low, and then he pulled my arms taut above my head. My growl in response only made the smirk curving his lips widen as he trailed his hand up the inside of my thigh. "Tell me what you need, Love."

His movements were maddeningly slow, my chest rising and falling rapidly despite him barely doing anything to me. Despite the cool winter breeze, there was a desperate need burning inside me. A need that only he could satiate.

"I need you to claim me."

A shiver of anticipation skittered down my spine at the hunger burning in his eyes.

Luke leaned down to pepper light kisses along my jaw, and his hand found the slick heat between my thighs, my hips bucking off the blanket as he drew his finger down my centre.

"Good girl," he growled, nipping my earlobe as he slid one finger inside of me. His groan as he felt just how wet I was for him made me want to squeeze my thighs together, but his knees forced me to keep my legs open, his grip on my wrists unyielding. I was at his mercy and I liked it.

I moaned when he added another finger, curling his fingers forward to stoke the pressure building within me. I was burning up, my hips rolling with his movements.

"You're so fucking beautiful," he murmured, brushing his lips over mine as I moaned and bucked beneath him. "And so wet for me, aren't you, sweetheart?"

All I could do was nod as he curled his fingers again, playing my body like a goddamn instrument.

"What was that?" His voice was a seductive purr as he released my wrists to move lower, dragging his tongue between my breasts. "I can't hear you."

He hooked his fingers, and I cried out, the words failing to form in my mouth. The pressure was building deep in my core, threatening to pull me under.

"So fucking wet and needy." He moved lower, his tongue trailing along the curve of my stomach and then lower.

His mouth joined his hands in their torture, and my body shattered as he sucked my clit into his mouth. I came hard, climax sweeping through my body, his name falling from my lips over and over. He didn't stop, his fingers pumping inside me as I ground my hips against his hand and rode the orgasm out.

"Come for me."

"I d-did," I panted, writhing beneath him, the pressure inside not letting up.

He licked and sucked the sensitive bundle of nerves before replacing his fingers with his tongue. Just when I thought I couldn't take any more, he looked up at me. His lips glistening as he twisted his fingers, and my hips shot off the blanket. "Come for me, Eve."

It wasn't a request; it was a command.

He dropped his head, dragging his tongue along my core before eating me out like a man possessed. His stubble rubbed against my sensitive clit, and the moment he added his fingers to his torture, I crashed over the edge once more. I repeated his name like a summons as I came again, my body going taut when a second wave of pleasure crashed into me.

I went limp as he lapped gently at my pussy, eliciting a soft moan when he withdrew his fingers. I didn't get the chance to recover because he crawled over me, my chest still heaving. The moon was still blurry when he leaned down to kiss me deeply. His tongue stroked against mine, the tip of his cock nudging my soaked entrance.

I didn't want a break. I didn't want the sensations setting my body alight to stop. I wanted him to take me, to claim me as his.

"Are you ready?" he murmured, pulling back to look at me. His silver eyes blazed with fiery passion as he interlaced our fingers and pressed my hands into the blanket, pinning me beneath his weight. His familiar scent of orange and pine enveloped me, and I felt nothing but safe in his arms.

"I'm ready," I whispered, feeling the magic levels slowly rise around as a breeze blew through the clearing. Beside us, the lake was unnaturally still, the moon's reflection lighting on its surface.

Love shone in his eyes as Luke studied my face, as if he was trying to memorise it. He looked at me like I was something to worship, his gaze never once leaving me as he lowered to slowly pressed his thick length deep inside me.

We groaned in tandem as he stretched me inch by decadent inch, the sting of body adjusting to his size chased by pleasure. Desire licked down my spine at the sight of his eyes rolling into the back of his head as he buried himself to the hilt.

Whatever he saw in my eyes made a growl build in his chest, and he unleashed himself on me. He drew his hips back, pulling out completely before slamming his cock deep inside.

"Fuck," I moaned, wrapping my legs around his waist. My nerves were on fire, my cum dripping down my thighs.

He shifted his position, hitting the perfect spot each time his cock slammed deep inside me. Each thrust drove my hips into the ground, stretching me to my limit in the most delicious way.

I was so caught up in the bliss coursing through my veins, the sound of his groans and feeling of him filling me up, that I barely noticed his lips skimming down my neck.

"I'm yours, Eve. Completely and utterly yours."

The moment his canines bit into my flesh, my body went taut like a bowstring. Then I snapped. There was a brief flash of pain, my scream echoing in the night as magic surged around us.

He squeezed my hands in a silent check in, a possessive growl ripping from his throat as he forced his teeth deeper. The bond swelled, as if coming to life within me.

Just like in London, the pain quickly morphed to pleasure as heat radiated from the bite through every inch of my body. I dug my heels into his back, each pound of his hips rocking my body. It was too much. The stretch of his cock. His teeth piercing my skin. His muscular body caging me in. The magic continuing to rise.

He released my hands once the pain subsided, one arm braced by my head while the other roamed my body.

"Fuck." I couldn't catch my breath. The sensations threatened to overwhelm me. His bond called to me like a siren's song.

He was my mate in every sense of the word. My rock, the steady presence that grounded me. But the fire that burned in me, the love that burned in me for this man was like no other. He'd walk through hellfire for me, and I'd follow him to the ends of the earth because he was my world. He was home, my safe haven.

He lifted his hips, allowing his cock to hit that sweet spot deep inside me, and a carnal growl vibrated in his chest at my gasp. Each thrust was a possessive claim that sent me hurtling over the edge. Stars danced in my eyes as I came apart beneath him, crying out for my mate as an orgasm ripped through me.

His touch was everywhere, his presence all consuming. I wanted to drown in him. I was his, to love and protect. But in that moment, I wanted him to use me, to claim me as his own.

The charged air made the hair stand on the back of my neck as it washed over us, the moonlight growing brighter as mist continued to fill the area. The heavens thundered, the ground beneath us beginning to shake.

Magic continued to rise as he picked up the pace, his thrusts punishing. I clawed at his back, a writhing and trembling mess beneath him as one orgasm crashed into the next.

My pussy pulsed around him. I couldn't tell what was Luke and what was the magic anymore as pure bliss engulfed my body.

He withdrew his teeth from my neck, silver eyes glowing. I ran my hands through his hair, capturing his lips as he claimed me with long strokes of his cock. The metallic taste of my blood on his tongue was surprisingly sweet. The power of his wolf called to me, my heart hammering as magic radiated between us. I could feel him, every part of him, memories of our time together flashing through my mind like a movie.

Water in the lake rippled as the moon completely lit up the clearing, glowing so brightly all I could see was Luke. It was just us, our dancing souls merging as the pleasure built. They intertwined, the bond solidifying in my chest as the moon's magic bound us together for every lifetime under the stars.

He claimed me with each thrust, the ground around us shaking as the earth splintered and a loud roar ripped from my mate's throat. We came together, his cock seated deep inside me, and his claws digging into my side, the fire building in my core erupting. My legs shook, my head falling back as I called out his name, warmth spreading inside me.

The bond snapped into place, plunging me into another wave of ecstasy. We stayed there, Luke's arms shaking as he braced himself above me until the aftershocks lapping at my body subsided.

With tears stinging the corners of my eyes, I looked up at my mate. The smile on his face tugged at my heart, and he reached down to brush his knuckles against my cheek, the magic surrounding us subsiding as the bond nestled in my chest.

*My mate.* Adoration coursed down the bond along with his voice in my head, my heart filled with so much love I thought it might burst.

The bond locked between us was unbreakable. I was his, and he was mine. Mated for life.

We lay there until the sky began to lighten. And when we

shifted to run back to the pack house together, the moon guided us home. Our spirits forever bound as one.

# CHAPTER 19

## LUKE

"I don't like this," I muttered, keeping a tight grip on Eve's hands as we stepped onto a plush red carpet.

With its ivy-covered walls and sprawling size, the Abhartach's mansion was just as imposing as its owner. Guests filtered ahead of us, climbing the steps towards the double doors where two vampires stood on as sentries, their long black cloaks pooling on the floor.

"This place…" Eve inhaled sharply, sticking close to my side. "It feels wrong."

She was right. The place felt like death. No matter how pristine Lars forced his staff to keep the place, the amount of blood spilled over the years had left its mark. It wasn't a scent; it was the lasting scars of his depravity that I could feel in my core.

"Our names are definitely on the list, right?" she asked, her throat bobbing as she glanced towards the two vampires guarding the door. One held a tablet, the glow of the screen illuminating his gaunt features, while the other with perfectly tousled black hair handed masks to guests.

"Yes, I trust Darius." I forced a shaky breath out, resisting the urge to look back as the scents of other Crescent pack members reached me.

Car doors slammed behind us as Alice, Dylan, and Josh arrived together; Tom was already inside. Eve and I the only ones who were glamoured. Our presence would tip Lars off if we snuck in, but my dad and other pack members would put him on edge.

According to Darius, a Royal emissary was in attendance tonight. He couldn't refuse my pack entry without causing a spectacle and raising suspicions. My mate and I, however, were still technically exiled.

At first, we thought the glamour didn't work. When Alice had told Eve blonde hair suited her, and I was still staring at her brunette waves, there had been some serious confusion. Turned out, the mate bond meant that we could see each other's true forms even if we were glamoured.

The bowtie felt suffocating, everything from the collar of my shirt and the cufflinks Dad had insisted on making my skin crawl. But each of Eve's steps revealed a glimpse of her toned leg. The fitted, black satin of her gown matched the theme of the ball—the neckline of the dress an enticing V with sheer lace panelling on the sides and back wasn't helping me rein in my temper, or my temptations.

Nervous energy coiled in my gut as we became next in line. Bright ruby eyes tracked our approach.

Eve's hair was pinned in a loose up-do, the faint hint of my bite mark still visible on her neck despite my sister's best attempts to cover it with make-up. It would fade in another few days; the more primal side of me didn't want it to.

"Name?" The vampire to my right tapped the tablet with his nail, his fangs peeking out.

"Kevin Fitzpatrick and Paula Donohoe," I lied smoothly, wrapping my arm around Eve's waist and flexing my shoulders.

She tensed at the sight of the doorbell embedded in a human skull. Shadows flickered around the ruby-encased eyeball in the other eye socket as it swivelled to look us over.

"Pockets?" he asked, his tone bored as he motioned for me to empty mine. He turned to Eve then, his pupils dilating as he took in the curves of her body. "And you?"

She shrugged, a smirk lifting her lips as she held out her hands. "I don't have any. It sucks being a woman."

The vampire motioned for his colleague to pat Eve down. The dark-haired vampire didn't get the chance, my hand shooting out to slap his away as a low growl built in my throat.

"Not happening."

A scowl twisted the vamp with the list's face, his foot tapping impatiently. "Sir, we have to—"

"Finish that sentence and I'll make sure it's your last," I snapped, my voice dropping low as I leaned in. "Unless you want me to make a scene, you keep your paws off my woman."

I did my best to keep the possessive side of me in check. Eve wasn't my property; she was my better half. But it was the kind of language Lars' disgusting coven would respond to.

The vampire I'd grabbed shook his head, plucking two masks from the table behind him. "Let them go, Marcus. We need to keep the line moving."

"Fine." Marcus motioned for us to pass, moving his attention to a Fae couple.

"Put them on before entering," the other vampire ordered, handing me a black mask. It was simple, with subtle rhinestone swirls on the surface.

I ignored him because many others were only putting their masks on inside. But as I took a step forwards, he grabbed my arm and nodded his head towards the top of the doorway. I followed his gaze, realisation smoothing my brow as I sensed tendrils of magic hanging in the air.

"Put the masks on, please." Gold lightened his eyes as he handed Eve her mask, white with silver glitter and stones that glittered in the light and feathers on the sides.

I knew Lars kept all but his closest vampires on the edge of bloodlust. Something told me I was face to face with Darius' contact.

I fixed my mask to my face before helping Eve tie the ribbon of hers behind her head. The vampire watched us carefully, inclining his head before inviting us inside.

The moment we crossed the threshold, I felt the spell strip the glamour from us.

"Did that just do what I think it did?" Eve's piercing blue eyes widened, panic rising in her voice.

"Yep, guess I know why these guys are so obsessed with masks." My lips brushed the shell of her ear, her body shuddering as I subtly slipped my hand under the slit of her dress to brush my fingers over the holster strapped to her thigh. The fake dagger was in place, ready to be swapped with the real one. "Stay close to me."

I pressed my hand against the small of her back, guiding us further into the foyer. The masks covered half our faces, and I had to hope that was enough. All the men looked the same, black suits and identical masks. The women were all dressed in floor-length gowns, their pale masks probably meant to symbolise innocence or something like that. Lars had a thing for innocence.

*Lars doesn't want them hiding their identity unless he controls it. That mask is to stay on your face all night, got it?*

Candles burning in the large, round iron chandelier cast the shadow of a pentagram on the marble floor. Black panelled walls of the foyer continued down corridors that split off in each direction. Red ropes cordoned off the two spiral staircases leading to both upstairs and to the floor below, each guarded by tall, hooded vampires.

The crowd filtered evenly in both directions, but something tugged me towards the right. The amber sconces only added to the sinister feel, as if we were walking into the pits of hell.

"Let's see if we can find the others before we spread out." I kept my voice low, my thumb stroking Eve's side as we followed the crowd down a dimly lit corridor.

I focused on the feel of Eve against me, the bond tethering us a constant reassurance, but I still wanted her as close as possible.

One bite from a vampire, and I could lose her—I wasn't going through that again.

The corridor gave way to a massive ballroom with rib-vaulted ceilings that stretched above us, intersecting in breathtaking patterns like a gothic cathedral. The canopy was adorned with golden designs that gleamed in the dancing candlelight cast by chandeliers suspended in the air, floating as attendees swept across the black-and-white chequered marble dance floor below.

Tables stacked with colourful drinks and appetisers lined the walls, including champagne towers and wine bottles filled with blood. Masked patrons gathered near tall, round tables with elaborate gold sculptures to match the details of the grand ceiling.

I pulled Eve onto the dance floor as the song changed tempo, spinning her into my arms and moving into the crowd. At the top of the room, a Fae band played on stage, one of their members stroking the hair of an emaciated vampire kneeling at the base of his feet.

*We need to find Tom.* Eve wrapped her arms around my neck, her hips swaying to the music as we moved around the dance floor.

I nodded, scanning the room.

Bile rose in my throat when I spotted chaise longues littered around the ballroom, and most corners were veiled by gauzy curtains. Shadows moved behind them on what looked like half-moon shaped beds, bodies writhing, and my hearing picked up moans coming from the nearest one.

Eve's lips popped open as she heard the same, the faintest hint of pink visible beneath her mask.

One corner didn't have beds or curtains, instead it had a spelled cube with faux glass. A vampire was on his knees, stripped naked with his hands bound tightly behind his back. I was surprised to see a human brandishing a leather bullwhip in there with him.

Eve felt me stiffen, leaning up on her toes to press a tender kiss to my cheek as she whispered. "I'm here, Love."

The bond hummed in my chest, and I swallowed, dragging my gaze back to the ballroom in search of my dad.

Instead, I spotted Lars. He stood by a large banquet table laid out at the base of the stage. I could smell death from where we danced; what was once a beautiful siren was now laid out like a meal. Her blonde hair fanned around her head like a halo, grey scales beginning to form on her mottled skin. Fresh blood trickled from her slit throat, her upper body suspended by magic so the blood pooled in a golden chalice. A mixture of side dishes and starters were scattered around her, along with napkins.

My stomach flipped, doing a second somersault when I noticed Lars picking up a napkin to wipe the edge of his blade clean. Silver glinted, his fingers caressing the intricate bone carved handle.

*Lars has the dagger.*

Eve's eyes widened when I spun her just in time for us both to see Lars hooking the blade back on a loop hanging from his belt. He hid behind no mask, dressed in a fitted tuxedo with those velvet lapels he favoured, matching his ebony curls and making his sharp, pale features stand out. Despite his put-together exterior, his blood-red eyes were a reminder of the monster that lurked within.

A hand gripped my shoulder, and I whirled around, pushing Eve behind me. I flashed my canines, but my shoulders relaxed when I recognised Dylan behind the mask, dancing with my sister in tow.

"Sorry," he murmured, pointing with the hand he had linked with Alice towards a lone figure holding a full flute of champagne near the corridor entrance. "We just got in."

The two guys cleaned up well, looking smart in their tuxedos. Alice's black dress was simpler than Eve's, strapless and flaring from her waist into a ballgown. I'd questioned if it was practical until she'd smugly reminded me that she could shift outside of the full moon and showed off the Converse she was wearing hidden by the poofy skirt.

I twirled Eve back into my arms, swaying to the beat as I tried not to draw attention to us. "Have you seen Dad?"

"I saw him walking off with the Royal emissary," Alice said, her sharp eyes searching the dance floor.

"We need to go to the bathroom." I paused, trying to choose my words carefully as I inclined my head towards a set of large wooden doors Lars was exiting through. "I think I left something of mine behind."

"Got it." My sister flashed a smile, masking her distaste as a scream that could either be pleasure or pain sounded from the nearest corner. "We'll find Dad."

"If we're not back or in contact within thirty minutes, come find us."

Dylan nodded, whisking my sister across the dance floor.

I took Eve's hand in mine, and we stepped off the dance floor, casting a subtle glance around the ballroom to make sure no one was paying us any attention as I led her towards the exit Lars had used. I eased the door open and slipped through, trying to act like I was luring Eve away. Fuck did I wish that was the plan.

I peeked around the corner to see Lars turning down another corridor. My shoulders crept up, the anxious knot of tension between them tightening. The mansion was an endless maze, and the further he went from the ballroom, the less the music would drown out our steps.

Luke nudged me forwards, the bond between us one of the few things keeping me grounded as we tiptoed after the ancient vampire.

Lars stopped in front of a closed door, and Luke pulled me back behind a large pillar. I watched through a thin gap between the pillar and wall as Lars glanced around, his sharp nose wrinkling. Luke's grip on me loosened as the vampire disappeared out of view, the door creaking closed behind him.

*Now.*

Luke led the way as we inched closer to the door, my heart in my mouth. A crest was carved into the door, two serpents wound around the moon and sun. Maybe an office? He pulled a small sachet of what almost looked like dirt, sprinkling it along the threshold. The wisps of hair framing my face fluttered as magic sizzled in the air, burning a hole in the silencing spell surrounding the room.

I pressed my ear to the door, and Luke followed suit, the muffled voices inside becoming clear.

"She's not happy, Lars. And you know that never ends well." Damien's voice filtered through the door, followed by the sound of pacing.

"It's not my fault your son irritated the witch. Be grateful he came home in one piece. I hear it was the Crescent wolf that gave him the beating, not her."

"I don't care about that," Damien scoffed, and my temper flared. Not because I cared for Ryan, but no child should grow up with a parent who doesn't care for their welfare. I couldn't imagine Luke's dad ever speaking about him that way. Tom jumped on a plane to save his exiled son. The two alphas couldn't be more different if they tried. "According to Henry, she's not interested in continuing with the projects. She just cares about this prophecy."

"If she fulfils the prophecy, her power would be unmatched," Lars replied, his tone growing bored. "Your experiments have been nothing but a failure. Besides curing your wolves of their weakness to nightshade, nothing has changed. My coven is still bound by the sun. A werewolf's bite still kills us. While I enjoy partaking, being reliant on blood is inconvenient at times."

"We've done our best. Your kind is harder to... test." The Faolchúnna alpha's scent grew stronger as he moved closer to the door, and I held my breath. "The agreement was that we would help her fulfil the prophecy if she promised to imbue some of that power unto our kind, and yours. The select few, so that there would be a clear hierarchy. I no longer trust her to do this."

"I agree. She has become rather... unhinged of late." I could hear Lars' smirk in his words. "She is occupied upstairs while the Royal emissary is here. Even she isn't stupid enough to risk heightening their suspicion, especially when we are weeks away from a blue moon. She claims this should help the prophecy come to pass. It's fated, so she claims."

"The two are mates, did you hear?"

My body went rigid, and silver bled into Luke's irises.

"Yes, apparently that was part of it. She was rather giddy when their bond was confirmed." Lars sighed, the floorboards creaking. "She's still seeking the dagger. I've been keeping it on me at all times, but if it would make you feel more at ease, here." Leather rustled and something clattered onto the table. "I know you have issues with control."

"That was mine to begin with. It went missing when the previous alpha passed away." A low growl rumbled, and Damien's words were laced with disgust. No matter how much he was aligned with Lars for business, he hated anything that wasn't his kind.

"Ah, yes. 'Passed away', sure." Lars chuckled, the sound hollow. "I saw his daughter drop it back in the city last year. Maybe you should spend less time worrying about the witch and pay more attention to your pack."

Metal dragged against wood, followed by pounding footsteps that grew louder as the Faolchúnna alpha approached the door.

*Run.*

I spun on my heel and sped in the direction we had come, or so I thought, but as we skidded around a corner and came face to face with an enormous portrait of Lars that I definitely wouldn't forget, I realised we were lost.

Luke cocked his head before shaking it, his brow furrowing. *He's gone the other way. We're safe.*

The portrait was in a small open area with a staircase leading up in one corner, the grand piano beneath it covered in a thin layer of dust.

A high-pitched giggle sounded in the distance, heels clacking against the tile floors followed by measured footsteps. I smelled them before they came into view, two Fae heading towards us.

Strong hands gripped my waist, spinning me around and shoving me up against the nearest wall. Luke's lips were on mine, his voice in my head as his body caged mine in.

*Follow my lead.*

His tongue parted my lips, his head blocking my view as he kissed me deeply. I couldn't understand why we weren't running until I noticed a third scent above us, at the top of the stairs. We were trapped and clearly in an area that was off-limits.

He slid his fingers over the thin lace on my sides, one hand moving to grope my ass while the other slid between us, dangerously close to the slit in my dress as the two Fae grew closer.

*Relax.* Luke nipped my lower lip, his fingers trailing beneath my dress. *We just need to put on a show, and they won't bother us. I imagine they're slipping away for the same reason.*

He pressed his thigh between mine, while my hands glided over his chiselled chest to cup his face. *And if they don't fall for it?* My heart was hammering in my chest so hard I was sure the only thing they'd smell from me was fear.

*Then we have this.* He brushed his fingers across the blade strapped to my inner thigh and then higher. His sharp intake of breath made my lips curve as he realised I had no underwear on. *Naughty. You did not tell me this before we left.*

*I didn't trust you to keep your mind on the job if you knew. The dress showed everything, and we didn't exactly have time to hit the high street.*

He confirmed my suspicions, a low growl rumbling in his chest as he cupped between my thighs, pinning my legs apart with his, his arousal pressing into my hip.

*You said to put on a show, Luke.* I regretted my teasing instantly when he teased my entrance, my moan swallowed in our kiss. *Not fuck me in the hallway.*

*Who said anything about sex?* He broke our kiss, a devilish smirk playing on his lips as he ran his fingers along the slick heat building between my thighs. *You turned up here looking like that with no underwear and without a single word to me?* Heat pooled in my core as he pressed the tip of his one finger in my pussy, the pad of his thumb brushing over my sensitive clit. My hips bucked to meet his hand, and I hissed a breath, far more concerned with his hand than the Fae growing closer. *This dress was made to fuck you in.* He slid two fingers inside me, slowly pumping them in and out as he trailed hungry kisses down my throat. *And I will, when we get home. All fucking night.*

"This way, I know where Lars keeps the good stuff." A Fae with his shirt half unbuttoned hurried into view, followed by a woman holding up her skirt. "Oh, what do we have here?"

The female's gaze landed on us just as Luke curled his fingers, putting pressure on my g-spot and drawing a moan from my lips.

My cheeks heated, knowing they could scent my arousal.

"Fancy some company?" she asked, her eyes shifting from purple to pink as she licked her lips.

Luke ignored them and slid his hand from my ass, his touch gliding over my breasts before his fingers closed around my throat. My pussy clenched around his fingers. He was putting on one hell of a show. Desire burned through our bond as he squeezed either side of my throat and drove his fingers deeper.

My eyes rolled into the back of my head as a heady pleasure spread through my body.

The male wrapped his arm around her waist as they swayed. He raised an empty bottle of something that smelled like bubble gum, his cheeks flushed. "I'm happy to share."

Luke looked up, his hand still torturing me beneath the dress as he levelled them with a cold glare. "I don't share."

"Are you sure?" The Fae stepped closer, but my mate's growl of warning stopped him. He raised his hands, his drunken grin widening. "Chill, it's just an offer."

*I'm going to kill him if he looks at you for another second.* He pressed down on my clit as he released my throat to cup my breasts through the thin satin material, nipping the tender spot on my neck where his mark lingered.

*Don't. Look at me.*

Luke did as he was told. His lust-filled gaze travelled over my body, snagging on my heaving chest as he increased the pace of his fingers. His body kept mine mostly hidden, the slit in my dress allowing him perfect access without baring me to the world.

"Suit yourselves," the woman muttered, grabbing her partner by the tie and hauling him into one of the many rooms.

The pressure in me built, Luke pressing his lips to mine in a bruising kiss. He muffled my moans, pressing his thumb against my clit as he hooked his fingers to drive me over the edge.

"Come for me, Baby," Luke whispered, the gravel in his low voice making my core tighten.

I obeyed, my legs giving way as I came apart for him. My back arched off the wall, his hard cock pressing into my hip while ecstasy coursed through my nerves. I collapsed against the cool stone, whimpering against his lips when he withdrew his fingers and aftershocks of pleasure rolled through me.

He gripped my hip with one hand to keep me upright, his hooded eyes locking with mine as he brought his fingers to his mouth and licked them clean.

I swallowed hard, my pussy clenching. That was hot. *Holy fuck.*

*Later.* He stole one last kiss from my lips, smoothing the split on the skirt of my dress back into place. *I promise. First, we have a problem to deal with.*

I wasn't entirely sure why he didn't stop after the two Fae left, but I just figured it was lust or the bond.

I followed Luke's gaze to find Ryan at the top of the stairs, his icy eyes fixed on us.

# CHAPTER 21

## LUKE

R*yan.* Eve stiffened, the glow in her cheeks fading.

*Don't say anything. Pretend you didn't see him.* I ran my hands down her arms, leaning in to whisper loud enough for him to hear. "We're not finished."

The more primal side of me wanted to claim Eve right there. I wanted to bend her over that piano and make her come for me over and over again until she was hoarse from screaming my name. But, I was a gentleman. Finishing her off while he was watching me had to be enough.

Eve's brow furrowed, but she smoothed her expression and painted on a smirk to rival my best. "I am."

"Bold." I nipped her earlobe, making a show of reluctantly stepping away and adjusting my trousers. *Good girl, let's see what he does. He should run to tell Daddy Dearest about us. Let him lead us straight to the dagger.*

The railing above rattled as he pushed away, Ryan running away with his tail between his legs like the coward he was.

I waited until his footsteps faded a little before rushing over to the staircase, motioning for Eve to follow. *Let's get a dagger and get the hell out of here.*

We kept our footsteps light, sneaking upstairs to find a landing with long corridors leading in three directions. Unlike the rest of the mansion, these had simple black walls with no creepy portraits. The stairs felt like a servant's entrance, as if we were moving away from the main part of the house.

*This way.* Eve tugged me towards the middle option where Ryan's footsteps echoed.

We set off slowly, the bare walls giving way to plain doors with gold numbers. I noticed the fifth number was crooked, exposing a peephole underneath. Pausing, I moved the number completely out of the way. My gut plummeted as I looked inside to find a small room with a hospital bed with machines beside it, wires hooked up to what looked like a very emaciated vampire.

*This is where they're keeping them.*

Eve glanced over her shoulder, dragging me onwards as Ryan's footsteps faded. *We can't lose him. Keeping what?*

*Vampires. Hybrids. Anything, I guess.* I hurried after her, rage boiling deep within me as I thought about my sister being trapped like that. *Like what Alice described.*

Her lips thinned, and she squeezed my hand as we half-walked, half-jogged along the corridor trying to be as quiet as possible.

When I'd visited with my dad, Lars had hosted us downstairs. It's exactly where I'd have looked, expecting the kidnapped paranormals to be in his dungeons. But the bastard was hiding them in plain sight, and I doubted the Royal emissary was going to ask to see the many bedrooms of the mansion. No, she'd see his normal human prisoners and his blood-starved recruits that were a well-known secret in the community. Like always, they'd turn a blind eye.

I'd stopped counting the ascending numbers because they just stoked the anger burning within me. The doors became less frequent after we took a left. A low growl rumbled from my mate as we reached a room with a window that allowed passersby to see in. It was just like the one I'd found but larger. Not a hospital room, but a testing facility.

We slowed, my shoulders dropping at the empty room. But it was the next that had my mouth hanging open.

Ryan's back was to us, his ebony curls dishevelled as he sat on a plastic chair pulled up beside one of the beds. He was murmuring; the words muffled by the glass and whatever spells were on the room.

*Oh my God.* Eve grabbed my hand, staring wide-eyed at the occupied bed.

Ryan's double lay there with his eyes closed, tubes coming from his nose and wires stuck to his chest as the monitor beside them beeped intermittently. He had an intubation tube down his throat, and a needle in his arm was hooked up to something that looked like it belonged on the set of a *Back to the Future* movie. The machine pumped sparkling red liquid into him, seeming to run it through some kind of cycle.

Cupboards lined one side of the room, above a counter that was stacked with different medications and vials. The room was white, clinical—a complete contrast with the rest of the Abhartach's mansion. Unlike the windowless rooms of the other captives, this one had curtains drawn across its windows and a set of double doors that led out onto a large balcony. The sky was dark; the moon obscured by the cloudy night. Not that it would help. We were just outside the full moon cycle, so my magic was subdued.

Eve shifted closer, her palm clammy against mine. *Is that a clone?*

I shrugged, noticing the way the patient's nose lacked the little bump Ryan's had. The harsh fluorescent lighting highlighted the deep purple under his eyes, but his jaw was also less defined. The realisation hit me like a ten-tonne truck.

*I think it's his brother.*

That night in Edinburgh came flooding back. I had focused

so hard on surviving Larissa's torture with my sanity intact that I'd almost forgotten about it.

I pulled Eve back from the window, moving so we were just out of Ryan's sight.

*Mary told me about his brother, Jake.*

She frowned, shaking her head. *Jake is dead. He died when they were kids.*

*That's what she said too. He was killed by a hybrid; that's why Damien and Ryan hate them so much. Ryan was a kid when it happened.*

*He told me that Jake drowned.*

*It happened by the creek?* I glanced towards the door, keeping my ears trained for the slightest movement. *Maybe that's their cover story? I can't imagine the alpha wanting to admit his son was killed by a hybrid.*

*But if he didn't die, why would Damien dedicate his life to eradicating hybrids and making his pack so powerful?*

Eve was right. The Faolchúnna alpha had dedicated his life to destroying hybrids. He was power-hungry, but that was extreme. There had to be a reason, something driving him to work with vampires he despised.

*What if that was just part of it. Larissa is a necromancer.* The blood drained from my face. *What if he wanted revenge, but also wanted to bring him back?*

Eve moved closer to see through the window once more, and I followed. The patient was the image of Ryan. If it was his brother, he would have been kept alive for years.

*Could it really be him?*

I hovered my hand over the handle, not entirely sure what my plan was. *There's only one way to find out.*

Shadows snaked around the end of the corridor, and I froze, shoving Eve down just in time as a blast of magic flew over our heads and smashed into the wall behind us.

"Ah, I should have known you'd come sniffing around." The cackle from my nightmares vibrated around us. Larissa stepped into view, clapping her hands together as she looked over my shoulder. Sarcasm dripped from every word. "Oh goody, the gang is here."

I followed her gaze to see my sister and the two boys at the opposite end of the corridor, true to their word to come find us.

"Stay back," I ordered, pushing Eve behind me as I planted my feet. There was nothing but me standing between the witch and the people I loved, and I'd die before letting her past.

Larissa's long blonde hair tumbled in waves down her back as she sauntered towards us, her black gown pooling around her like the shadows she commanded. Despite Lars mentioning she was told to lie low, she obviously didn't plan on listening to the ancient vampire. She looked incredible, deadly.

"I know," she flashed a pearly-white smile, smoothing her hands over the curves of her waist. "I'm dressed to kill."

# CHAPTER 22

EVE

**L**arissa's laugh was vicious, amusement lighting up her face as Luke pulled me behind him. Luke may have been next in line to be alpha, but I wasn't letting him face her alone. I stepped up beside him, ignoring the growl of warning that rattled in his chest.

The door burst open, Ryan nearly tearing it clean off its hinges. "What the fuck are you doing here?" His anger turned to fear as he spotted the witch beyond us, his throat bobbing. "Larissa."

"I got bored. I couldn't find the dagger I *know* Lars has hidden somewhere. Then I stumbled across these two delicious love birds, and here we are." She canted her head, her lilac eyes sparking with something sinister. She could dress herself in the most beautiful gowns in the world, but nothing could ever hide the evil beneath. "But perhaps I can kill two birds with one stone."

"No one is dying tonight," Ryan cut in, glancing behind him. "This isn't the time or the place, Larissa. My father is already on his way."

"Good, I need to have a chat with Damien about the lies he and Lars have been spinning."

"You can't kill us until the next full moon," I muttered, my nails morphing into claws as we faced the witch. "Unless you've officially lost the plot. By all means, fuck up the prophecy."

"Your mate has a smart mouth, too. I thoroughly enjoyed making him scream." Her nostrils flared, as if she could smell him all over me. "I wonder how prettily you scream."

"Say that again, bitch. I dare you." I took a step forwards, but Luke's hand snapped around my wrist to stop me with a growl. My skin crawled at the thought of her hands on him.

"You need to get *your* bitch under control, Luke. Or else she'll end up walking herself across the veil sooner rather than later, and neither of us want that."

"I don't know. I'd quite enjoy it." Nadine joined Larissa from a corridor. The redhead's feline eyes narrowed at the sight of me, her pretty face twisting into an ugly scowl.

"Nadine. I told you to fetch my father." Tension bracketed Ryan's mouth, pink creeping up his neck as he kept glancing back at the machine that was beeping more frequently.

"Who is that?" Alice asked, her eyes widening as she looked between Ryan and the man in the bed. "Oh my God. It's true. Your brother is alive."

I did a double take. "You knew?"

"There were rumours... I never thought it was actually true."

Ryan froze, the muscle in his jaw feathering. "Get them out of here. You were on security tonight. What the fuck do you call this?" An angry vein in his forehead throbbed as Nadine looked at Larissa. "You do *not* work for her."

"I don't work for you either, Ryan," she replied dryly, rolling her eyes as if he was a toy she'd grown bored with. "Damien sent me to make sure Larissa behaves until he gets here. He's busy with Lars."

"Well, I better not disappoint them." Larissa cast her hand out, her magic connecting with the window beside us. I dived out of the way, tucking and rolling as her spell sent it crashing to the ground in a shower of tiny shards.

Ryan raced back inside, barely slamming the door shut behind him before Larissa blasted it off its hinges. I scrambled to my feet just in time to see a ball of fire smash straight through the wood and slam into his gut. He crumpled, the force of her magic sending his body into the air. He hit the doors leading onto the balcony with a thud, slumping onto the ground as the doors burst open and cold air rushed inside.

The witch sent another spell our way, and we kicked into action, Josh and Dylan leading the way as we raced back in the direction they came from. I skidded to a stop, pain shooting through my ankle as I smacked straight into a wall of magic. Luke rebounded off the same magical barrier beside me. We were trapped.

My mate and I shared a look, and I nodded. *Get them out.*

Alice hesitated when she saw us fall back.

"Don't stop," Luke's voice was a booming order as all three werewolves stopped. "Try all the numbered doors. They're holding the captives here."

I kept an eye on the advancing witch while Luke focused on commanding his pack.

"Get as many as you can out, but be careful. They have vampires that look like they've been starved."

"We're on it." Josh nodded, tugging Alice with him when she lingered.

Dylan took up the rear, casting one last worried glance over his shoulder before he reluctantly obeyed my mate's wishes. "We'll send Tom and the others to you."

Magic charged the air, a swirling mass of light and shadows destroying the remaining partition wall between the treatment room and the corridor. The building shook, the floor beneath us creaking as plasterboard exploded into the air. I shielded my face, clinging onto Luke as my vision blurred until the dust showering us cleared.

One leg of the hospital bed snapped, metal groaning as the height of the bed dropped on one side.

Ryan rushed over to it, blood pumping from his temple. He righted the bed, placing a gentle hand on the patient's arm. His eyes shone silver, the muscles of his back and shoulders flexing beneath his dress shirt as he glared at the witch.

"You can't do this."

"Oh, I believe I can." Larissa lifted her dress as she stepped over a pile of rubble. "I'm the only reason he's still alive. He's played his part. Now it's time for your father to learn what happens to men who tell lies."

"It's really him," I gasped, staring at the man who was Ryan's brother. Alive, barely.

His cheeks were hollow, his limbs lacking so much muscle his skin clung to bone.

Ryan clenched his fists, his eyes glassy. "Yes, it's Jake. My father managed to save him, and Larissa promised to bring him back."

"That was almost fifteen years ago. You can't..." Luke shook his head, staring at the bed, appalled. "He's not alive. He's no better than a ghost."

"No, I've brought him back for playtime. Isn't that right, Ryan?" She tossed the ball of energy between her hands, cocking her head to one side.

Ryan's sombre expression was all the confirmation I needed.

I couldn't process the truth. My heart twisted at the thought of Ryan playing with his big brother in this room, growing up while Jake had one foot in the grave. Stolen fleeting moments. I couldn't imagine how painful that was. But then I remembered he knew what happened to my parents. And while he wasn't responsible for their death, he hid the truth from me and groomed me for their experiments. He was a tortured little boy who didn't grow up because his brother never did.

"That's unnatural. It's *inhumane*." Luke made a noise of disgust as he planted himself between me and the witch.

"He's not a human," Larissa countered, a smirk lifting the corner of her lips. "But his time has come to an end. The dagger is in the building; I'll have it by the end of the night. With the Royals sticking their nose in, it's time for me to tie up loose ends."

Wind whipped through the room, and the balcony doors rattled, the air growing so cold my breath fogged in the air. My hand instinctively moved to the dagger strapped to my thigh.

"You can't kill him." Silver pooled in Ryan's eyes, a growl ripping from his throat.

"Wait, what?" Nadine looked between them, panic rising in her voice. "I thought you were just going to torture the hybrid. This wasn't the deal."

"The *deal* was that I'd gain you favour with Damien. I didn't say how, or when."

"You shallow bitch," Ryan snapped at Nadine, planting his feet shoulder-width apart as he guarded the bed. "Sleeping with the alpha's son wasn't enough?"

"Evidently not." Larissa's laugh grated like nails on a chalkboard, shadows swirling in her palm. She felt stronger, her control of the shadows a sign Béibhinn was lending her power. "My magic is the only thing keeping your brother alive. Your father broke his side of the deal, and now it's time for me to collect." Magic charged the air as she sent the shadows after Ryan's brother.

"No!" Luke launched himself across the room, forcing Larissa to redirect the spell.

Fear straightened my spine as her power slammed into Luke's chest, the bond vibrating in mine as his body hit the ground with a sickening crack.

The roar that ripped from my throat was raw, carnal fury. A red mist descended, rage pulsed within me as my magic soared. She had tortured my mate, haunted his nightmares, and almost robbed me of the chance to complete the bond. I wasn't letting her touch a single hair on Luke's head ever again.

I leaped at her, my form shimmering as I shifted mid-air. My jaw elongated, my roar becoming a snarl.

Larissa's dress caught on rubble as she tried to back away, my paws gouging through a wall of defensive magic as she threw her hands up.

I dropped to the ground, the sound of Luke's groan while he got to his feet only spurring me on as I went for her again. This time my teeth were aimed right for her jugular.

She twisted, my bottom teeth sinking into the fleshy muscle of her shoulder while my canines ground against her collarbone. Her shriek sent a shudder of excitement down my spine.

Chaos broke out around me, Nadine diving on Luke at the same time Ryan barely dodged a spell Larissa sent his brother's way. The legs of the bed buckled, the base giving way.

Ryan's eyes widened in horror. He dived to stop it, but he was too late, the mattress flipping as the bed collapsed.

Larissa's cackle became a scream as I ripped my teeth free, tearing a piece of her pale flesh with me. Her blood was sour on my tongue as I spat the clump of muscle and skin out.

The machine started beeping faster, the pitch rising with urgency. I turned my attention to Nadine, bounding across the room to put myself between her and my mate. Out of the corner of my eye, I could see Ryan on his knees. He cradled Jake's head in his lap, muttering "no" over and over again as he tried to put the needle pumping spelled blood back in his brother's arm. His hands were slick with blood. My pity withered as I saw the parallels, how he looked just like me when I found Kate.

Damien's voice boomed, and I looked up to see the alpha running over the remains of the corridor wall. Horror contorted his features as dropped to his knees beside his sons.

Nadine froze, backing away towards her alpha.

Ryan didn't protest as his father shoved him aside, looking every inch like the lost little boy he was.

Damien clutched Jake's face between his hands with a tenderness I'd never seen the Faolchúnna alpha display. "No, no. This can't be." He brushed his son's dark curls back, snatching the needle off Ryan with a deadly glare, as if it was his fault. He stared at the machine that was screeching before looking at Larissa, his voice cracking with desperation. "You have to fix him. Fix him now!"

The necromancer shook her head, her brow creasing in the most pathetic, fake display of pity I'd ever seen. "I'm afraid it's too late."

"You saved him once. You can do it again." The alpha hugged his son's head to his chest as he fumbled with the needle. "Ryan! Do something," he ordered, jabbing his index finger at the spelled machine that was no longer pumping what smelled like a mix of blood and a magic that felt wrong, as if it wasn't meant to exist in that form. "Stay with me, Jake. I'm right here."

The werewolf's chest was still, the sluggish beat of his heart slowing.

"It's your fault," Damien spat at his youngest, utter hatred lacing his every word. "You failed him the day of the attack, and now again. You're a pathetic excuse for a werewolf. I wish it had been you—"Jake's body convulsed. His heart skipped a beat. The alpha rushed to lower him to the floor, starting chest compressions as if he could save his son's failing heart.

Larissa's lilac eyes glowed as she stood back and watched them scramble to save Ryan's brother.

Lars joined her side, the pupils of his ruby eyes dilating at the sight of the blood. "This is quite the mess." His voice was low as he turned to the witch, his lips pursed. "How do you suggest I explain the noise to our guests downstairs?"

"*I* suggest that you don't try to hide something from me in future. Fear is not the same thing as loyalty, Lars. Your coven betrays you all too readily."

Luke took my hand, slowly pulling me back towards the door. One of Jake's weak ribs cracked under the alpha's desperate attempts to kick-start his son's heart.

The vampire raised a thin eyebrow, his tone cooling. "Careful, Larissa. We're one and the same."

"What the hell is going on?" Tom's voice pulled my gaze away from the carnage. He stood in the destroyed doorway, the wooden remains snapping under his weight as he strode inside. He looked to us for an answer, shock crossing his face when he noticed Damien on the ground. The Faolchúnna alpha's shoulders shook as he clutched his son to his chest. "That's not possible."

Ryan's gaunt cheeks were pale, his knuckles white as he squeezed his brother's hand. The room fell silent as Jake's eyes fluttered open to reveal silver-ringed irises, a shuddering breath slipping from his lips. The werewolf's body stilled, the machine flatlining as his head dropped into his father's lap.

Damien's scream of anguish pierced the silence. The raw sound of heartbreak tugged at my heart, but fear dragged its icy claws down my spine as the Faolchúnna alpha turned on us. There was nothing but blazing rage behind his cold eyes. His upper lip curled with a snarl, his words dripping with the promise of revenge. "You did this."

# CHAPTER 23
## LUKE

Damien's pupils were dark, endless pits of hatred, the silver of his irises glowing as he gave in to his wolf side. He couldn't shift outside of the full moon despite his desire to change that, but a werewolf could lose themself to their base instincts, and I could tell by the growl thundering in his chest that the Faolchúnna alpha had given in to the grief. My bond tightened as Damien's icy gaze met mine. There was only one thought behind them: revenge.

An engine roared to life, followed by Alice's voice and the crunch of footsteps on gravel drifting from outside. Lars shot through the doors in a blur of motion, leaning over the stone balcony just as something below shrieked.

The vampire cursed, racing through the empty space where the wall once stood and disappearing down the corridor. I could hear Dylan and Josh too, hope swelling within me at the sound of them rescuing some captives.

Any thoughts of following Lars to protect the others vanished when Damien laid his son onto the ground with care, the bands of muscles across his shoulders tensing so much the back of his suit jacket split when he rose to his full height.

There was no time for reason or explanations as the alpha launched himself at us. Eve got to him before I could, her paws slamming into the alpha's stomach and shoving. He stumbled back a few steps, gripping her scruff and yanking. She tumbled to the side with a yelp.

I didn't know what experiments he'd been playing with, but even an alpha shouldn't be that strong in his human form.

"Get back." My dad crossed the room, placing himself in the middle.

My gaze snagged on Eve's shredded dress pooled on the floor. The witch's lilac eyes followed mine, widening as she spotted the dagger. It was the wrong one, but I needed to distract her as my dad faced down the alpha.

We both dove for the dagger, my fingers closing around the bone hilt. Her nails dug into my wrist, biting into the skin there as she tried to wrestle it free.

"Give that to me," she hissed, fire exploding from her fingertips and searing my skin.

I gritted my teeth, twisting to slam my foot into the witch's chest and dislodge her grip. The stench of burned flesh turned my stomach, sending me back to the endless nights she tortured me until I lost consciousness. I shook the images from my head, focusing instead on the lessons it had taught me. The ability to withstand her pain. I took a deep breath, planting my foot against her solar plexus and digging my heel in with one last shove.

Her grip loosened, and I snatched my wrist free, rubble digging into my back as I rolled out of reach. A blast of power glanced off my shoulder, and I scrambled to my feet, my lips curving at the sight of the fury twisting her mouth.

"I'm not as much fun when you can't have me doped up on nightshade, am I?" She growled and my smile widened. I was no match for a witch with Royal blood, but sometimes raw power wasn't the only thing that mattered. Sometimes strength wasn't about the physical.

Eve and my dad fought to my side, my mate taking a lump out of the alpha's leg while my dad wrestled him to the ground. Nadine lunged at my mate, her red hair streaking like flames as they crashed to the ground.

"Back off, Damien. They did not do this." Command rang in Dad's voice as Damien's hands wrapped around his throat.

Ryan hung back, crawling over to his brother's side.

I caught Larissa watching, her eyes dancing with amusement. She didn't just lack empathy; she looked like someone watching long-laid plans falling into place.

"You," I whispered, the bond in my heart vibrating as Eve threw her head back and howled. A call for backup. Alice's answering call echoed from outside.

Larissa turned to me, running her tongue across her teeth as if their pain and the chaos was some kind of turn on. "Oh, I see the cogs turning." She rose to her feet and brushed the dust off her gown, flames licking at her fingertips.

It wasn't a hybrid who had attacked Ryan's brother. If he saw a wolf as a child, it could have been one of Larissa's hounds. She knew she needed to find a hybrid for the prophecy. Damien was a young alpha who already had fucked up ideals. What better way to nurture that than give him the ultimate reason to hate hybrids?

"You did it." I gripped the dagger tightly in my hands, something about the magic imbued in the blade bothering me. If it wasn't Béibhinn's dagger, then why did it feel like it called to me? "You orchestrated all of this."

A loud growl ripped from my mate as she threw Nadine off her, sending the Faolchúnna wolf crashing into the cabinets. Something fractured on impact, Nadine's head cracking back against the metal counter and sending the vials stacked on top tumbling onto the floor. They crashed around her in a shower of glass, Nadine's eyes shuttering closed as she slipped out of consciousness.

"Good boy," Larissa purred, a malicious smile lighting up face as she watched Ryan crouch over his brother's dead body.

I swear, she looked like she wanted to bottle his tears. No matter how much I hated Ryan, his brother was innocent in all of this. I remembered the crippling pain of thinking I'd lost Alice as if it was yesterday.

"Did you really think a man was behind everything? That *he* was pulling the strings?" Her laugh was a callous rasp, shadows joining the flames building in her palm. "No, dear boy. He's simply my sword. Men like to think women are easy to manipulate, but they're mistaken. A weak man's hatred can be channelled and controlled so easily they barely remember where is started. They just want to feel in control, superior. Their ego is their downfall."

As I watched Damien grapple with my father, fuelled by hatred and rage born of pain, I could see the truth in her words.

"Now, as much as you deserve a prize for figuring that out," she purred, wiggling her fingers as the shadow-infused flames grew and sparks flew from her fingertips, "I'm afraid that dagger you're holding is mine."

She lunged, shadows slicing through my side as I spun away and leaped over a pile of rubble to put some distance between us. The dagger hummed in my grip.

"Not the girl." Larissa flung her arm out, a wall of power sending Damien stumbling back as the alpha tried to launch himself at my mate. "She needs to be kept alive."

I spotted the dagger hilt peeking out of his trouser pocket.

*Eve. Damien still has the real dagger.*

Eve's head swung in the Faolchúnna alpha's direction, bloody saliva dripping from her mouth as she nodded. She kicked off her strong haunches, launching herself across the room.

At the same time, Larissa sent a stream of shadow towards me. My arm hair was singed as I rolled out of the way, catching a glimpse of Ryan's figure retreating down the corridor, his brother's frail body bundled in his arms. There was no sign of my sister or any backup, the noise outside rising as shouts erupted.

*I think the captive vampires are on the loose.*

I couldn't be sure though, Lars' new recruits wouldn't be much better behaved. But as another blood-curdling scream echoed, I knew reinforcements weren't coming. We needed to get out of here, and I wasn't leaving my mate behind.

Eve had Damien pinned to the ground, her jaw snapping at his throat. His fist connected with her chest, the sound of my mate's ribs crunching made my heart pound in my ears. Larissa's shadows surrounded me, the countertop digging into my lower back as she pinned me there.

"Give it to me," she ordered, shadows licking the fingertips of her outstretched hand. The handle of the dagger vibrated in my hand, as if recoiling from her.

Shadows bit into the skin of my fist, pain radiating through my nerves as they cut through tendons and muscles to force my hand to open. The dagger clattered to the ground, and Eve's head snapped up.

*No!*

She barrelled into Larissa with so much force the witch's head snapped back when they hit the ground. They rolled and landed with Larissa straddling Eve. The witch was so caught up with pressing the blade against my mate's throat that she didn't notice my father snatching the real dagger from Damien's pocket.

The Faolchúnna alpha did though. A guttural growl ripped from his throat as grabbed my father by the shirt and slammed him into one of the balcony doors. Wood splintered and glass cracked as they fell outside. They wrestled for the dagger, Dad flipping it so that the blade pricked the alpha's chest, a patch of red blooming on his torn shirt.

My heart was in my mouth as Damien gripped the hilt, his blood-stained hands covering my dad's as the two alphas fought for control. Instincts urged me to race after them, but the mate bond sparked at Eve's shrill howl. I turned to see my mate's blood welling where dagger met skin.

In my mind, I was back at the graveyard in Edinburgh, watching Larissa carve a blade through my mate's chest. I was in

Dublin, watching blood bead against the dagger as Larissa pressed it to Eve's throat. I was in my makeshift cell, pain lancing through every inch of my body as Larissa tore open unhealed wounds.

Shadows surged around Larissa, the magic binding me slipping.

There was no choice.

I threw myself at the witch, my claws slicing into her forearm as I wrenched her arm away. She hissed, shadows lashing at me as I pried the dagger from the witch's hands and flipped it on her.

Blood spattered my face; the steel blade now jammed into her side. I revelled in her howl of pain before rigging the dagger out of her flesh and tossing it into the rubble.

*Luke!* Eve kicked Larissa off, her eyes wide. *The balcony.*

I was already on my feet, racing towards the two alphas as Damien slowly positioned the dagger at my father's heart. They teetered on the edge of the balcony where a chunk of the stone barrier was missing, their feet sliding on the crumbled pieces beneath them.

My heart seized as Dad's sombre gaze locked with mine, his eyebrows drawn together in quiet acceptance.

"No."

I rushed forward as Damien roared and shoved my alpha, sending them tumbling over the edge. Fear dug her nails into my hammering heart as they disappeared. I reached the balcony ledge too late, my fingers grasping air. They hit the gravel with a loud thud, blood pooling around them turning the grey stones russet in the moonlight.

"Dad!" My legs buckled and I fell to my knees, pieces of the ruined balcony cracking off as I gripped the edge.

Time moved in slow motion as Damien rolled over to reveal my dad beneath him.

His tuxedo jacket hung open to expose the dagger's hilt and crimson blood spreading from where his heart once beat for his pack, for his family.

A scream of anguish tore from my throat as I stared down at

the limp body of the man who had raised me. The man who had taught me everything I knew, my alpha. The air left my lungs, something cracking deep inside me as the silver in my dad's eyes guttered out.

# CHAPTER 24

### EVE

I was frozen to the spot, watching in horror as the alphas tumbled over the balcony. Luke's knees cracked against the ground as he doubled over, gripping the ledge. The bond twisted when his agonised cry pierced the night sky.

My ears rang as I raced across the room, my paws sliding on rubble and debris. I stopped beside Luke, my heart pounding as I saw Tom lying below.

I threw my head back and howled, a keening wail.

Luke's pain coursed down the magic tethering our souls, throbbing in my chest as I felt the alpha's life slipping away. It wasn't like the mating bond; it was a deeper, communal sense of deep loss that washed over my body and robbed me of my breath. As if we had lost the magic binding our pack together.

Luke was on his knees yelling, begging for his dad. His tear-streaked cheeks glistened in the moonlight watching over us.

"No," my voice was a coarse whisper as I shifted back into my human form, the soles of my feet meeting the cool stone. I dropped beside Luke, a deep ache settling in my heart. "Oh God. Please, no."

But I knew. I could feel it. Tom's blue eyes stared up at the starry sky, his heart still. The Faolchúnna alpha was nowhere to be seen.

His cries stopped as I touched his shoulder lightly. Luke stared down at his father, likely in disbelief of the nightmare we were living in.

Josh was the first of those below to find the body. He stopped mid-stride as he stepped into view, carrying an unconscious young man in his arms.

"Luke, look at me." I tugged on his arm, trying to pull him away from the edge. "We need to get out of here."

He didn't budge, his hands balling into fists as he watched his family discover the body.

"Tom!" A lump formed in my throat at the pain in my friend's voice as he laid the rescued wolf down and sprinted over to his alpha. Josh kneeled beside Tom's body, his shoulders sagging. "Fuck. No, this can't be happening."

Dylan was next, his eyes widening at the sight of Tom lying in a pool of blood. He looked up at us, his throat bobbing, and he raced back towards the house. "Alice! Alice, stay inside."

*Alice. Helena.* My heart shattered, tears streaming down my cheeks. And Max. My stomach heaved at the thought of Tom's little boy.

I glanced behind us as quiet footsteps broke the silence. Larissa snatched the dagger from the rubble. I didn't move to stop her. The witch slipped away without so much as a backward glance, shadows swarming from the corners of the room to follow her.

Luke was motionless as I cupped his face, forcing him to meet my gaze. When he did, the sorrow in his beautiful hazel eyes knocked the air clean out of my lungs. I could feel it down the bond: a grief that threatened to pull him under. "We have to get out of here."

Dylan walked back outside, murmuring something in Josh's ear before they switched places.

I pressed my forehead against Luke's, keeping his face trained on mine. The crunch of Dylan's shoes on the gravel punctuated the silence. I flinched as the wet sound of the dagger being pulled from Tom's chest came from below.

Dylan's shoulders were rigid as I peered over the edge to meet his gaze, trying to communicate my silent thanks. He nodded, wiping his eyes as he slipped the dagger into his jacket pocket and folded Tom's arms across his chest.

"Luke." My voice was soft as I tugged on the sleeves of his suit. He was covered in dirt and blood from the fight, his hair dishevelled. But despite his muscular frame and battle marks, he had never looked so fragile.

He cleared his throat, blood-crusted hands shaking as he reached out for me. "I can't," his voice cracked, sorrow drenching every word. "I c-can't leave him."

"Never." I pressed a kiss to his damp cheek, taking his large hand in mine and squeezing tightly. "Dylan has him. We're going to take Tom home, okay, Love?"

He shook his head, the lost expression on his face slicing through my heart. He was frozen, his body trembling as shock began to set in.

Only when Alice's shriek came from below did he move, his face crumpling as he watched his sister wrestle against Josh. He held her back for as long as he could before Alice shoved past him, her bare feet sinking into the gravel as she sprinted over to her father.

She collapsed beside him, her screams drawing guests from inside the mansion. She clutched her dad's limp body and wailed, her voice vibrating with a raw pain that I hadn't heard since the night I held Kate.

His sister's cries drove Luke to his feet, his movements slow and his hand tightening around mine as he looked over the balcony one final time.

I grabbed my dress from the destruction. The skirt was ripped, the black satin covered in creases, but something made me put it on. Werewolves had no shame in being naked after shifting, yet I didn't want to greet Tom like that for our last time. Maybe it was the human side of me, maybe grief made no sense.

Luke was silent as he zipped up the back of my dress. There was a finality about the way he pressed a soft kiss to the crescent-shaped scar on my back before placing my hair back into place. I knew our lives would never be the same again.

Corridors that were once a maze led us straight to a staircase. We descended straight to the foyer, guided by the grief in our hearts. Fae, vampires, even the Royal emissary stepped aside to let us pass. There was no sign of Damien or Lars, no doubt hatching a cover story somewhere in the depths of this godforsaken place.

The moment Luke stepped outside, Alice's head snapped up and her delicate features crumpled as she broke into a fresh wave of tears.

Luke ran to his little sister, and she collapsed into his arms as he joined her by their father's side. My throat constricted as I watched him console her despite his own grief, her hands trembling as she clutched his lapels. There were no words, only a tidal wave of grief.

Dylan and Josh stood by my side, giving the siblings space to mourn. Onlookers murmured softly, but their words were white noise.

*Help Alice.*

Even in through our link, my mate sounded broken and hollow. I stepped forwards, gently peeling Alice off him. She clung to me, her arms wrapping around my neck as Luke shrugged his jacket off and draped it over her shoulders.

Only when Luke nodded did his two friends approach. They flanked my mate as he bent down on one knee, gently closing his alpha's eyelids. Lifting Tom into his arms, he gently kissed his dad's forehead, a single tear rolling down his cheek.

"It's time to go home."

# CHAPTER 25

## LUKE

I was numb. Numb to the world, to my mind cruelly replaying how Helena's heart broke right in front of me when we told her the news. Her screams would haunt me, the sound of a lover mourning the other half of their heart was a certain kind of grief that I would never forget. Alice was a shell of herself, glued to my side since the moment she collapsed in my arms that night. As if I was worth holding onto.

Max ran past, the pants of his black suit swamping the red car shoes he'd insisted on wearing, the dagger in my heart twisting.

My little brother. The innocent child who idolised me. Fatherless. He'd never know what it was like to grow up with our dad. He'd been robbed of those memories. Would he even remember the way our dad laughed? The way he loved so loudly?

All because of me.

I chose Eve over my dad—over my alpha, and I'd do it again. But the guilt weighed on my shoulders, threatening to drag me under. And I wasn't sure if I wanted to fight it anymore. I'd prove the voices in my head right.

Despite what my dad claimed, I wasn't worthy. I never was.

*Luke.* Eve placed a hand on my arm, her touch feather light. *It's time to go.*

She waited another moment before taking my hand in hers and pulling me up. The sympathy shining in her eyes made me want the floor to open up and swallow me, as if this was a nightmare I could escape. Every look of pity from a pack member, every condolence, forced home the reality. My father was dead.

I couldn't wrap my head around it.

As I looked around the pack house, at the many pictures plastered on the walls with my dad laughing, moments captured throughout the years, it just didn't seem real. He was everywhere from the old markings on the wall where he'd charted our heights growing up to the secret carving of our names that I knew was under the dining table. His scent was everywhere, all over the home of our pack. Because he was the pack, he was home to us.

Helena and Mary had cooked up one hell of a spread, except food that should have smelled delicious only turned my stomach. I'd barely kept anything but water and whiskey down the past few days. The house was packed with pack members and friends, all exchanging stories about Dad. It was a sombre celebration, but it felt wrong. A part of me wanted to run around and tell them to stop, stop talking about my dad like he was gone.

I kept expecting him to walk in the doorway, but he didn't. And he never would again.

"Luke." Eve adjusted my tie, cupping my jaw. She tilted my head down, forcing me to look at her, to face those piercing blue eyes that could see into the depths of my soul because it was hers. "We need to head out there first."

"I can't," I whispered, resting my forehead against hers as another wave of grief washed over me. "I can't do this."

"You can, and you will. Your dad was the best alpha any pack has ever had, and we're going to give him the send-off he deserves."

I hissed out a breath, fighting back tears.

"Your dad would want you to do this. He loved his kids more than anything, Luke." There was a certainty in her tone that I wished I could bottle because the only thing that still felt real to me was the bond tying us together. "Do this one last thing for him."

*Breathe.*

My hands found her waist as I took a deep, long breath in. I held it there, counting to six, before exhaling slowly. Just like I'd walked her through that night in the park. Except now she was the one holding me together.

Craig walked over, surprising me by pulling me into a crushing embrace first. "I'm so sorry, Luke. Your dad did so much for me and Eve. I'll never forget it."

Eve murmured her thanks and a promise to see him at the wake as she squeezed her friend tightly, both sharing a sombre look of understanding. They knew loss.

Darius and Jonas found us as we stepped outside, the bonfire crackling near where Darren was prepping more food for after the ceremony.

"We're so sorry for your loss," Darius said, extending his hand. "Tom Whelan was an incredible alpha, one who always had our respect. He will be sorely missed."

I shook his hand, swallowing the lump rising in my throat.

Jonas was less composed than his partner as he clasped my hand, pulling me into a tight hug. "I'm sorry, Luke. Your dad was a great man," he whispered, his molten eyes swirling with emotion as he released me and moved to embrace my mate. "Please, let us know if there's anything we can do."

They knew the full story. I'd sent Dylan and Josh to the Dark Night soon after we returned home to make sure the true story got out there before Damien could spread his lies. I wasn't letting the villain write the ending to my dad's story.

"We'll see you out there," Eve said, her eyes glassy as she inclined her head.

Murmured well wishes faded into the background as she led me away from the pack house, where fires burned and friends commiserated. Once they saw me enter the forest, they would soon follow.

The moon followed us, her light filtering through the canopy of trees beginning to regain their leaves as we walked through the forest trail in silence.

Helena had decided not to wait weeks until the full moon for his burial. Not only because she couldn't join the hunt anyway, but because of the impending prophecy. Legend claimed that a wolf's soul should be released before the next full moon. She didn't want to risk that being true if Larissa were to come for us then.

Another layer of mounting guilt pressed down on me as the trees gave way to a clearing lit by spelled firelight that danced on torches dotted around the perimeter. Moonlight flooded the area where we always started our pack runs. The place where I'd shifted with my dad for the first time as a kid, and the place his spirit would run alongside me one last time when the full moon came to pass.

Eve's hand tightened around mine. The pyre stood tall at the centre of the clearing, my dad's body laid on top under the glow of the gibbous moon. Four coloured fires burned around the pyre, one positioned at every corner with offerings for each of the elements.

He was so still, a calmness to his expression. Gone was the blood, the dagger safely stashed away. Dressed in one of his favourite navy suits, his arms crossed over his chest with his hands clasped. I saw his cufflinks as I moved closer, adorned with our family crest.

The trees behind us rustled, and I turned to see Helena walking into the clearing. She gripped Alice's hand, while her other arm kept Max balanced on her hip. Her long flowing dress was navy to match her husband, sequins sparkling on the bodice like the stars above us. My dad's wedding ring hung on a chain around her neck, sitting right over her heart.

Max didn't cry for me like he usually would, instead his lower lip trembled at the sight of our dad lying at the top of the pyre.

Alice lifted him off her mam, gently cooing in his ear to settle him. "It's okay, Max. Dad is sleeping, remember? He's gone to be with the big wolves now."

He nodded, and my heart cracked a little more. Losing my dad wasn't the hardest part, it was trying to live without him. He was always the voice of reason who knew exactly what to say. I'd always aspired to be like him, even in my rebellious years. And now I was lost.

Tears clogged my throat, my hand growing clammy against Eve's.

She lifted my hand to her lips, brushing a kiss across my knuckles before turning to my little brother. "Hey, Max, let's go look at the snowdrops."

Helena walked over to the base of the pyre where I stood, while Alice carried Max over to the nearest tree where a ring of snowdrops grew around the base.

"It doesn't feel real. We said goodbye every time he left, just in case. I always knew marrying an alpha would come with its fair share of trials, but I never thought I'd lose him so soon." She spoke so softly it was barely audible over the gentle breeze. "I know you lost your mother a long time ago. You were even younger than Max. He's going to need you to help him through it. We're all going to need you."

I shook my head, tears stinging the corners of my eyes. "I'm not him, Helena. I can't do what he did. I can't lead like that. I'm not ready. I was supposed to have years left to learn from him."

"I remember him saying something similar when the time came. So, I'll tell you the same thing I told him: you will do what you have to. You'll find a way, and so long as you lead with your truth, your pack will follow." The fire that blazed in her eyes matched the heat of the auburn curls tumbling over her shoulders. She rarely wore it down, but Dad always said it was his favourite like that—wild. "I know you're scared. Scared to fight. But if we let fear control us, then they've already won."

"Was he ever scared?" I stared at the four fires, knowing that soon they'd come together to send my dad over the veil.

Helena laughed, playing with the chain around her neck. "Of course. He didn't try to hide it, either. He led with his heart on his sleeve. You just don't remember seeing it because you idolised him so much."

"Really?"

Voices rose in the distance as people filtered into the forest.

"The night he went to take down Damien and split the pack, he was terrified. You were only a toddler, and he'd already lost so much. Grief and fear are old friends; the two go hand in hand," she said, linking her arm with mine. "But if he let fear win, the Crescent pack would have never come to be. And all of this"—she motioned at the trees around us stretching into the night sky and where Max chased Alice and my mate around with a drooping snowdrop—"wouldn't exist. Fear has its place, but if we listen to it and let it stop us from standing up for what is right, we risk missing out on the most beautiful future."

"You sound just like him."

The voices grew louder as people stepped out into the clearing, Darren and Mary leading the way.

Helena dropped her head onto my shoulder, squeezing my hand when I placed mine in hers. "That's what happens after so many years together. I suppose his wisdom had to rub off, eventually. I was the hothead when we were dating."

Her joke tugged at the corner of my lips. "I hope the same isn't true for Eve."

"Oh, sweetheart. It will be, and you two will have the most wonderful life together. I can feel it."

She was a human, but Helena had strong instincts. My dad often trusted her over Darren when it came to decisions. Some humans were destined to be a part of the paranormal world, like how Craig had taken so well to being a vampire.

I could only hope that she was right about us.

"It's time."

# CHAPTER 26

LUKE

A mixture of pack members, friends, and members of the paranormal community that my dad had helped over the years formed a large circle around the clearing with the alpha at the centre. The four firepits cast a flickering light over their sombre expressions. My throat tightened as I noticed there were so many gathered to see our alpha over the veil that they formed rows going back beyond the tree line.

I stood beside Helena at the front of the circle, facing the base of the pyre. Eve was to my right with Dylan and Josh just beyond her. Helena gripped Max's shoulders as he stood in front of her, Alice to her left. Family gathered to say one final goodbye.

My chest tightened as I looked up, the sight of my dad lying there something I would never come to terms with. He was too young; he had so much life left to live.

Eve's hand rested lightly on the small of my back, tracing imaginary shapes over my spine to keep me grounded.

Except they weren't just shapes. She was writing 'I love you' over and over again.

Despite the fear and nerves knotting my shoulders, each familiar face in the crowd brought me comfort. Darius, Jonas, Craig, Mary and even Russell stood among those gathered to pay their respects, the Edinburgh alpha having jumped on a plane when he heard the news. Jeremy stood beside him, his frame far less frail, but his expression haunted as he watched the flames.

My mouth was dry; I didn't have the right words. I wanted to back out, to pass the honour of speaking onto Darren. But I couldn't. I had to do this for my dad.

"Thank you for gathering with us today. We are here to mourn a man who was not just our alpha, but a beloved husband, a father, and a friend," I began, swallowing hard to force the lump in my throat down. "Tom Whelan was an incredible man, an outstanding alpha taken from us too soon. So, tonight we mourn a deep loss that has rocked our community."

You could hear a pin drop in the silence as every single person present hung their head in respect. It shouldn't have shocked me. I knew he was well liked, but for everyone from vampires to Fae to show up—this kind of turnout was unheard of.

Helena inclined her head, willing me on.

"Together we mourn the man who was not only one of the greatest alphas to ever lead an Irish pack, but the man who formed the Crescent pack, chosen by the moon and not blood. He led us with dignity, kindness, and his heart." I wrung my hands, choosing each word carefully as the weight of doing him proud sat firmly on my shoulders. "He died doing just that, protecting his pack."

Murmurs of agreement spread throughout the crowd, especially our pack, each Crescent wolf's eyes turning silver.

"I don't want to dwell on his death." I struggled to get the last word out, my mind warring with the reality in front of me. "He deserves his life to be honoured, his achievements to be heard. We want to remember him as he was, full of life and positivity."

Helena nodded, her knuckles white as she clutched Alice's hand while Max hugged her waist. Eve's love flooded the bond, her silent encouragement ringing in my mind.

*Keep going, Love.*

"When I came to my dad with the news about Alice, I

couldn't understand why he wasn't losing it like me." My lips twitched as a few laughs broke out around us. "He was so calm and positive despite everything seeming so bleak. When I challenged him on it, he said something that has stuck with me ever since. 'Even in the darkest of times, we must find a reason to smile'. I have many stories about my dad, but the past few days have taught me that there are many I've never heard before. So, to honour my dad and his legacy, I'd like to invite anyone with a story to share to step forwards."

In true Irish fashion, despite everyone having a story, no one stepped forwards. Darren grunted as Paula gave him a not-so-gentle shove, scratching the back of his neck as he walked over to me.

He pulled me into a tight hug, clearing his throat as he clapped me on the back before turning to face the crowd. "Tom was my best friend," he began, the way his voice wavered tugging at my heartstrings. "We grew up together, and while I could tell you *many* crazy stories about our nights out and his college years —my drop out years. I want to share a story that's close to my heart. We have all cried for him. We grieve for him, but I want to tell you who our alpha really was."

Everyone listened with rapt attention as Darren delved into the story of Eve's parents, a few gasps echoing as he explained that Shane had come to Tom about fearing for their unborn child's life if the baby was a hybrid. He told us how my dad had counselled Shane, helping him and Eve's mother escape to Scotland to keep their child safe.

Eve shifted beside me, and I glanced over to find tears streaking down her face, her jaw clenched as she fought to keep her control.

"I don't think it's a coincidence that it was his son who brought her into our lives," Darren projected his voice, blood rushing to my cheeks as he pointed to me. "Tom saved my niece's life, and now I get a future with her thanks to his family. Out of all the stories and things he's done for me, I think this sums up exactly what made Tom special, and why I knew he was destined to become alpha." Darren wiped his eyes. He was usually the joker, the life of the party, but he was lost without his partner in crime. "That's... That's who he was at his core. It didn't matter who you were or where you came from, our alpha cared. He wanted to help. That's why he dedicated his life to being a doctor alongside raising his children. Even while leading the pack, he was still pulling hospital shifts. That's who my best friend was, not just a leader, but a person with a heart of gold that would do anything for the people he loved."

I reached out to grasp his arm, my cheeks wet. "Thanks, Darren."

He nodded, wringing his hands as he walked back over to his wife, who welcomed him with open arms.

I didn't have to worry about what to say next because once Darren finished speaking, the floodgates opened. I lost count of the number of people who stepped forwards to share their stories and memories. Everyone from colleagues, pack members, even Mary. By the time the line of people wishing to pay their respects ended, my cheeks were wet and Helena was gripping little Max's shoulder so tightly he wiggled out of her grip with a scowl.

I grabbed him before he could reach the base of the pyre, scooping my little brother into my arms. "Max." He kicked in my arms, but I held firm, letting him reach up to stroke our dad's arm gently. His brow creased when the alpha didn't respond, and I struggled to hold back the sob that stuck in my throat. "He's gone, little man. Come on, it's almost time to say goodbye."

Max nodded, and I pressed a kiss to the top of his head, walking back over to join Helena and address the crowd once more.

"Thank you all for sharing your stories. I know coming here today was a statement in itself. I'm sure my dad would have been grateful for your support, as am I." I kept one arm wrapped around Max, the other resting on Helena's shoulder. My mate's presence was a constant behind me, her pride coursing down the bond and lending me the strength to continue on without letting the cracked pieces of my heart shatter entirely. "Tom will always be a special member of our pack, the founding member, a wonderful alpha, and a friend to all. My dad spent his time honouring us, and now it's time that we honour his life and lay him to rest."

I nodded to Alice, my stomach sinking as I noticed her lip was cracked and bleeding. But she steeled herself and stepped forwards alongside her mother to join us at the front of the pyre. Four torches lay against the base of the wooden structure, one for each of the fires forming a diamond around it.

Eve followed, taking my brother's hand in hers after I set him down on the ground. Max watched with wide eyes as I handed out the torches to each family member, my mate taking his. We shared a long look before fanning out, each of us standing behind one of the small fires.

The coloured flames represented the elements coinciding with the offerings beneath them, along with different crystals and herbs forming a ring around each pit. Fire was a rich red, earth a leafy green, air a silver white like the moon, and the flame representing water in front of me was cobalt.

"Each of the offerings to the moon were chosen by our family tonight. Helena's choice is a candle from her wedding ceremony to Tom. May their love burn for an eternity here and in the afterlife," I explained, my throat bobbing as Helena lit her torch with her fire. This was the last part of the ceremony, the finality of it all slamming into me.

*Breathe.*

My mate's quiet voice anchored me.

"Max has chosen a white feather to represent air, knowing our father's spirit will be with him when the time comes for him to claim his powers." Eve lit their torch, Max's bright blue eyes— my dad's eyes—transfixed by the silver fire as it flared. I tore my gaze away. It would be me who had to teach him to shift when the time came, the realisation that I would have both the privilege and responsibility making my mouth go dry. "Alice has chosen sand from the beach where our dad often took us on hot summer days. It was actually the first location she shifted, and where she first ran under the moon with him."

Alice lit her torch, embers sparking as the green fire took hold. The sadness in my sister's eyes mirrored my own as I stepped towards the fire crackling in front of me.

"My offering tonight is water taken from the lake on these very lands. A spot that was always my safe haven on the lands he claimed for us, for the Crescent pack he founded." The water in the bowl at the base of the blue flames was bubbling from the heat as lit my torch. "It's where I went to think after his lessons, the place I found solace and calm. He taught me integrity and resilience—attributes I hope I can carry with me now that he's not here to guide us."

We turned in unison towards the pyre. Tears stung the corners of my eyes as I faced my dad, knowing this was my last action, my final moment with the man who had taught me everything I knew.

"Tom Whelan, you will always be the greatest man I've ever known. It was a privilege to call you my dad, our alpha. Until our next lifetime," I promised, my hand trembling as I lowered the torch until the cobalt fire latched onto the kindling. The other three followed, Eve holding Max's hand at the base of the torch to make sure he was a part of the ceremony. The flames spread, different colours mingling as the fire expanded and merged. "They will forever be in our hearts. May they run free for eternity and the full moon guide them always."

Helena clutched the ring around her neck as the flames engulfed the pyre, her eyes shining with tears. "May you run forever under the freedom of the moon."

Tendrils of flame stretched towards the moon as we watched on in silence. The crowd began to disperse back to the house for the wake, but my mate stayed rooted to my side.

A breeze cut through the clearing, fanning the flames. He was gone. My dad was gone, and I was to be alpha. The responsibility I'd sworn I didn't want had become something I so desperately wanted to do justice. I wanted to be an alpha he was proud of, the one he envisioned. But as a deep chasm of pain opened in my chest in his absence, I wasn't sure if I had it in me.

I rish werewolves fully embraced our native funeral traditions. The wake at the pack house continued into the early hours of the morning; food, more stories, and drinks followed Tom's burial. The storytelling became disjointed and chaotic as Guinness became spirits and shots. The stories grew more colourful and stronger by the hour. Not even my werewolf powers could offset the amount of Fae wine ingested. Tears of grief became tears of laughter as we shared in our pain.

I couldn't remember how we ended up at the Dark Night when the sun rose.

Dylan shielded his eyes, hissing like a vampire as the sun's rays hit his face. "Make it stop."

"Drama queen," Darius muttered, speeding across the room in a blur that made my stomach lurch, the liquid inside sloshing around. He lowered the blinds and strode back over to us with far too much energy.

I'd never seen Darius drunk, but after witnessing Jonas' rendition of Shania Twain's "Man! I Feel Like a Woman!", I could understand why one of them might want to keep a sober-ish head. One drop of blood with a vampire that intoxicated could have soured the mood quickly.

Luke and I were curled up at the corner table on the love seat, away from everyone else at the bar. I sat with my back against the wall and my legs across Luke's lap, my boots long since kicked off on the floor beside us. His hand rested on my thigh, something he'd taken to doing since Tom passed, as if he was afraid I might vanish.

"Talk to me," I murmured softly, running my hand through his hair.

The deep-purple bags under his eyes had nothing to do with the drink; Luke had barely slept since his dad's death. "I'm fine."

"The bond says otherwise."

"I'm... I'm here, okay? That's the best I can do right now."

I swallowed, my mind going back to that night in Lars' mansion as it often did. Back to the moment when Luke chose to tackle Larissa off me instead of helping his dad. I couldn't help but wonder if he'd left me with her, if he'd gone outside to help Tom sooner, if we would still be sitting here today mourning his life.

Vampires must sober up faster than werewolves, because Craig seemed unnaturally bright-eyed as he plonked two plastic cups filled with water in front of me and Luke. "Drink up, buttercup."

"How are you so peppy?"

"I fed this morning. It's kind of like getting your blood pumped—or my blood, I guess." Craig shrugged, flashing his fangs. "We metabolise the blood fast, couple that with a fresh dose diluting it, and we're flying. It's pretty awesome. I could have done with this when I was a fresher." He pushed the water towards my mate, his expression growing serious. "Drink it, you'll feel better."

"Isn't it a bit early for an intervention?" Luke shoved the water aside, pouring himself another glass of whiskey.

"You smell like a brewery." Josh stole the water for himself as he sat down in the chair across from us.

Alice joined him, some colour having returned to her cheeks. "He's right."

"You've all been drinking with me all night."

"Yes, last night. Not the last four days." Jonas was the voice of reason, concern furrowing his brow as he pulled a second table over to make room for everyone. They'd closed the bar for the day... or night—both, probably. So we were alone and could talk freely.

Luke rolled his eyes, the muscle in his jaw ticking as he turned to me. "Are you in on this?"

I didn't need to answer, the bond between us tensing the same way my chest tightened whenever Luke let his mask slip. He was hurting. It was understandable, but no amount of drowning his sorrows was going to change the fact that his dad was dead.

"It's normal to celebrate at a wake," Craig said, pulling over a chair. He sat with his legs on either side, his arms folded across the back of it, shuffling closer to me as Dylan decided to join us too, despite our proximity to the window and warmth of the sun peeping from beneath the blinds. "I'm all for celebrating life and death, but I'm worried about you. I know I'm probably the newest recruit here, but I know my bestie enough to know that she's worried, too."

My mate stared into the depths of the amber liquid as if it would give him the answers to whatever was on his mind. I could feel the guilt weighing on him, and I didn't need our bond to know he was blaming himself. That was his M.O. and I knew Luke's blueprint inside out. I desperately wished I could silence the voices in his heads, the doubts, but the only person who could take control was him.

"I'm not sure what to do," he said quietly, running his finger around the rim of the half-empty glass. "My dad was the one with all the answers, and now he's... gone. I feel like I've forgotten how to breathe."

"First, you grieve. Then, you honour your father's memory and lead your pack. Not because you're his son, Tom would have let you do whatever made you happy. But because you were destined to lead your pack, and they need you. Your family needs you. And you might not think you're worthy, but that's not your choice," Jonas said, his golden eyes softening. "You don't have to do it alone. That's what your friends and family are for."

Luke shook his head with a heavy sigh. "It wasn't supposed to be like this."

My heart twisted at how broken he sounded.

"It's a lot. Becoming alpha is rarely under ideal circumstances. It's the nature of the job," Dylan said, but backtracking when a growl rumbled from my direction. "I mean, the Irish packs have been unstable since the split."

I know what Helena had said about the dangers that came with the position of alpha. There were risks, and somehow they scared me more than what we were about to face because even if we overcame Larissa and Damien, what other threats were coming down the line in our future?

"Life itself comes with risks." Darius sipped from a glass of what smelled like blood mixed with cranberry juice. *Gross.* "You can't predict the future. You can't hide from it either. Tomorrow is going to come whether you want it to or not. So, whether you're an alpha or a human, you put one foot in front of the other."

"My dad always seemed so sure of himself."

Jonas shook his head, a wry smile tugging at the corners of his lips. "He wasn't always that way. He had years of experience by the time you remember him being alpha."

Luke's hand flexed on my leg, and he shifted in his seat. "What if I fuck up? Everyone's counting on me."

"Being alpha doesn't mean you're immune to mistakes," Alice chimed in, her gaze far away as she pulled the blind back and peeked out at the rising sun. "Dad made plenty, and he admitted to them. He could have searched the Faolchúnna pack lands when I was taken. I understand why he didn't. It would have caused a pack war. But every choice has a consequence."

"Do you think he was wrong?" I asked, the question slipping from my lips before my sluggish brain got the chance to vet it.

She paused for a long moment. "No. We spoke about it a few times, and I could tell he regretted the decision in hindsight. But he could only make calls based on the information he had."

"I think Tom was a natural born leader, but there's more to being alpha than that." Josh pried Luke's hand off the whiskey glass, swapping it out for an orange juice while Craig poured a coffee. "There's no such thing as the 'perfect' alpha. Tom led his own way. You'll find yours. We don't need you to be your dad; we need you to be yourself. As for the rest, we'll figure it out."

Footsteps echoed on the stairs, tension uncoiling in my shoulders as Alec came into view. The pale vampire had made an appearance at the wake to pay his condolences, though he left much earlier than other vampires.

*Come to think of it, was he the reason we'd ended up here?*

Alice's expression brightened, and I noticed that his tie was askew. Yes, she had suggested we head to the Dark Night once the celebrations subsided at the pack house. And now I knew why.

Alice and Alec. Never mind giving them shit about their names, Luke was going to lose his shit when he realised what was going on. Not just because werewolf-vampire relationships could be dangerous, but because that was his little sister.

I lifted the water to my lips to hide my smile. Dangerous or not, Alice deserved some happiness after everything she'd been through.

"There's someone at the front door," Alec said, inclining his head in greeting. I didn't miss the twitch of the corner of his lips as Alice caught his eye.

"We're closed." Jonas settled back against Darius as the ancient vampire slid an arm around his waist. It was rare to see them so relaxed, normal. It was nice. "Tell them to come back tomorrow."

"I did. They're refusing to leave. And I don't believe they can hear me either."

I sat up straighter, rubbing my throbbing temples. "What do you mean?"

Alec wrung his hands. "I think they're possessed."

ALEC LED the way to the CCTV room, which was located in an off-limits area I'd never visited before. Monitors lined the main wall of the dark room, some in colour and others in black and white. A long desk stretched beneath the monitors with neatly stacked files and paperwork, along with two fully kitted out computers.

We filed in, and Alec took a seat on one of the leather chairs as he pulled up an image on the computer screen. All the monitors flickered, switching focus to the alleyway entrance.

A hooded figure stood outside the rusted, glamoured door. Alec zoomed in to reveal a black box in their hand, complete with a ribbon and what looked like the fuzzy outline of an envelope attached.

"All she will say is that she's here for the Crescents."

Luke's arm wrapped around me as I shuddered, dread knotting between my shoulders.

Alec turned a knob on one of the keyboards to switch to a different camera view. My stomach plummeted at the familiar voice.

"I am here to deliver a message to the Crescents," Fiona's voice buzzed through the speaker. She looked up at the camera, her pixie-like face staring back at me through the screen.

"Fiona," I gasped, leaning in to get a closer look.

My mate's fingers dug into my side.

She'd stayed back with the Faolchúnna pack because her parents refused to leave. We'd been getting updates from Fiona via Mary, but it had been months since I'd seen my friend.

Any response Alec gave on the recording just resulted in her repeating her message. The live view showed she was still there, standing in a black funeral dress and flats with her legs bare despite the cool night.

"We need to get her inside."

Jonas pressed a button on the wall, his voice deathly calm as he made the order. "Take the girl inside. Do not use force."

"Wait." I pointed at the screen, my brow furrowing as I watched her make the same request again. Something about her movements didn't feel right to me. "This might not be Fiona."

I watched as the doorway on the screen shimmered and morphed into the true entrance of the Dark Night, two demons stepping out into the alleyway.

"Hold," Jonas ordered, lifting his finger off the intercom. "Follow me. Alec, keep monitoring the situation."

The vampire shared a long look with his partner before leading us out of the room, and along the dimly lit corridors of the Dark Night. I rushed to keep up, Jonas' long legs eating up the distance as he led us down a set of stairs and back to the double doors covered in intricate Celtic images.

My heart thumped as we passed two bouncers stationed there. Fiona stood outside the glass door, wispy blonde hair peeking out from beneath her hood. She shook her slowly head, the movement stilted and unnatural. Two demons were stationed either side of her, their nostrils flaring as if they sensed the same thing as me.

Something was wrong.

"Sir?" The demons backed up as we approached, their black-clawed hands, usually stuffed in their pockets, ready to grab Fiona if needed.

Jonas raised his hand in a silent signal for them to remain on standby.

"Fiona?"

Her head snapped up, the movement so rapid that vertebrae crunched. The same face I remembered stared at me, right down to the dusting of freckles on her cheeks. Except her eyes were black, inky pits.

She opened her mouth to reveal a set of blackened, rotting teeth. A stale stench assaulted my senses, my stomach doing a set of somersaults when I noticed her tongue was missing.

*Get back.*

There was something different about Luke's voice as he slipped his shoulder in front of mine. He stepped out, putting himself between me and whatever that thing was—because it certainly wasn't my friend.

The demons on either side of her tensed, their suave suits straining against the bulging muscles of their hulking figures. They kept one eye on Jonas, waiting for his command.

She offered the black box to us, the skin on her bony hands thinning. The straw-coloured hair that matched Fiona's slowly faded to white, her cheeks hollowing.

It was tied with a black silk ribbon; the glossy casing glinting in the morning light as the sun rose over the city.

"Careful," Jonas warned as Luke reached out, ruby flecking his gold irises. "It could be a trap."

Luke hovered his hand over the box, his fingers threading through the air surrounding it, searching for magical traces. I couldn't sense anything from the box, but the girl was steeped in it. The kind of unnatural magic that sapped energy from the world around it.

The *thing* watched him, her rosy-pink lips turning blue and then a deep purple. Skin stretched on her fingers, breaking away from the nail bed to expose bone as she thrust the box towards him.

Luke stepped back, bumping into me as he narrowly avoided the box hitting his stomach. "Place it on the ground, please."

She shook her head, a spider's web of veins becoming visible on her pale face with the movement, as if every action caused her to decay.

"I have an idea." The slightest movement of Jonas' hand kicking his staff into action.

The vampire's form blurred as the two demons grabbed her,

pulling blades from their belts. Metal sliced through bone and flesh. A loud shriek pierced the air as the box dropped to the ground, along with the girl's hands.

We leaped back, Luke flinging his arm out in front of me. I clutched my stomach as its contents threatened to reappear, bile rising in my throat.

Jonas stood by one of the demons, cleaning off the curved blade with a handkerchief and brushing down his slacks. "Disgusting." He leaned down, hooking the hilt through a loop in the bow, examining the box at a distance.

I stared at where her hands once were, shards of bone and sagging muscle sticking out of where her wrists had been severed. There was no blood, but whatever this was, it was long dead. Her skin greyed, another scream ripping from her peeling lips.

One of the hands twitched on the ground, shadows seeping from where it lay.

"Inside, now." Luke gripped my hips, pulling me back towards the doorway.

We rushed back into the Dark Night, Jonas dangling the box in front of him. I watched in horror as the thing rushed at the door that closed behind us, banging at the glass and wailing like a banshee until the shadows engulfed it. They singed its flesh, stripping it away until only bone remained. The skeleton let out one final scream from its gaping mouth before collapsing on the ground in a pile of bones and ash.

"What the fuck was that?" One of the demons asked, his amber eyes flaring. I recognised him as the one who had let me in on the first day here.

Luke released me as Jonas dropped the box on the floor, circling it like a wolf and its prey. "A message."

"If it was spelled, the wards would have stripped them," Jonas said, handing the blade back to his bouncers. "It's safe."

I joined Luke's side as he crouched beside the box, carefully undoing the bow. Nervous energy coiled in my gut as he pinched either side of the lid and flipped the box open.

Inside the box was a glass heart nestled in plush satin. No, it wasn't just glass. I could smell the blood, make out the veins beneath the glare of the lights above us. It was a real heart.

He peeled open the envelope to find a purple piece of paper with a note scrawled in cursive. I read it aloud, my heart thundering with each word.

"Dearest Eve, my deepest condolences on the passing of your dear alpha. The fates can be cruel in their workings." My voice wavered, a mixture of fear and anger bubbling inside me. "You know in your heart that the prophecy will soon come to pass. Your efforts to prevent it are in vain; the stars have already aligned. Come to me with your mate on the full moon to seal your destiny, or else you will forfeit your pack and everything you hold dear. I expect a response by the new moon. Until then, Larissa."

Jonas had his phone to his ear. His calm exterior rattled as he put Darius on speaker. "We need to get in contact with Fiona and her family immediately."

"What's that?" Luke asked, turning the page over to reveal another note. "It's the address where she wants us to meet on the full moon. Uaimh na gCat, Rathcroghan, Rathcave, County Roscommon."

I reread the address, snippets of childhood memories resurfacing. "Isn't Rathcroghan one of the archaeological sites? I remember visiting it on a school tour when I was a kid."

"Alec is making contact as we speak," Darius answered, fear creeping into the ancient vampire's voice. "Please tell me I didn't hear that correctly."

"You did. It's also called Oweynagat." Jonas shook his head, his pupils dilating as ruby particles swirled in the depths of his golden eyes. "A cave where the two sisters were buried. Otherwise known as the gateway to hell."

"Absolutely not."

I sighed, rubbing my forehead as a tension headache brewed behind my temples. "We've been talking about this for days, Darren. It's the only way."

He paced around my kitchen, much like my dad used to. The pack house still felt full of life, whereas our home felt empty. It was too quiet once people stopped popping by to pay their respects. Everything felt strange without him. Each morning, I came downstairs hoping to see him sipping coffee at the kitchen table. When Helena cooked, I half-expected my dad to waltz in and sweep her into his arms or mess up Alice's hair as he walked past. Memories replayed like ghosts everywhere I looked.

Max's first day back at school broke me. When he arrived home with his little backpack and test results, his blue eyes searching for their matching pair, the way his smile faltered was a knife to my heart all over again.

Darren shook his head, tension rolling through his shoulders as he looked at his niece—as if my mate wouldn't side with me. "I trust your instincts, Luke, but seeking them out is a mistake. I'm not trying to undermine you here. I just don't want to see either of you—or anyone—getting hurt."

"We can't avoid the witch forever. They're going to come for us either way, so we might as well make the first move." Eve shrugged, taking a sip of her tea before sinking back into the kitchen chair. "If we refuse, she's going to come for the entire pack."

We were one day away from the new moon, and I had yet to get everyone on board with our plan. We'd been talking for hours. Liz and the other wolves had returned home to their families, and Helena was upstairs putting Max to bed. Even Dylan and Josh had headed to the gym to blow off steam, with Alice tagging along. My friends didn't need convincing; I had their unwavering support.

Only Mary and Darren remained, and the latter was like a dog with a bone. I understood his reluctance, but Eve and I were in complete agreement. We were not going to sit around like ducks waiting for the Faolchúnna pack to come for ours. Death was a curse, and I was so sick of feeling like it followed me like a shadow.

"By agreeing to meet her at the cave, we guarantee two things. The Faolchúnna pack will be with Larissa and not here, so I can do my first run under the full moon and step into the role of alpha without them attacking. I can't accept the role until the full moon peaks, which gives Damien over a day to come for us if we don't make this deal," I explained, my words clipped because I was repeating the plan for what felt like the billionth time. "And they won't punish the pack because of us. If we face them, we take only the wolves old enough and trained to fight."

Our exile was lifted after the night Dad died. While the Royal emissary didn't see Larissa, she witnessed enough to know that there was something far more sinister going on. I didn't know what my dad said to her before his death, and I wasn't going to hunt her down to ask.

"If we let them come for the pack, they'll surround us. They have us outnumbered, especially with those zombie wolves Larissa summons." Eve took a sip of her tea, her responses calmer and more measured than mine. "It will only end in bloodshed. I've seen her raise a whole damn graveyard. I don't want to bring that to your doorstep."

"*Our* doorstep," I corrected, giving her knee a squeeze under the table.

Darren opened his mouth to argue, looking to Mary for support. She shook her head with a resigned sigh.

"So, let me get this straight. You're going to *trust* the witch is telling the truth about not attacking?" He arched a bushy eyebrow, throwing his hands into the air when I didn't react. "You're walking in there to die!"

"No, we have the real dagger. We're going in there to *fight*."

Mary pulled the box containing the dagger over to her. It was lying in the box that had housed the fake one, the silver blade glinting in the light. She'd spent half the afternoon staring at it.

"You recognise it." I tilted my head as I watched her trace her fingers over the bone-carved hilt.

"The dagger was my grandfather's, gifted to him by the Edinburgh alpha years ago." There was a nostalgic wistfulness to her tone as she replaced the cover. "It was passed down through the generations. Damien didn't even know about it because the dagger was a family heirloom rather than pack property. I had it until last year; I lost it when everything kicked off the night I helped rescue Craig. I didn't know how important it was. My dad never got the chance to tell me before he was killed."

My throat bobbed, and I wondered how much my dad never got to tell me.

"Darren." Eve's was voice quiet but firm, and she reached across the table to cup his hands. "Even if we avoid her this month, Larissa will just come for us again. She'll never give up. She's a necromancer; I'm not entirely sure she'll even stop in death."

"We can't outrun the prophecy anymore, the medium said as much." I sat up straighter in my seat and motioned for Darren to sit back down. His nostrils flared as he stared at me for a long moment before reluctantly following my request. "We either face Larissa on our terms once and for all, or we go through this every month. And if she attacks each time, soon we'll have no pack to protect. I will not have their blood on my hands."

"They're right, Darren." Mary braced her elbows on the table. "Luke is becoming alpha. They can't live their life on the run. I know you want to protect Eve, but this isn't the same as it was with Shane. There's so much more on the line."

His jaw feathered at the mention of his brother's name, expression softening. "I don't like this."

"I don't like it either," I agreed, my tone growing sombre. "Damien is more unstable than ever. He's out for blood, and I'm not giving him an excuse to come for our pack. I won't have bloodshed on our land, and I refuse to spend our future fearing for our lives."

"We're still outnumbered when it comes to taking them down." Darren folded his arms across his chest, his brow furrowed. "We can hold them off for you two to get to Larissa, but not for long."

"I know. That's why I've called in reinforcements."

Darren's eyebrow arched towards his greying hairline.

"I may not be alpha yet, but after seeing how many people turned up for my dad's funeral, it gave me an idea. He had so much respect in the community. I'm unproven, but I'm still his son, and that has to count for something." I swallowed hard, rolling my shoulders as anxiety seized the muscles there. "It might not work, but I've reached out to other packs in the UK, while Darius has put out word to other vampires, asking for help."

"That's a dangerous decision." Mary leaned forwards, concern wrinkling the corners of her eyes. "Damien and Lars will find out, as will Larissa."

"It felt right. I can't explain it, but I just know it's what he'd want me to do. He's always told me to ask for help and not do everything alone. I'm finally listening. If I'm wrong, then I'll stand over it."

Darren glanced at the clock and dragged his hand over his face with a heavy exhale. "I trust you."

The corners of my lips twitched. "Good, because we've already sent our reply."

"Of course you have." He glowered, but there was no malice behind it. No matter how worried or scared he was, I knew he just wanted to protect us. "I better head home before Paula skins me alive. We're not done talking. This plan has holes that need ironing out."

I nodded, my chair squeaking against the tiled floor as I stood. "I'm not trying to freeze you out of this, Darren. I need you—*we* need you."

"Come here," he grunted, walking over to Eve to pull her into a tight hug. "You really are your father's daughter, you know that?"

She embraced him just as tightly, curiosity sparking in her eyes. "Why?"

"Because he was responsible for my first grey hair, and now here you are adding more."

Mary laughed, rushing to cough as a cover-up when Darren shot her a glare before tiptoeing into the hallway to avoid waking Max upstairs.

Eve's smile warmed my heart despite the purple circles under her eyes. She hadn't slept properly since finding out that while Fiona was safe, her mother wasn't. After we alerted Fiona, she found her mother unconscious downstairs with a bottle of nightshade on the ground. It was only thanks to Jonas and Darius that she would survive because they caught her so soon. According to my mate, Fiona wanted to leave the Faolchúnna pack ever since Eve fled, but her parents were blindly loyal to Damien. Eve swore they were good, kind people, but I couldn't parse that with their decision to stay, choosing to believe their alpha over their own daughter.

"Get yourself to bed, kiddo," Darren murmured, patting her head as Eve stifled a yawn and waved him out the door.

"I'll be two seconds," Mary said, rummaging around in her handbag. She was staying with Darren, along with Fiona and her family while Fiona's mother recovered.

My mate nuzzled into my chest, her arms looped around my waist as Darren waved and hopped into his car—a flashy old Porsche he'd painstakingly resurrected from death's door. He could barely squeeze his broad frame into it, let alone a booster seat for his kid. Paula often joked it was his second wife.

"I'm gonna head to bed." Eve covered her mouth as she yawned again and pressed a gentle kiss to my cheek. "Night, Mary," she said with a small wave, before stepping back towards the stairs. "I'll see you upstairs."

"Goodnight." Mary's smile faded as Eve turned away, waiting until she hit the landing before holding out a white envelope to me. "This is for you."

My palms grew slick as I spotted my name scribbled on top in my dad's handwriting, tension coiling in my gut.

"Tom came to me the night before he died. He'd been having nightmares, and he was worried there was something to them. I told him he was being superstitious." Mary sniffed, pressing the envelope into my shaking hand. "I've never wanted to be right so much. He asked me to give this to you if something were to happen to him."

I turned the envelope over in my hand, the blue wax seal on the back stamped with our pack crest.

"Do you know what it says?"

"No, I didn't open it. Your dad wasn't scared when he came to me. He seemed almost at peace," she whispered, her voice thick with unshed tears. "He told me not to come to the Abhartach mansion that night, as if he knew what was going to happen."

Darren beeped impatiently, cringing and raising his hand in apology when he remembered half the neighbourhood were in bed.

"A medium told Eve that death was coming," I admitted,

tracing my thumb over his penmanship. "She thought it was about us. Maybe it still is."

She patted my hand, her breath fogging in the cool air as she stepped outside. "Listen to what he has to say. Your father loved his family more than anything."

I barely registered her leaving or the roar of the engine as Eve's uncle sped away. My gaze was glued to the envelope in my hands.

The kitchen was empty when I walked back inside and sat at the head of the table in my dad's old seat. A part of me wanted to fetch Eve, or even Helena, but something deep in my core said not to—as if this was supposed to be one last moment between us.

I cut through the wax seal with a knife, my hand trembling as I slid a folded piece of paper from the envelope. The sight of his writing and the way his scent lingered on the page brought tears to my eyes.

*Luke, my son. If you're reading this, then the worst has come to pass. Ever since we landed from London, I keep having these nightmares of falling, of ravens visiting me in my dreams. Helena thought I was losing my marbles, but I couldn't shake the feeling that my time was up.*

*I don't know how, when, or why. But what I do know is that it wasn't your fault. Whatever reason your brain has cooked up to blame yourself, it's not true. I've always known that when my time comes, it will be at the hand of Damien. I was told this many years ago by a psychic, and given the way life has come so full circle recently, I believed it to be true. I should have killed him all those years ago when the Faolchúnna pack split; it would have saved us both so much heartache. Kindness was always my downfall. As yours is your lack of self-belief.*

*You're going to be alpha now and that comes with a lot of responsibility, but also power. Your instincts will be heightened, and while you don't believe yourself right for the job, I know I've raised a strong, fair man who is more than capable of leading the Crescent pack. Don't walk in my shadows, Son. Step into your light.*

*I've spent a lot of time in contact with Cassandra. Mary worked with the sphinx back in Cambridge to examine the prophecy, and we think there might be a loophole. It has to come true, but it may not play out the way you think. Wielding that blade will grant Larissa the power she seeks, but it can also take power away. Eve is the key. Trust her judgement, trust in your bond, and trust that love is the purest form of magic.*

*Alice will get a letter from me too, as will Helena, so you don't need to pass any messages on. Just look after them, be there when they need you, and teach Max to grow up to be like his big brother. Because you are a good role model, Luke. You're worthy of this position, and your mate. Promise me that you will embrace it and live every moment of life to the fullest—the good and the bad.*

*I'm incredibly proud of you. When you step up as alpha, know that I'm always there with you in spirit, and in your heart.*

*Love you always,*

*Tom*

I didn't notice Eve standing in the doorway. I couldn't see anything through the tears in my eyes as they fell freely and my shoulders shook. The bond between us throbbed in my chest as she crossed the room and wrapped her arms around me, holding me tightly as choked sobs racked my body. I clutched the note, the last piece of my dad, and let grief wash over me.

# CHAPTER 29
## EVE

I woke to an empty bed. Thankfully, one call to Jonas was all it took to find Luke. Benji had called the vampire because apparently my mate's impending alpha status had gone to his head, and he'd broken into the boxing gym.

Between escaping evil wolf packs and outrunning witches, I still hadn't got around to passing my driving test. Calling Fiona up for a lift had brought up a sense of déjà vu.

"Thanks again for this," I said, twisting to look at her as she pulled up in front of the boxing gym in her trusty Mini. "I know it's early."

She shrugged. "I haven't been sleeping much anyway, so I was awake when I got your text."

"How's she doing?"

"She's healing physically." Fiona sighed, rubbing her forehead. "*Mentally*, I'm not sure. She's angry, blames herself for not seeing the truth, but also my dad for not seeing the signs when he was much more involved in the pack's dealings. I'm just grateful she's okay and that we're out of there."

I squeezed her hand on the gear stick. "I'm glad you're out too."

"Let me know if you need a lift back, but I'm guessing your

mate has you covered." She gestured to the lone car parked out front with a small smile.

The first signs of dawn's pale blue pierced the inky sky, birds beginning to chirp in the trees lining the football pitch backing onto the gym, reminding me that it was early—too early.

Benji must have been keeping an eye on the security cameras, because the door buzzed and clicked open as soon as I touched the handle.

The gym was eerily empty, but the sound of music blaring filtered up into the reception area. Someone was blasting Green Day below, and the bond flexed as if drawing me to him.

I wasn't sure what I'd find when I descended the stairs. Luke had been riding a rollercoaster of emotions since Tom passed away. One minute he was angry, the next he was sad, and then worried about his ability to lead as alpha. I was doing my best to support him through it. I knew grief; I knew loss. But what I couldn't help with were the voices in his head that told him he would fail as alpha. No matter how many times I reminded him of his strengths, my words of encouragement could only do so much. Only he could silence those doubts.

The boxing ring in the centre of the room was empty, as was the punchbag in the corner. Luke's mark was there, though. Two busted punchbags were propped to one side, the stuffing falling out of where the covering was torn.

Muscles flexed across the span of my mate's upper back where he stood in the weights area, two heavy dumbbells pressed above his head.

I caught his eye in the mirror.

"Eve?" He spun, his taut biceps lengthening as he lowered the dumbbells to his sides. "What are you doing here?"

"I woke up and you were gone."

"I couldn't sleep." He hung his head and placed the dumbbells down onto their rightful place on the rack, knowing better than to abuse the weights, even if Benji wasn't there to catch him.

He crossed the room in long strides, pulling out his phone to lower the music. He was shirtless, his workout shorts hanging low around his hips. Despite them being loose, they left very little to the imagination. I never thought I'd be the girl to tell a guy what to wear, but if I ever caught him in the gym with others around dressed like that, *I* was going to be the possessive one.

"I'm sorry," he said, his hazel eyes softening as he grabbed my waist. Sweat beaded his brow, his chest heaving from the workout. "I was tossing and turning all night. There's only so long I can stare at you sleeping before it becomes creepy. I needed to get the stress out of my body or else I was going to lose my mind."

We had one day left until the full moon peaked and Luke was to become alpha. One day until we would face the prophecy together.

"I'm not mad at you for hitting the gym instead of the Dark Night, but leave a note next time. Or text, you know? It'll save me the heart attack."

He arched an eyebrow, the corners of his lips lifting.

There was a time where I'd have worried he was slipping away from me, losing interest. An younger version of me would have been panicking about the relationship, constantly wondering if I was the problem, if he was going to get sick of me and leave someday. Because everyone left me. Except they didn't, I knew that now.

It wasn't the mate bond—that was just a bonus. So much had changed in the last few months. I felt like a different person. Instead of worrying that my friends or partner would reject me, I watched them fight tooth and nail for me. I'd learned to fight for myself, too, and that I was worth fighting for. They chose me over and over again, and I knew regardless of the mating bond that Luke would choose me in every lifetime.

"It's been almost two weeks since I sent word, and we still haven't received a single reply. None of the packs responded, not even Russell. Even Maya has dropped contact," he said, his shoulders caving in under an invisible weight. "I don't understand."

"We still have time."

"And if they don't show? We both know that our pack alone doesn't have the numbers."

"Darius and Jonas will back us," I said, snatching up a set of gloves beside the wounded set of punchbags. "You can't give up before we even try."

He hung his head with a sigh, bracing one hand on the wall while he took a sip from his water bottle. "I'm trying. Every bone in my body wants to barge into the Faolchúnna manor and rip Damien's heart out in revenge. Another version of me would have done it too." His biceps tensed, his hazel eyes blazing as they met mine. "But that's not the 'alpha' way. I keep being told that I need to think with my head, to not let my temper get the better of me. When all I want is to avenge his death."

"You will." My mouth dried at the intensity in his gaze, my own sweeping over his chiselled body. Suddenly I really wanted to be that wall. "One more day, that's all we have to wait."

Luke rolled his eyes, his sweat-beaded chest rising and falling with a deep sigh. "Patience isn't my strong suit."

"Come on." I shook my head as if it would get my thoughts in line, tossing the boxing gloves at him. Turns out we both needed to let off some steam. "You're stressed, but we don't need your first business as alpha to be replacing Benji's gym equipment."

He pushed off the wall, catching them in one hand with ease. "I'm not fighting you."

"Excuse me? It never stopped you before. You put me on my ass so many times it was bruised."

"I'm sorry I never got to see that." He winked, mischief sparkling in his eyes.

My stomach fluttered, but his smooth mouth wasn't getting him out of this one. "Tough. Fight me properly and maybe you will."

"I used to hold back with you, Eve. You were learning. My goal wasn't to kick your ass."

"And they say chivalry is dead," I scoffed, tossing my phone down on a weights bench. "I appreciate your concern, but I can take care of myself."

His brow arched at that double meaning. "Oh, is that so?"

Luke turned his water bottle upside down, pouring a small bit of water on his hair. He shook his head off like a dog, splashing me in the process.

I leaped back and scowled as he straightened with the biggest grin.

"Oops."

"Get in the ring," I ordered, tugging my sweatshirt over my head, so I was just in leggings and a tank top.

His charged gaze raked over me as he slowly backed towards the boxing ring, biting his lip as I tugged on the boxing gloves. "We're bossy today."

"You're not the only one who's stressed." I followed him, taking the steps leading up to the raised platform.

His abs flexed as he ducked under the ropes and climbed up with ease. "I can help with that."

"You can stop shit-talking and actually fight, or are you afraid you taught me too well?" I teased, keeping to the opposite side of the ring as we circled each other. "Your alpha powers haven't kicked in yet."

"I don't need any help getting you on your knees."

My mouth popped open, heat pooling in my core.

Luke's distraction worked. He shot forwards, and his fist connected with my shoulder before easily spinning away from my retaliation.

I staggered back, a low growl rumbling in my throat. "That was cheating. You can't do that when we're fighting the others."

"I can't use my charm and good looks?" He feigned surprise, bouncing on the balls of his feet as he took up a defensive position. "I use anything I can to gain the upper hand on the battlefield."

"Oh, well in that case." I opened the strap of one glove with my teeth, removing it before grabbing the back of my tank top and pulling it over my head. His answering growl as I flung it at him only made my nipples harden beneath the thin material of my sports bra. Thanks to him soaking me with water, the white pale pink material was almost translucent. "If you're gonna play dirty, so can I."

"Eve…" He licked his lips, allowing me to put my glove back on before he circled once more. His movements were slow, purposeful, a predator homing in on his prey. "I thought you wanted to fight, not fuck."

I rushed him, ducking as his right hook swung towards my ribs. My glove connected with his stomach, and I twisted away just as his glancing blow caught my hip.

He doubled over, his eyes narrowing.

"I warned you not to take it easy on me."

"Fine, but remember, you asked for it," he warned, his voice husky as it dropped low. His eyes flashing silver was my only warning as he closed the distance between us.

I managed to block his first blow, but his jab connected with my side and sent me stumbling back a step. I'd known he was taking it easy on me before, but I'd massively underestimated just how much. I kept my eyes on his power hand, but it was fruitless because where I slipped, his footwork was careful and sure. I tried to remember to keep my weight forwards, my punches growing tired as his became harder.

Even though I told him not to hold back, each time he backed me up against the ropes or landed a hook to a vulnerable area, he stopped to let me regather myself. A gentleman, even when he was kicking my ass.

He moved fluidly with a blow ready to follow each one of mine. Any punches I dodged, there was a counter move that caught me off guard.

By the time we broke apart, I was covered in a thin sheen of sweat and panting. His speed was something else. Even with my hybrid abilities, he was running rings around me.

"I need a breather." I raised my glove, gripping the rope behind me as I struggled to catch my breath.

"Nope." Luke advanced, sending a jab towards my chest.

I dodged at the last moment, the muscles in my calves screaming as I raced to the other side of the ring. "Just five minutes."

He was in front of me, one gloved hand pushing my stomach as he walked me back until I hit the padded corner. With a wicked smirk, he caged me in, bracing his hands on either side of me. "You're the one who said don't go easy on me."

He shifted closer as I slid my hand between us, gripping him through his shorts.

"I thought you said you wanted to fight, not fuck?"

I grinned at the defiance flashing in his eyes when I used his words against him, but quickly found myself crushed against the padded pillar, his mouth capturing mine in a deep, heated kiss. Heat radiated from where our bodies met, and he pulled back just enough to murmur against my lips. "Regretting that decision yet?"

*This man is going to ruin me.*

I mustered all my energy while he was distracted, putting it into my right hook as I swung at his ribs. He winced as my blow landed, giving me enough room to shove his chest and slip away.

He caught my ankle, sending me crashing to the floor. My gloved hands slipped against the canvas, giving him the chance to pin me there. He leaned over me, pinning my arms down with his forearms as he growled in my ear. *Only if you want me to.*

Blood rushed to my cheeks. I could feel his arousal pressing against my ass as he kept me trapped face-down with his bodyweight. "You're not playing fair."

His lips brushed the back of my neck, sending a shiver of

anticipation skittering down my spine. "I don't think you want me to."

The gravel in his tone made me squeeze my thighs together.

He slipped his gloves off, lifting his hips just enough for him to grip my waist and flip me. The moment my back hit the floor, he was kneeling over me. His fingers closed around my wrists as he pinned my gloved hands above my head with one hand while the other slid over the planes of my stomach, his fingertips brushing the swell of my breasts. Desire pulsed down the bond as he watched the way my body arched beneath him.

"Not so mouthy now." He leaned down to place light kisses along my jaw as his hand rose higher. He pinched one of my taut nipples through the thin material, and I jerked beneath him, my breath coming in short pants.

"Is this your victory speech?"

"No, but you are definitely my prize." The nail of his index finger morphed into a claw, and it took him seconds to rip through the material of the bra to free my breasts.

"It wasn't a fair fight. You can't tackle someone in boxing."

Luke gripped the top of my leggings, moving down my body as he tugged them to my knees. "You're also not supposed to be fighting in a see-through top. Seeing your tits while I'm trying to land a punch is more than a little distracting. You can deny it all you want, Eve." My name was a sin on his lips as he sliced his claw through my underwear, cool air making me shiver. His grip on my wrists tightened as he bared me to him. "But your body says otherwise."

The hard outline of his arousal was visible after he released my hands and leaned back, his claws vanishing as he ran his hands down my sides. I let my head fall back with a moan while he drew one finger through my slick centre.

His hum of approval made heat flare through my body. "I spent so many of our training sessions wanting to do this."

He sank one finger into me, my knees pressing against the inside of his as he kept my legs pinned. My nails dug into the gloves as I fumbled to tear them off, the sensation of being forced to take the intrusion without being able to spread to accommodate him making me writhe.

"I'm too tight, I can't—"

He added another finger, then dropped his mouth to my breasts, flicking his tongue over my nipple.

"Hm?" His hum sent vibrations through my body, making me clench around his fingers as he moved them torturously slow.

"The club opens s-soon," I moaned, grinding my hips against the palm of his hand, desperate for more friction. He read my body, dipping his head between my thighs to lap at my clit. I gripped his hair as the pleasure built with each lash of his tongue. All of the pent-up tension in me wound tight like a coil, ready to snap.

He lifted his head, silver dancing in the hazel depths of his eyes as he crooked his fingers. "So?"

"They could see us," I hissed through gritted teeth, my upper body jerking off the floor.

He picked up the pace, driving his fingers deeper and stoked the pressure building inside me until I came apart with a cry of ecstasy. He never took his eyes off me, his fingers working me through the aftershocks as I rode out the orgasm.

I groaned softly when he removed his hand, and my body slackened beneath him.

"Let them."

Then he flipped me over as if I weighed nothing. I put my hands out to stop myself from falling, my knees hitting the soft padding of the boxing ring as he pulled my hips up so that I was on all fours.

"Luke!" I caught sight of the clock in front of us ticking closer to opening time. I couldn't tell whether it was panic or desire that had me moaning as he pressed his arousal between my legs. My yoga pants were tangled around my ankles as he held me by the waist, his nails biting into my sides, my legs still trembling from my climax. "What if someone sees?"

"Let them."

The mirrors all around us reflected the sight of him bending me over in the centre of the ring, pulling his shorts down to free his hard cock. My pussy clenched, adrenaline and desire rushing through my body as he leaned forwards to whisper in my ear. "Let them hear how sweetly you come for me. Let them see how well I take care of my mate."

His groan as he pressed into me emptied my head of all thoughts but him. My back arched at the delicious stretch as he forced his cock deep until he was fully seated in me. He gave me a moment to adjust before beginning to fuck me with slow, deep strokes.

"Fucking hell," he groaned and dragged his nails down my back, his firm grip pulling my hips back to meet his each time. "You take me so fucking well, Love."

Any protests I had about being seen died as he filled me up, unintelligible moans spilling from my lips. He wrapped my hair around his fist, pulling my head back so I was forced to watch us in the mirror as he claimed me with punishing thrusts. My cries of pleasure echoed throughout the gym, my eyes locking with his as he fucked me like it was our last chance. And when we came together, I saw stars.

# CHAPTER 30

## EVE

Luke waited until afterwards to tell me that the club was closed during the full moon. I should have known his possessive streak wouldn't have risked anyone seeing him fucking my brains out.

By the time we got home, everyone else had already headed to the pack house, even though it was before nine in the morning. We wanted to get everyone there as early as possible to prevent any underhanded attacks from the Faolchúnna pack. Larissa and Damien had a history of kidnapping. This time, we weren't taking any risks.

Luke had even suggested having people stay for days leading up to the full moon, but they had lives and jobs. We settled on the morning of the first day of the full moon, just at the cusp of when full-blooded werewolf powers kicked in. There would be no pack run until the following night when Luke would step up as alpha.

Green countryside flashed past as my mate sped along the country roads, houses giving way to thickening forests now that spring was in full swing. I stared out the window, his hand on my thigh as I sat in a content haze watching the world go by. A small smile played on my lips as my mind wandered from our workout session to the way he'd covered me in his hoodie before carrying me to the car, just like the night he rescued me in the park. Except this time, our hearts beat as one.

Warmth radiated through my chest at the memory. My fond thoughts faded as the mood inside the car shifted and Luke's hand tightened on my leg. I looked over at him as we turned onto the drive to the pack house, but his gaze was firmly fixed on the winding road.

"Are you okay?"

The fingers of his hand on the steering wheel flexed. "Something's not right."

My buzz from the morning wore off as we neared the bottom of the driveway, and he rolled down the windows. Immediately, my senses picked up a mixture of different scent signatures—ones that weren't werewolf or human.

*Damien wouldn't hit during the daylight. He's not that stupid.*

A muscle in his jaw feathered. *He just lost his son for a second time. Grief makes the best people do things out of character. He may have stopped caring about appearing to follow the rules.*

We pulled up in front of the house where all the pack cars were already lined up and killed the engine. My heart hammered as we got out of the car, and I flinched as he slammed the car door shut behind him.

Luke loved his car. There was only one reason he'd manhandle it. To send a message: the alpha was here.

His silver eyes smouldered as he stared at the house, tension rolling through his shoulders. I could feel the anger radiating off him, along with a tug on the bond as he fought the urge to shift. If I wasn't so worried about what we were about to find inside, it wouldn't have been fear making my stomach somersault.

Luke stalked forwards, his eyes narrowing as voices drifted from behind the house. *Stay by my side.*

*I'm not a dog.*

*Just don't go running into anything.* His warning in my head was stern, but a hint of amusement coursed down the bond between us.

A howl echoed, followed by a scuffle as birds fled the nearby trees. We both froze, and dread clawed at my shoulders as it came again.

I was about to follow Luke as he skirted around the corner of the house towards the stables when the front burst open. Alice's tiny figure appeared in the doorway. I automatically scanned her for blood, but she was grinning from ear to ear.

"Luke!" His sister yelled as he jogged back towards me, his brow creasing in concern and then confusion. "You have to come see this."

"See what?"

"Come on." She waved for us to hurry up, practically vibrating with excitement as she tugged him inside.

I was right behind him, Alice's hand pressing the small of my back to usher me through before she closed the door behind us. I could see the fireplace from the hallway, but no one was enjoying the crackling fire. The half of the open-plan living room within my view was completely empty, and there were no footsteps thumping upstairs.

"Alice, what's going on?" He glanced around, trying to get his sister to stand still. "Has Darren checked the perimeter? There were a bunch of different scents outside. I can hear the—"

"Just shut up for two seconds," she scolded, taking his hand and tugging him into the living room.

My wide eyes mirrored his as we stepped into the living room. It was empty, but the garden wasn't.

The double doors leading outside were wide open. Pack members laughing and chatting were scattered throughout the garden. But it wasn't just their voices and scents. No, there was a deep Edinburgh voice rumbling. Not only that, I also saw my best friend's blue hair bobbing around outside, alongside another vampire that I recognised.

"Lawrence and Russell are here," I whispered, emotion

clogging my throat as I saw their familiar faces lift at the mention of their names.

Alice led us closer, looking like she might actually burst with happiness as we stepped outside.

Luke shook his head slowly, rubbing his chin. "It's not just them."

The moment my shoe touched the grass, someone launched themselves at me. Maya's familiar magic washed over me as she squealed and hugged me tightly. "Eve!"

"Maya," I breathed, laughing as I squeezed her back. Her magic tingled my skin, the softness of it so at odds with my recent experiences with witches. "You don't know how good it is to see you."

She released me from the embrace and shook her head. "Once we got Luke's message, there was no chance I was staying back. Cassandra said she wanted to come, but she's a little tied up with something at the moment."

"We cleared it with her parents first. They're still over in Canada doing research." Valeria joined us, her hand linked with her daughters.

"Not that she'd have stayed back without their permission," Gabi said, her eyes brighter than the last time I'd seen her. Her long black hair fell in waves over her shoulder, brown skin glowing in the sunlight. "Maya was booking plane tickets before Dad even agreed."

"As if your father had the final say." Valeria tutted, nudging Gabi's arm. The humour in her eyes faded when she inclined her head, her voice growing serious as her magic simmered around us. "You helped our family when we needed it without even knowing us. We will always remember and honour those who stand up for us."

I didn't miss the way my mate glanced away, clearing his throat. As much as he might want to believe the people there turned up for his dad, he had to face the fact that he too had earned the respect of people. Him accepting that he deserved it was another battle.

Darren pulled Ezra into a conversation, and I found myself overwhelmed as I looked around at the crowd that had formed. People sat talking in different groups, mixtures of every paranormal creature you could imagine. Fae, sirens, vampires, even griffins. We had more than doubled our numbers.

Russell was sitting at the end of the picnic tables, beer in hand, as he regaled a bunch of kids with tales about the Highlands. I could see a few of his wolves weaving through the trees lining the forest and chasing some of our younger shifters, including Sorcha, who would be held back from the fight tomorrow.

"I can't believe this." Luke rejoined my side after being pulled away by someone who knew his dad. His face was fixed in a permanent expression of surprise as he scanned the crowd. "There are wolves from the meeting with Edmonstone that turned. Hell, there are vampires who don't even work alongside Darius normally who have a bone to pick with Lars here. There are even a few Fae and a demon my dad helped years ago."

"How did he help a demon?"

"He saved his girlfriend—she was human." He scratched his head, exhaling a deep breath. "I wasn't expecting this. When we got no responses, I just presumed that was it."

Callum walked over, his red hair pulled back into a man bun. Except it looked like he let one of the kids do it, and I was pretty sure I saw Max stealing one of the girl's hairbrushes in the background.

"We did reply. They must have been intercepting the responses," the Scotsman said, rolling his eyes as he spotted his brother laughing in the background. "Jesus, he really is in full swing."

I shrugged, the energy around us infectious. "Let him. It's nice to see the place filled with laughter again."

"Eve's right. Everyone here has agreed to face danger

tomorrow. They deserve to blow off some steam." Luke held his hand out to Callum, smiling as the werewolf shook it firmly. "Thanks for coming, I know my dad would have appreciated it."

"Kid, I knew Tom, but that's not why we came. And I think if you look around, a lot of these people aren't here for your dad." Russell slung his arm around his brother's shoulders as he joined us, his expression softening. "You're going to make a fine alpha. I just hope we all get to celebrate it after."

Darren bounded over, pulling me into a one-armed hug. "I can't believe I'm saying this, but I think you guys made the right call."

Jonas spotted us from where he sat with Darius on a log near one of the fires. Alec had made his way over to the door to talk to Alice. Everyone hadn't just showed up, they were mingling. All of us working together was exactly what the likes of Damien and Larissa didn't want. Larissa fed that divide because together we were dangerous. We were a threat to their sordid plans. Hope blossomed in my chest, tears stinging the corner of my eyes.

"Don't jinx it," Luke muttered, his hand finding mine by his side and linking our fingers.

More heads were beginning to turn towards us. Mary and Helena were directing some werewolves on how to wind the fairy lights around the gazebo. I recognised a few of their faces from our meeting with the packs in London, along with a few Luke had shown me pictures of before who were from the different provinces throughout Ireland.

Russell coughed, clearing his throat with a chuckle. "I know you're kind of new to this, but around now is when you give a speech."

Luke's head snapped up. "Now? I'm not even officially alpha."

"But you are," Dylan cut in, greeting me with a warm hug before turning to my mate. "You were the moment your dad died. There is no one else, and nor should there be."

"I don't see the moon in the sky right now, do you?" Russell joked, nudging Luke, who was going paler by the second. "You don't need her powers to say the words that everyone needs to hear."

I squeezed his hand, realising the Edinburgh alpha was right. Everyone was looking to my mate for guidance, it was now or never. Their presence was a show of faith, but we needed to give them something to fight for.

Josh nodded, patting Luke's shoulder as if he was both commiserating and egging him on at the same time. "You're ready, and we're right here."

An younger version of me was cringing somewhere in the background as I grabbed a fork off the nearest table, clanking it against the glass beside it.

I didn't have Luke's commanding presence, but I had their attention. Luke was about to be alpha, but he wasn't the only one who needed to step up.

"First, thank you to each and every one of you for coming," I began, struggling not to trip over my words under the weight of their stares. "Most of you probably don't know who I am. My name is Eve O—" I paused, forcing my shoulders down and lifting my chin. "My name is Eve Donohoe. I know our letters detailed Larissa's plan. I am the one the prophecy speaks of. Which sounds very grand, but all it means is that I'm a descendent of Cadhla and I've a target on my back. As my mate, Luke forms part of the prophecy too."

Luke's voice boomed across the garden much louder than mine. "Tomorrow, Larissa expects us to hand ourselves over or face bloodshed."

A ripple of angry murmurs broke out. It was good. We needed anger; we needed people willing to stand up and fight.

"If Larissa fulfils the prophecy, it will allow her to harness the powers of Béibhinn's dagger, granting her access to all of the elements." Pride swelled in me as Luke stood taller with each word. "She will be almost unstoppable, and this could have catastrophic effects on both werewolves and vampires bound by the original curse."

We decided to keep the truth about the dagger to ourselves. While I trusted everyone here in good faith, it was our secret weapon and needed to stay that way.

"When I reached out for help, I did so based on my father's reputation. I am not him, but I can only hope that I prove myself worthy of the risk and sacrifices you have made by coming here." Luke scanned the crowd, somehow mastering the same skill Tom had—the ability to make everyone feel seen, speaking to a crowd but also at an individual level all at once. "I will run through the strategy this afternoon once we make sure everyone gets settled. After, please come and speak to me. I want to thank each and every person individually for their show of faith." The sun may have been dazzling above us, but the moon shone in his eyes as Luke spread his hands. "Tonight, we bond in a celebration of life, share stories and experiences, learn about one another. Tomorrow, we fight."

# CHAPTER 31

## LUKE

I'd been nervous to complete the bond with Eve, but also excited. It felt like one of those monumental moments. But standing in the forest clearing with the full moon above us once more, knowing I was about to be named alpha, was a different kind of nervous. These were the nerves that coiled in my stomach and made me skip my breakfast that day because I couldn't keep anything down.

Not only was I becoming alpha in front of my pack, the other alphas and their packs had requested to run with us. I was drowning under the pressure.

Our plan was in place. Gabi and Lawrence would stay back with Helena, any humans, and the kids. Along with staff from Château Minuit and some of the London wolves, their job was to protect the Crescent pack lands. Fiona and her mother would stay too, though I was surprised when her father asked to come with us to fight. I guess he wanted revenge, and I could respect that.

I didn't think Damien would try to attack and risk splitting his numbers, but it was a base we decided to cover. The rest of us would head to Oweynagat to face Larissa and her army of undead wolves, along with Damien and Lars.

"Ready?" Darren stood at my side, my dad's closest friend.

The buzz around the clearing only added to my nerves. So many Crescent pack members had known me since I was a baby, and here I was, about to step up and become their alpha. I was on the cusp of turning twenty-four, an adult by all arguments, but standing there waiting to step into my dad's position, I'd never felt more like a kid.

I shrugged, trying to ease the tension out of my hunched shoulders. "Nope."

"Your dad wasn't either," he said, clapping my shoulder with a grin. "But he turned out pretty good."

"Yeah, he did."

I stared at the spot where his body had burned. All that remained was a dirt patch in the centre of the clearing, the fire burning tonight much smaller than the one for his burial. We'd cleared away the firewood and let the wind take his ashes after three days, as was the tradition. The ground beneath should have been scorched, but plants were already budding through the soil along the edges. New beginnings, as if his soul nourished the earth.

"We need to get started if we're to get to Rathcroghan before midnight," Eve said, glancing up at the sky above us. Fear and excitement tinged her words in equal measure as she took my hand. "It's time."

The full moon hung above the clearing, her moonlight bathing the Crescent pack as if she too knew it was time to call in a new age. She was a ticking clock, binding my magic and my future. Supposedly becoming alpha during a blue moon was good luck. It was hard to believe that when it was also a celestial event that would facilitate the prophecy coming to pass.

I clutched Eve's hand, all too aware that this was either our last night together or the beginning of the rest of our lives.

Darren cleared his throat, but the chatter continued. He scowled. "For fuck's sake. That always worked for him."

"Everyone," I raised my voice, my eyes widening as they all fell silent despite me not being much louder than Darren at all. A breeze whipped through the trees, the shadows they cast piercing the moonlight illuminating the clearing. "It's time to begin."

The smile that spread across Darren's face was one of pride as everyone circled around the fire.

I scuffed the grass with the toe of my shoe, struggling against the urge to shrink into my shell as all eyes landed on me.

"We're gathered here this evening to welcome in a new alpha. While we grieve the loss of Tom, our fallen alpha, it is time to enter the next era." Darren stood by the fire, performing one last act for his old friend as he motioned for me to join him in the centre. "Can the next in line for alpha please step forward?"

I held my breath for a moment, waiting for someone else to step forwards. Anyone had the right to contest the role, we just hadn't scheduled in time for a debate. There would be no fight to the death for the role of Crescent alpha, it was one of the many archaic traditions that my dad dropped when forming the pack.

My feet didn't feel like they were attached to my body as I stepped out to join Darren. I could see Helena and Max, along with other human members of the pack and children that were allowed to come watch just for this bit. It wasn't the norm, but I needed my family around me.

"Tonight, we have a new beginning. A new alpha, ready to step into the role and lead our pack," Darren said, his hand resting on my shoulder lightly. "We all know Luke. Many of us were there for his first run under the moon."

*Breathe.*

Eve's voice was the calm to my storm. I forced myself to take slow breaths despite my racing heart. I wanted to remember these moments.

"When Tom told me he named Luke after our alpha at the time, the leader of the original Faolchúnna pack, I thought 'Cute name, but they're big shoes to fill'," Darren joked, flashing me a grin as a chorus of laughter rang out around us.

Part of me wanted to punch him, another part appreciated

him trying to bring some levity. My dad didn't have any brothers, but Darren was my uncle in everything but blood.

Silver flames flickered, and I remembered Dad telling me that during this childhood the fire for the Faolchúnna pack was blue. But he wanted the Crescent's fire to be silver like the moon, white being a symbol of hope, burning strong and bright.

"I should have known that the kid would grow into every bit the man to reflect his namesake. Watching Luke become the man before us today was a privilege, and I have no doubt that he will honour his namesake in how he leads."

My throat tightened as I met his glassy eyes, his sincerity catching me off guard.

"I've been prepared for this all my life, but I'm not sure one ever feels entirely ready to become alpha," I said, deciding to begin with the same kind of honesty I planned to carry forwards.

"Family and my pack are the most important things to me. I promise to lead with bravery, strength, but most of all kindness. The Crescent pack is my dad's legacy, and I can only hope that I do him proud."

I could feel the pull of the moon in the sky above us, her magic calling on the wolf inside me. The others could feel it too, silver beginning to bleed into the irises of werewolves, while hybrids also grew restless.

"Luke Whelan lays claim to the position of alpha," Darren decreed, raising his hands to the sky. "And the Crescent pack accepts. By the grace and power of the moon, may he guide us through the darkness under her light."

The fire crackled, silver flames swelling to soar towards the starry sky. My wolf stirred, the magic inside me stirring in unison.

I focused on Eve, my gaze locking on her blue eyes as the bond between us flexed in my chest and pride coursed from her end.

Magic rushed over my body like a wave before bursting into something raw, a fire ripping through my veins as a kaleidoscope of colours danced in my vision. My body contorted, bones cracking as if it was my first shift.

My paws dug into the ground, and when I opened my eyes, it was like I was seeing for the first time. Everything was brighter, clearer, sharper. I could feel a difference in the strength of my muscles, and a lightness in my feet. But most of all, I could feel them—all of them. My pack.

The moon seemed to glow in approval as she granted me her magic, moonlight brightening and spilling across the entire clearing as the fire swirled in unnatural movements.

When I looked across at Eve, she was holding Helena's hand, both teary eyed. Helena inclined her head with a soft smile, a sombre mix of grief and pride in her eyes. I may not have ever called her my mother, but she had raised me alongside my dad. She was the approval I needed for the role, not the moon's.

My shift was the catalyst. All around me, the wolves gathered began to morph into their wolf forms. Each wolf raised their head and howled to the moon in a show of approval.

I padded across the lush grass to Helena, my heart stirring as Max's eyes widened, and he reached out to poke my snout with a small giggle. I butted his hand with my nose before looking up at Helena, gently nudging her side.

"You'll be great," she whispered, gently scratching behind my ear. "Just like he was."

I closed my eyes for a long moment, only opening them when Eve's presence tingled by my side. She was the last wolf to howl to the moon, her striking blue eyes shining as she lowered her chest to the floor. The others followed suit, and I froze as I realised what they were doing. They were bowing, not out of servitude, but respect.

Each step I took towards my rightful place at the edge of the forest felt like I was stepping into my purpose. When I threw my head back and my first howl as alpha pierced the inky night, magic surged. I launched forwards, the moon glowing above us as I sprinted into the dense forest.

The ground shook as thunderous paws hit the forest path, my pack of wolves falling into place, followed by our visitors. Darren, Eve, and Alice ran behind me. Their eyes glowed in the night, quiet encouragement each time I looked back.

I weaved between the trees, excitement coursing through my body as the forest stretched ahead. The trees beginning to get their leaves were a reminder of what could come and new beginnings as I leaped over roots and undergrowth. A chorus of yips and howls followed me as the pack raced behind, sending birds and small mammals scarpering as we tore through the forest.

My mind slowly filled with noises within. I could hear the pack. My pack.

Not their every thought or ones slipping through like Eve, but messages they were projecting. Having minds other than just my mate's linked to my own during the full moon was going to take some getting used to.

A breeze tickled the back of my neck, and I turned my head, almost losing my footing as I saw something dart between the trees alongside me.

It was barely a wisp of magic in the air, but I knew it was him. I could feel him deep in my bones and all around me, the departing alpha running one more time with his pack. Tears stung the corner of my eyes as my heart twisted, my dad's scent reaching me as I led the pack through the forest.

*Goodbye, Dad.*

I howled into the night, the raw sound ripping from my throat both a sound of celebration and mourning. Answering calls came from behind me, their minds opening up with an outpouring of support. That night, I led the Crescent pack for the first time, my dad's spirit running alongside me in a final farewell.

# CHAPTER 32

## EVE

The tyres of Luke's car sank into the dirt path as we pulled up to Rathcroghan, a group of hundreds of archaeological sites in a tiny medieval village called Tulsk. We drove straight there once Luke's first alpha run was complete, squeezing everyone into as few cars as possible.

Oweynagat cave was located just outside of the village, where a narrow boreen gave way to sprawling fields, broken up only by old stone walls and hedging. It looked so normal at a glance, but there was no question that this was the right spot. I could feel the magic the moment we got out of the car; we were walking on ancient land.

Cottages were dotted along the country roads on our way here. In fact, one stood only a stone's throw away from the cave. My heart thumped in response to the magic surrounding us. I couldn't imagine living so close to it all the time. Then again, if the occupants were human, all of the history attached to these places was mostly myths that served as bedtime stories.

"Is this really where Cadhla buried her sister?" I asked, hovering nervously by Luke's side as the others parked up. The narrow road didn't give us much room.

"Based on our research, I think it might actually be where she killed Béibhinn." Luke shrugged, his eyes narrowing towards the nearest house. "If she's possessing or working alongside Larissa, it would make sense that she'd want to complete the prophecy here."

Josh appeared in the house's garden, walking over to join us. "There are humans in there, but they've been spelled to stay asleep. Dylan is checking the other ones nearby along with Maya who is adding protection spells just in case things get out of hand."

I swallowed, knowing exactly what the spells were for. Lars and his blood-starved vampires, if they were here.

Luke nodded. "Good, at least they'll be safe."

My brow furrowed as I wandered to where a wire fence nailed into wooden posts cordoned off the road, and a small gate led into the field. Rolling fields stretched around us, circles and mounds in the grass, all signs of ancient burial sites. The land was steeped in magic, the back of my neck tingling.

I could see the cave, a small entrance in the ground surrounded by rocks beneath a hawthorn tree. It was pitch black inside, as if even the moon herself couldn't touch the darkness within.

"It's so empty around here. There's no way Damien's entire pack is in there." I pointed to the cave, the entrance barely wide enough to squeeze through on all fours.

Dylan jogged over, his breath fogging in the night air as the wind whipped around us. "If these are the gates of hell, it's underwhelming."

The temperature plummeted, our breath fogging in the night air as the ground beneath our feet seemed to rumble its disapproval.

His eyes widened and he backed up, glancing around as if looking for the source of magic. "Sorry, my bad. I didn't mean it."

Luke ran his hands over the metal gate as the rest joined us, everyone staring around our surroundings with confusion. "You're right, something is off. They should be here. Larissa would have spelled the humans, but there's no way she came alone."

As our alpha led us through the gate, we had our answer.

The image in front of us shuddered, a glamour stronger than anything I'd ever seen before dropping away to reveal the Faolchúnna pack's glowing silver eyes. They were gathered around the cave in their human forms, backed by a row of the undead wolves at the rear, wisps of their shadowy coats swaying in the wind. Lars' coven stood on either side, their crimson eyes devoid of any warmth. Damien was at the front, with Lars by his side, and Ryan stood slightly behind, in his rightful place.

The moon hung in the sky, watching, waiting as time ticked closer to midnight.

"Were the theatrics really necessary?" Luke rolled his eyes, muscles flexing across his shoulders as he stepped over the gate in one smooth motion and led our pack onto the field.

"Nice of you to finally join us." Damien's voice dripped with disrespect, but I enjoyed the way the smug look drained from his face as he saw not only the Crescent pack following Luke, but the other wolves and paranormal creatures backing us. "The agreement was that you would come alone."

"Our agreement was with Larissa." Luke cocked his head, his fierce gaze fixed on the man who had killed his father. "I don't see her here, and she certainly did not come alone."

"Larissa is inside preparing for the ritual." Damien's upper lip curled into an ugly scowl.

"Hiding, you mean."

The Faolchúnna alpha's head snapped towards me. "Excuse me?"

"She's hiding, letting you fight her battles." Luke sneered, his hands balling into fists by his side. "And you're stupid enough to let her pull your strings."

"You're young, Luke. It's a pity you'll never get to learn." Damien's sigh was bored as he stepped forwards, his nails morphing into claws. "I'm not here to defend Larissa. I'm here to kill her."

Shock rippled through those around us, but it was quickly followed by a series of growls and hisses of disgust as Damien continued his tirade. "Don't worry, I'll let her complete the ritual first so you and your mate can join each other in the afterlife. Then I can take back your pack that rightfully belongs me," the Faolchúnna alpha's voice was gloating, a cruel smirk lifting his lips as he stared at the dagger strapped to my thigh. He was the only one outside of our group who knew it was the last remaining key to the prophecy, and that Larissa had a fake. "I'll take all of the power she harnesses and use it for good, so that scum like you cease to exist."

Lars' upper lip curled back to reveal a sharp set of fangs when the ancient vampire finally used his voice. "It's time we right the balance."

A deep growl rumbled in Luke's chest, our bond vibrating as silver bloomed in his hazel eyes.

"Your idea of good is steeped in misguided hatred." My hand tightened around the hilt of the dagger sheathed on my thigh. Maya had spelled it to shrink or expand based on whatever form I was in, so I wouldn't lose it. Which was a good thing because there was no way we were reaching the mouth of that cave without a fight.

"You don't wish to restore balance, only power." The change in Luke since our hunt under the full moon was visible in the set of his shoulders to the command of his voice. "And they were never your pack." Luke stepped towards the rival alpha, those behind us doing the same. "They left before you *stole* the position of alpha. That's all you are, a fake trying to hide behind wealth and power that isn't truly yours. You're cowards."

I glanced over to see Mary's eyes glistening with steely determination. Luke wasn't the only one coming for revenge that night. Embers I'd pushed down flourished in my gut, the burning desire to avenge not only Kate, but my parents too. They had stolen too much from us. It had to stop.

"You're so much like your father," Damien spat, pure hatred twisting into a mask of fury. "Hybrids took my son from me. Your father stole part of the pack. I'll take great pleasure in righting both those wrongs tonight."

The air shimmering around the Faolchúnna alpha's body was our only warning before he launched forwards. He shifted into his wolf form in mid-air, his black coat glinting under the moonlight as he raced towards us.

Magic levels soared as every wolf on both sides followed suit. Within seconds, I was running beside Luke's sandy wolf form as we charged towards the cave.

*Stay away from the vampires. Leave them to Darius and Jonas' team as much as possible.* Luke's pack order echoed, the bond between us quieter than when he was speaking to me alone. *Your instincts may be unsettled by the presence of so many alphas and vampires, but they pose no threat. Do not attack any of those who stand with us today. Work together. Protect one another.*

Howls of defiance rang out around us as Luke led the charge towards the line of Faolchúnna wolves ahead.

*Eve and I need to get to the cave. If something happens to us, retreat immediately.*

We met the Faolchúnna wolves in a clash of snapping teeth and claws. I connected with the wolf in front of me, sinking my teeth into the shoulder of someone I didn't even recognise. They howled, swiping at my legs, but I tightened my grip and whipped my head to the right, throwing them aside. I wasn't here just to fight; we needed to get to the cave. We had to trust that the others would hold the fort.

It was chaos, spells flying over our heads as vampires blurred and blood burst as a Fae ripped a burning vampire's head clean off its body. My stomach lurched as blood sprayed from their headless neck, but I didn't have time to recover from the image that would be seared into my brain for life.

Ryan was the next wolf I hit, and one hesitation from him was all it took. My nails dug into the soft earth as I lunged at him, my jaw clamping around his throat. We rolled onto the ground, my jaw locked tightly as my teeth sank deeper. He howled and writhed against me, sharp claws biting into my skin as he kicked.

All I could see in my mind was Kate. Her dead eyes empty, devoid of the joy for life that once sparkled there. He might not have dealt the final blow, but her blood was on his hands.

A zombie wolf smashed into my side, its decaying teeth catching my hind leg. I yelped, releasing Ryan's neck enough for him to tear himself free. By the time I freed myself of the shadow wolf, shoving it into the path of Alec, Ryan had bounded off into the distance.

The green field was covered in blood and scorched earth where spells had rebounded. It filled my senses, the noise almost overwhelming as blades clashed with claws. The broken bones of a wolf's leg landed in front of me, the stench of rotten flesh turning my stomach as the shadow tendrils wound around the bony remains and guttered out.

A red wolf crashed into me, Nadine's teeth grazing my throat as we hit the ground. The hilt of the dagger still strapped to my hind leg dug into her side as we flipped, and the wolf side of me hummed at the sound of her pain.

She couldn't spew her usual vitriol in her wolf form, but the hatred burning in her eyes spoke volumes as she struck again. She went for my jugular every time, untrained, and clearly operating from the pit of anger that was her heart.

I pounced on her back, grass clumps flying into the air around us as I forced her face down into the grass. Her blood was sour on my tongue as I sank my teeth into the back of her neck, growling while she struggled against me in a clear request for submission.

Nadine twisted in my grip, and it was her own undoing, the motion tearing a flesh from her neck as she pulled away from me.

I spat the muscle and skin aside, watching as she shrieked and writhed in pain. *That's for Kate.*

She would heal, and I didn't have time to stick around for round two. She wasn't worth my time.

A howl sounded nearby, the call I recognised as Alice.

*The cave, Eve.* I told myself, trusting that someone would come for her.

I forced myself to run in the opposite direction, but I couldn't resist a glance over my shoulder. Both Dylan and Craig headed to help her with a wolf from the Faolchúnna pack. Josh fought in the distance, facing down a group of the undead hounds alongside Jonas and a Fae who made the earth crack around them and thick vines burst from the fissures.

The mating bond throbbed in my chest, and I whirled around to see Luke nearing the cave opening, and the Faolchúnna alpha tackling him from behind.

# CHAPTER 33

## LUKE

**P**ride swelled in my chest as I watched Eve tear into Nadine and put her in the ground. She was fierce, brave, and beautiful. Gone was the timid, unsure woman I'd found in the park. I'm sure Kate would have been proud.

My paws pounded the turf as I sprinted towards the cave, trusting Eve was hot on my heels. As much as I wanted to fight alongside my pack, they needed us to stop Larissa. And with the full moon close to reaching its peak, we were running out of time.

The land around the burial sites had become a battlefield, a bloodbath bathed in moonlight. The Crescent pack fought tirelessly alongside vampires, witches, and other paranormals. Helping one another, fighting for the same goal.

Magic tingled along my spine, the hairs on my neck standing on end as my instincts urged me to turn at the last minute. I caught sight of Damien just in time, ducking my head out of the way of his open jaws as heavy paws hit my back.

I skidded to a halt and dropped my chest to the ground, momentum sending the alpha over my head. He twisted, kicking off me to spin in the air. Pain shot through one shoulder as his claws gouged my skin, the alpha landing in a crouch in front of me. Bloody spittle dripped from his teeth, his lips peeling back in a vicious snarl.

I couldn't speak to him in this form, but we were past talking. There was nothing I could say to convince him that a hybrid hadn't killed his son and that Larissa was playing him. He was blinded by anger and grief, and sometimes people who thrived on hatred wanted to believe the lie that fits their ideals.

Lars approached, his pupils shot with bloodlust as he cast aside a centaur's lifeless body. Guilt threatened to drown me, knowing that someone on our side had lost their life, wolf or not.

The vampire's form blurred, and I whirled to see him headed towards my mate.

*Eve!* I dived to the side as Damien rushed me, my teeth snapping around air as I narrowly missed one of his legs. *Lars is to your left.*

The Faolchúnna alpha landed a nasty bite to my side while I was distracted, watching Darius join Eve just in time to intercept the ancient vampire. I leaped away with a groan, my breath coming in short pants as I fought to breathe through the pain.

The moon may have lent me her powers, but Damien also had those perks. We circled one another, and for each blow I landed, he would land another. We were too closely matched, and I found myself cursing her for granting him alpha powers when he was nothing but a fraud at heart.

One thing I had on my side was youth. Inexperience may have cost me a few blows, but I was faster and more lithe than the Faolchúnna alpha. I tackled him to the ground. I pinned him by the throat, my front paws ripping into the flesh of his chest until I saw bone.

By the time he lodged his hind paws beneath me and bucked me off, skin hung loosely from his chest. It made him look like one of Larissa's pets.

It also really pissed him off.

A howl of defiance ripped from his throat as Damien lunged at me. We were covered in dirt and blood as we thrashed on the ground. I lodged my canines in the back of his neck, digging deep into the muscle there. The alpha jolted beneath me, his legs giving way. He flipped onto his back, taking me with him and slamming his bodyweight into me as my back hit the ground with a thud.

Air left my lungs, something important crunching in my spine. I felt one of my front legs go numb for a moment, and that was all he needed. My healing abilities kicked into gear, but the Faolchúnna alpha was on me. Sharp pain radiated through my body as his jaws closed around my throat, his teeth sinking into my flesh.

My chest was heaving, my magic reserves going towards the healing robbing me of some strength as I clawed at Damien. He forced his teeth deeper, my lungs burning as he cut off my air supply.

*Get up!* It wasn't Eve in my mind, it was Darren. I could see him tearing the ground up to cross the field to get to me.

The edges of my vision blackened.

Damien released, blood gurgling from my lips as he ripped my throat open in the process. My powers were struggling, desperately trying to stem the blood flow.

*Luke.* Panic coursed down the bond as Eve's voice tied me to the present, her fear so strong I could almost taste it. *Stay with me. Don't you fucking dare give in.*

Images surfaced in my mind of Damien grappling with my dad. The malice on his face as he shoved my dad off the edge of the building. My dad bleeding out on the gravel, staring up at the moon that had forsaken him. Raw, white fury rose within me.

My vision blurred and time slowed as the alpha pulled his head back, jaws poised towards my heart.

I would not die at the hands of the man who had taken my dad—our alpha—from us.

Magic surged, my wolf side fighting back and drawing on every ounce of my strength as I tucked my tired legs against his chest and shoved. It was enough to knock him off balance, and I took my chance.

I roared as I rolled out from beneath him, the sound echoing throughout the battlefield and rumbling the ground around us. I was on my feet before he could right himself, and this time it was me driving him into the blood-smeared grass.

I didn't hesitate as he twisted and exposed his chest to me. I didn't care if his jaws sank into my shoulder, I had one target and one only—to end this for good.

I clamped my jaw around his still-healing ribs, ignoring the pain as they shattered with the pressure and splintered in my mouth. Damien screeched, his claws slicing into me. I shoved my muzzle through the pectoral muscle remaining there and locked my mouth around his heart.

Out of the corner of my eye, I spotted Ryan's figure to my right. I braced myself for his attack, but it never came. Damien might have been too busy fighting to hear Larissa's admission back at the Abhartach mansion, but Ryan wasn't.

He pulled up as I sank my canines through the thin tissue holding his dad's heart in place. He took one look at Darren approaching and backed up.

I held his beating heart between my teeth, watching as the Faolchúnna alpha's eyes widened. Broken bone shards dug into my gums, and I tore his heart from his chest, cutting off his piercing shriek of agony.

Someone howled, but I couldn't pull my gaze away as Damien's body convulsed beneath me. I stepped back before dropping his still-warm organ and watching it roll towards its owner's head. The Faolchúnna alpha stared at his heart in disbelief until the silver in his eyes dimmed for a final time.

The Faolchúnna alpha was dead.

Dylan and Josh appeared by my side, motioning towards the mouth of the cave where a white mist was forming. It rolled across the grassy plains, the glowing eyes of more undead wolves appearing in the distance.

*Go.* Josh turned his head towards where Eve was racing away from a vampire and towards the cave entrance. In the distance behind her, Darius was squaring up to a retreating Lars. *You need to get Larissa.*

Mary ran alongside Eve, guarding her as I approached. We skidded to a halt at the cave entrance, all three of us panting heavily. Craig joined us too, his T-shirt and mouth covered in blood. Even his blue-tipped hair was flecked with red.

The corners of my mate's eyes creased with relief. She nuzzled my neck, a low growl rumbling in her chest where worry radiated through the bond as she spotted my healing throat. *Don't ever do that to me again.*

*We're not out of the woods yet.* I shook my coat out, grimacing as a chunk of pink skin dropped onto the grass. I wasn't sure if it was mine or Damien's.

"You need to get in there, guys," Craig said, glancing over his shoulder as someone yelled for backup. "I'm coming with you. Alice is going to follow in a second."

I didn't like the idea of anyone else risking their lives down there, but we needed numbers. Larissa was powerful, and if our plan didn't work, all we had was brute force.

*Gentlemen first.* My joke fell flat as I eyed the narrow mouth of Oweynagat, wondering if wolves built it because I couldn't imagine humans crawling in and out.

I dropped down low to the ground, slowly inching my way through the hole beneath the hawthorn tree. Rocks snagged my stomach as I wriggled through the rubble. Once I was inside, the cave opened up slightly but not enough for me to stand up to my full height.

The magic outside was nothing compared to the suffocating levels within the cave. As if power emanated from the very surface of the walls.

I heard Eve crawling behind me as I finally reached an area tall enough to stand.

"Why the fuck would they build a cave like this?" Craig's voice echoed.

My eyes adjusted to the complete darkness, attention snagging on carvings in stone lintels of the roof.

*Do you think it's really where Queen Medb was buried?* Eve paced in a small circle, her paws sinking into the damp ground of the cave floor.

I tilted my head, stepping back to let Craig stand. *A lot of the research we pulled together said so. With magic like this, I wouldn't be surprised. It's very likely where the sisters from the curse are buried.*

Relief loosened my shoulders as Alice joined us, battered, but relatively unharmed. I led the way down a rift passage that seemed to narrow into a dead end.

*I don't think this is right...*

My paw passed through a veil of magic to reveal a wider tunnel, this one lit by torches lining the walls. Their flames made something sparkle in the rocks, and the magic on this side was even stronger.

The moment I passed through the barrier, pain shot through my body as I shifted against my will. I landed on my knees with a groan, back in my human form. Magic thrummed through the earth beneath my hands. *Maybe this was built by wolves.*

"What the hell?" Craig's voice sounded distant, as though we were standing on two sides of a mirror.

I could feel Eve's worry as she rushed through afterwards, stumbling as she was also forced to shift mid-stride.

"We're okay," I called back, watching both my sister and Craig look around bewildered as we seemed to vanish in front of them. I pressed my hand through to show them, the veil of magic parting like a curtain. "Come through, it's just some sort of protection spell."

I took my moment while the two of them hesitated to cross, pulling Eve into my arms and claiming her lips in a hungry kiss born of desperation and love. She melted against me as I fisted her hand in my hair. We were both breathless by the time we broke apart.

"Just in case." I drew my knuckles across her cheek, trying to memorise her smile. "I love you."

She bit her lip, emotion shining in her bright blue eyes. "I love you too."

"Is this really the time?" Craig finally stepped through, wincing as the magic washed over him.

"We don't know how much time we have left," Eve whispered, taking a deep, shuddering breath. "Any of us."

A melody drifted from deeper into the winding cave. I shuddered, something about the woman's voice setting my teeth on edge. The magic of Oweynagat was ancient and potent. A warning to stay away?

"I can see why it's called the entrance to the underworld."

The veil of magic behind me buzzed, as if someone was pounding on it. I turned to see Alice trying to step through, but her paws hit an invisible wall.

She shifted back to her human form, smacking her fist against the barrier, but it wouldn't budge.

"Guys?" Panic rose in her voice as she tried again, the veil acting like an impenetrable wall. "I can't get through."

"Craig, why are your eyes blue?" Eve asked, staring at her best friend with wide eyes. "Where's the gold gone?"

I pressed my hand against the veil, expecting it to part for me again, but my fingers hit what felt like stone. "What the fuck?"

Eve and Craig took turns trying, both paling as we realised there was no way back. And when I reached towards the well of magic that usually resided within me, it didn't answer my call. We were trapped.

# CHAPTER 34
## EVE

Something felt wrong. I could feel the wolf within me, but it was like when I was weakened by nightshade. The power was there, but I couldn't tap into it.

"Whatever that magic is, it's stripped us of ours. I can feel my wolf side, but I can't seem to access it." Luke turned to the veil, his voice calmer than the storm of panic rising in me. "Alice, we can't get out. Go get the others out of here."

Alice shook her head. "I'm not leaving you."

"That's an order." Command rang through Luke's voice, his throat bobbing as his sister's lip trembled. "Go, tell the others and get to safety until we can handle Larissa."

Her wounded expression tugged at my heart as she shifted back into her wolf form, taking one last look at the wall before sprinting back through the cave.

Craig dropped his small backpack on the ground, handing out the change of clothes we'd packed earlier. I'd just finished dressing when the answer hit me.

"It's the prophecy."

Luke and Craig turned to me, the fire burning atop the torches flaring as I spoke.

"Undead, hound, ancient magic, bloodline..." I listed them off, gesturing to myself before pointing to my mate. "And moon bound."

He reached out to brush his fingers over the dagger strapped to my thigh. "Trinity tied by the blade."

The humming was incessant, sending tendrils of dread winding down my spine as magic danced over the surface of my skin. The potency of the magic contained within the cave was suffocating.

"We need to get to Larissa before Damien can tell her about the real dagger," Craig said, my attention snagging on his eyes again. "She's a necromancer. We don't know how quickly he will figure out how to contact her."

"Your magic..." I reached out to touch his face. His skin was still cold, and his heart didn't beat, but his cheeks were gaunt. "How long can a vampire survive without his power?"

Luke's eyes widened. "I don't know. We need to get to Larissa and kill her. The cave seems to want the prophecy to come true."

"Then we need to make sure it's on our terms."

I loosened the dagger from its sheath, lifting my top to slide the handle down the waistband of my leggings. The blade bit into my back and I hissed, the silver searing the skin there. But at least it was hidden.

Luke's jaw feathered when I flinched, his fists clenching and unclenching.

"Come on," I urged them, starting to lead the way deeper into the cave. "We need to get out of here. I'm not losing another person to that witch."

The walls of the cave curved, the humming growing louder. Luke cut in front of me, crouching behind a large boulder as the tunnel gave way to a large cavern.

Runes and drawings covered the walls, ranging from ogham carvings and ancient Gaeilge, to symbols I remembered seeing in the *Liber Umbrarum* back in Cambridge. The roof of the cave stretched to a peak with a small skylight. Silver light filtered through the gap; the full moon almost perfectly aligned as it basked the centre of the cavern in its glow.

Larissa stood at the centre of the cavern, her blonde hair tumbling in waves over a long black cloak that swept the dusty ground as she moved. There were lines drawn in the dirt in the shape of a triquetra bound in a circle, with stone offering bowls evenly spaced around the outer arc. Similar to when we sent a fallen wolf to the other side, except this was no burial. There was no pyre.

She kneeled at one of the spokes beside an empty bowl, humming the same haunting tune that stirred a mix of white and black shadows to life as the final offering. Spirit. The necromancer's forte.

Craig inhaled sharply, rubbing his chest with a frown.

"What is it?"

"I can feel it calling to me. I know I'm technically dead, but something tells me I'm walking a very fine line between the realms right now," he explained, his eyes narrowing towards the witch. "And I'm not ready to go."

Luke gripped the boulder, his fingers making dents in its surface as he ran through our plan that was feeling more holey by the minute. "We need to get close enough to take her down without her expecting it."

"Are you going to come out to play or hide all night?" Larissa turned towards us. Her right eye was the normal lilac, but the iris of her left eye was a swirling, misted silver. "I *do* love a good chase."

The fake dagger hung from the belt around her waist. Beneath the cloak, she wasn't dressed for ceremony. No, her corseted black top and leather pants made her look like she was a warrior, ready to fight. And we were the only thing between her and the power she craved so dearly.

Luke stood first, Craig and I quickly joining him. Her red lips curved into a wicked smile as she stalked towards us.

"I see you did not heed my summons," she said, motioning to

our blood-spattered appearance. Her hands may have been spotless, but they weren't clean. "It's unfortunate. Life and death hang in such a precarious balance. At least you managed to make it on time. If you had been late, I would have been rather upset having to track you down again next month."

"We're done running."

"Good. In that case..." Larissa reached out, her fingers flexed as she twisted her wrist and magic flared to life in her palm. She pulled her hand towards her, as if tugging on an invisible string. "Let's get started."

I grabbed Craig's arm when he stepped forwards, but he didn't stop.

"What the hell are you doing?" I rushed to plant myself in front of him, my stomach plummeting as I saw his blue eyes were now completely clouded over—his face was expressionless. He took another step, driving me back with a strength far beyond his normal vampire abilities.

A jolt of magic shot through my hand, sending me stumbling back into Luke's arms.

"Stop it!" I watched in horror as Craig walked like one of her pets into the trinity knot carved into the dirt, dropping to his knees at the centre of one of the three interconnected arcs of the symbol.

The sight of him kneeling at her feet made my blood boil, a growl building in my throat.

Fire flared to life, following the lines carved around him before burning out. As soon as the flames vanished, Craig's eyes were back to their original blue.

"Eve?" He tried to step forwards, banging into an invisible barrier. He paced along the perimeter of the lines surrounding him and cursed. "I'm trapped."

"Join him," Larissa ordered, pointing to the two remaining arcs in the symbol. "Join him now, or I start with draining his blood." A silver chalice appeared in her hands, covered in carvings similar to those on the walls of the vast cavern. She placed it down at the centre of the triquetra. "He's already struggling with the magic binding this place. Perhaps I should speed him along as a kindness."

The moment she produced the dagger from her cloak, I was moving.

"Not him first," I growled, gritting my teeth.

*Eve, don't. Once we're in there, we're trapped.*

Luke's panic coursed down the bond, but I swallowed hard and continued until I was at the centre of the arc next to Craig.

*I'm not losing another friend.*

A sense of helplessness twisted in my chest, partially my own but also Luke's as the flames phoenixed once more. I felt the magic lock into place, caging me in position.

"Look how obedient your little mate is?" Larissa sneered, flipping the dagger in her palm to point the blade at Luke. "So many nights we spent together, and you're still as obstinate as ever."

Ice cold fury swept through my body at the way her eyes lit up, as if she was remembering the nights spent torturing him. The dagger pressed against my spine grew warm, the sting of the silver fading compared to the vengeance I was ready to unleash.

The witch crossed over to me, her magic prickling around my legs. She forced my knees to buckle, and I refused to give her more than the slightest of grunts as I hit the ground. The hidden dagger forced me to keep my back at an awkward angle, but I stared up at her, refusing to break. I had one chance and one chance only to save the people I loved, silver creating welts on my back would never compare to the pain of losing them.

Luke was already moving before she pressed the tip of the dagger to my cheek, just enough for a single drop of blood to fall like a tear.

"You're a sick, twisted bitch," Luke spat, his shoulders tense as he stepped into the last remaining arc.

This time when the fire flared to life, it was silver flames that threaded through the lines of the trinity knot like a snake as the magic levels around us soared. It was a mix of old and new, but only evil emanated from where Larissa loomed over me.

"It's nice to finally meet you, Eve," she said, her voice softer with an added lilt that I'd never heard before. She tilted her head slowly, moving the dagger below my chin to force me to look up at her. "I've been waiting a very long time for this."

Shadows stretched from the edges of the cavern, rolling along the ground like thick fog.

"Béibhinn."

"The one and only." She grabbed a fistful of my hair, pulling my head down to examine the back of my neck. Fear locked my muscles as she sliced through the top of my T-shirt just enough to see the crescent-shaped scar between my shoulder blades: the mark of her sister's bloodline. "After all this time, I've finally found the key."

I held my breath, my heartbeat blaring in my ears as I waited for her to spot the dagger.

A snarl ripped from Luke's direction, pulling her attention away. My head slumped as she released me, my shoulders shaking as I forced myself to sit up straight once again.

"Don't worry, darling. I'll be coming for your heart in a moment." Her sparking fingertips my only warning before she slammed her hand into my chest.

I howled in pain, the air leaving my lungs as pain lit up my nerves. Béibhinn dug through the flesh like it was butter, her magic tugging on the bond nestled in my heart. The dagger pulsed at the base of my spine.

"I can feel her, you know? Her magic is there. It's like a little beacon drawing me to you. Calling me to right her wrongs."

I gripped her wrists, digging my nails in hard enough to draw blood. Her shadows snaked around my arms, tightening until I released her so they could bind my wrists in my lap as she delved into my chest cavity.

Stars danced in my vision as she twisted the bond so far I thought it might snap. The pain intensified, her shadows pulling my arms taut as I cried out in agony. It wasn't my ancestry calling to the witch; it was her blade hidden behind my back.

# CHAPTER 35
## LUKE

**B**éibhinn's magic tore at the mating bond, pain forcing me to my knees as she tortured the woman I loved the same way she had tortured me. I could handle pain. I could withstand the abuse, but watching the witch's claws embedded in my mate's chest, while her shrieks of pain bounced off the cavern walls, was a torment I couldn't stand. I'd endure Béibhinn and Larissa's cruel acts a million times over to stop my mates screams.

"Eve!" I roared, slamming my fists against the magic binding me in place.

Craig's face was a mask of disbelief as he clawed desperately at the barrier between them. "Leave her alone."

A sinister smirk curved her lips as she gave our bonds one last twist before releasing it like an elastic band. I clutched my hand over my heart, relief slackening my shoulders as the witch removed her claws, the sickening squelch making my stomach roil. Fear licked down my spine as Eve's body slumped, blood pouring down her chest. The metallic smell marred her sweet scent.

*Eve. Look at me, Love.*

She lifted her head, her red cheeks soaked with tears. *I'm*

"I think I shall start with you," the witch mused, her focus shifting to Craig as she licked the dagger clean. Her eyelids shuttered closed, and she cocked her head. When they reopened, both irises were a glowing mist. "No, that's incorrect. The hybrid must be marked last."

The lighting around the cavern brightened as the moon moved closer into place.

Was she was arguing with herself or Larissa? All I knew was that we were running out of time.

"Your kind were my favourite." She pinched Craig's chin between her fingers, leering at him with a dark hunger in her eyes that kept switching between lilac and white as if there was a battle for control.

Craig crawled as far back as the magical barrier would allow, his upper lip curling in disgust. "I can't say the same for you."

Her shadows surged towards him, pulling his wrists behind his back and binding them.

"I was going to make your death come quickly, but I think I'll mark you first and then leave you to bleed out." A loud crack echoed as she landed a slap on his cheek. She sliced through the neckline of his torn T-shirt with the dagger, the material flopping aside to reveal his bare chest. "Love and loyalty will bring you nothing but pain."

Eve's chest was still heaving as her body struggled to heal the wound. Tears streamed down her cheeks as the witch pierced her friend's skin with the dagger, dragging it over his chest to carve three runes.

Craig's face was grey, but he gritted his teeth and didn't make a sound despite the pain contorting his features.

"I'm sorry," Eve sobbed, wiping her cheeks with bloody knuckles. "I'm so sorry."

Béibhinn's shadows released him once the final symbol was completed, and he sagged forwards.

"I'm okay," Craig bit out, his raw voice cracking. Blood

seeped from the markings, and his hands shook as he dug his nails into the ground.

He didn't have a heartbeat to slow, but I knew he was quickly losing his vampire foothold in the land of the living.

"It's her fault, you know. If Cadhla hadn't stolen what wasn't hers, none of this would have ever happened. It's her fault you're here. She started the chain of events." She sighed, raking her nail down Craig's cheek before shaking drops of his blood off the dagger into the chalice. The cup sizzled as the blood hit the surface. "My path was written. I had a future, a husband to be. I was willing to follow the plan laid out for me. But my sister decided that her desires were worth more than my happiness. The myth you love so much even tells the truth about her stealing my one true love from me—my own twin—and yet she's the one who is celebrated?"

"Because she hurt you, and in turn you burned villages to the ground. The cause doesn't justify the means," Eve growled, her hands balling into fists by her side. "I'm sorry that you were cheated on, but that's a really lousy reason to create a curse. Cadhla is celebrated because she created our kind to stop your murderous rampage and bring Ultán to rest. She killed her lover to protect others."

"She was my *twin*," Béibhinn hissed, whirling on my mate. "My other half. Our souls began as one. You should understand that. It was the ultimate betrayal in her lifelong mission to steal everything from me. She didn't just steal my lover; she stole my chance at a better life. She didn't kill Ultán as a kindness. She was disgusted by what he'd become."

Eve shook her head, sweat beading her brow as her powers fought to knit the skin of her chest back together and mend her broken ribs. "No, you stole your own future by killing Ultán the first time. You let yourself drown in the darkness. Cadhla was not responsible for the very acts of revenge that destroyed the future you wanted so much. She was willing to sacrifice her own happiness to save others."

"You're wrong. Her misguided belief in love is the reason you three will die tonight." Anger contorted Béibhinn's face as she stalked towards Eve.

"No, you just don't understand something you've never experienced. You think you created vampires with a spell born from love, but it didn't bring him back the way you wanted because you don't understand true love," I cut in, pulling her attention away from my mate. "Because if you truly loved Ultán, you wouldn't have killed him. I'd pity you if you weren't so vicious. You're just like Larissa. What you sought was power."

"Let me have him," the witch purred in an otherworldly voice, her eyes turning two different colours once more as she twirled the blade in her hands. "You grow distracted. The moon is close. Let me show them why their love is only a weakness."

Lilac bled into her irises, Larissa's cat-like gaze narrowing towards me. "All this talk of love is making me sick. Do you know what it's like to be born to lead, but to have that power ripped away from you?"

"Leading and power aren't birth rights. They're earned."

"And you think you've earned it?" She scoffed, grabbing me by the throat and lifting until my toes barely touched the ground. Her strength was not of this world as she held me there, her shadows burning as they lashed over my skin and pinned my arms down by my sides. "My dear boy, you led your pack straight to the gates of hell. I can feel the death above us, and their blood is on your hands."

I struggled to take a breath, her fingers closing around my throat as she slowly pressed the dagger into my chest. Her shadows singed my T-shirt, turning it to ash that showered the ground. Hatred flared in her eyes as she gouged one line in my chest, running her tongue over her teeth as I cried out and strained against her grip.

Each slice of the blade across my skin sent pain radiating through my body, making my lungs seize. I couldn't move, bound by her shadows that suspended me in her grip. The dampness of blood trickled over my stomach as she painted my chest in runes. I struggled against the shadows, the image of Eve before me blurring as she cut off my air supply completely.

"Stop!" Eve screamed, tearing at the invisible barrier between us as fear constricted the bond between us. "It's me you want."

"Not everything is about you." Larissa rolled her eyes towards the moon. She released my throat, her smile growing at the sound of Eve's cries bouncing off the walls. "The prophecy could not be completed without them. Then again, it's not surprising that a descendent of Cadhla would think it's all about them."

I collapsed in a panting heap when her shadows released me, rocks biting into my knees. The weak sense of my magic stirred deep inside, and I realised why we were stripped of our powers. If we could all heal, they'd never be able to complete the spell. That's why she chose the burial site; it was somewhere that robbed us of her powers.

Wait. Larissa wasn't using the elements, only the shadows Béibhinn lent her from the afterlife.

*She's weakened. Larissa's powers are blocked too.*

Eve's eyes widened as she snuck one hand behind her back. *So she can't heal?*

I nodded, glancing up at the moon that was almost perfectly in line with the window to the night sky.

"Craig," my mate whispered, crouching as close as she could to the line of the trinity knot that kept her separated from the vampire who was swaying with fatigue. "Stay with me."

Blood pumped from his chest wounds, and his supply wasn't endless now that he'd been robbed of his vampire abilities. It pooled on the ground, finding a path between the rocks and dirt to the lines carved, a river of his life force heading straight towards the base of the chalice. I gasped when the first drop hit the base of the cup, defying gravity as it climbed up the metal.

"Last to be marked, but first to die." The witch turned to Eve, letting a few droplets of my blood fall into the chalice to mix with Craig's as she passed. The colours switched between her eyes, white mist mingling with purple as the ancient twin and the scheming witch echoed together in one voice. "We've waited so long for this moment."

Eve stared up at the witch, fiery defiance flaming in her eyes and her chin lifted. "So have I."

"I'm glad you've finally accepted your fate." She gripped Eve by the hair, smirking as she stroked the blade over where the flesh had almost knitted over the wound completely. Eve groaned, but didn't fight her grip. "It's a poetic tragedy that love is your downfall. You must thank Cadhla when you see her on the other side, if you can find each other in the afterlife."

Eve stiffened, her fists balling by her sides as the first line was cut into her chest.

*Your dad was right. He said I'm the key, but it's not just me. It's both of you, friendship and partnership. It's love. Her key to the prophecy is death, but ours is love.*

The witch chanted, magic sizzling in the air and sparks skittering across the cavern walls as the flames of the torches swelled. "Life-source of the undead, the true heart of a hound."

Lightning forked through the air above us in the cavern, an invisible wind whipping her hair around her face as the shadows spilled from her like a billowing cloak and rushed across the surface of the triquetra. Glowing silver eyes manifested from the darkness, summoned undead wolves prowling towards their creator to take their places at the point of each arc in the symbol.

The moon moved to cover the skylight, blocking out the stars and flooding the cavern with her light.

"Ancient magic spilled, bloodline and moon bound. Trinity tied by the blade of magic intertwined." The witch's skin paled, silver fissures spreading through her face like veins as she carved the final symbol, turning her head at an unnatural angle. "Damien?"

My heart skipped a beat. *No.*

Eve caught my gaze, a lifetime's worth of love and promise

shining in her eyes as she drew the dagger from behind her back while the witch's blade hovered over her heart.

*I love you.*

"Wielded by the blessed can history unbind." Eve finished the prophecy and plunged the dagger into the witch's chest.

*No!*

Larissa's mismatched eyes widened, but it was Béibhinn's howl of fury that tore from her lips as she drove her blade right through my mate's heart. Pain seared through the bond, the floor shaking as ancient magic crackled in the air around us.

"Eve!"

I lunged at her, but flames flared along the barrier, an invisible power blasting me to the ground. The same happened to Craig, both of us trapped, watching helplessly as the witch twisted her blade, pushing her magic through it to still my mate's beating heart.

The cry that ripped from me wasn't human; it was a carnal roar of defiance as I watched Eve's lips part and blood trickle down her chin.

# CHAPTER 36

EVE

The moment I heard Damien's name leave her lips, I knew it was my only chance. I wasn't ready, but I never would be ready to say goodbye to the life I'd built. Tears clogged my throat, fear sending a shudder down my spine as I watched the realisation spread across Luke's handsome face.

*I love you.*

My fingers wrapped around the hilt of the dagger, the magic within it vibrating beneath my touch.

"Wielded by the blessed can history unbind." I finished the prophecy, pulling the true dagger from behind me and stabbing the silver blade deep into the witch's chest.

*No!*

It was Béibhinn who howled as she drove her blade into my heart. I kept my eyes fixed on Luke, the man who had taught me not only how to love, but how to be loved. To be open, vulnerable, and fearless.

"Eve!" Fear and anguish coursed down the mate bond as Luke threw himself at the barrier, both him and Craig fighting desperately to get to me.

My body jerked as pain flared to life, magic spreading along with the agony radiating throughout my chest, as if the witches were forcing their magic through it.

*Eve, don't let go. Don't you dare leave me. You're strong and powerful. Fight back.*

Beneath the pain, there was a sense of elation as Béibhinn's hands trembled. The moment I realised the key was love, I knew I could save the others. Tom's words from the letter floated in my mind, his voice so clear it was almost as if he was right beside me. *Love is the purest form of magic.*

For Béibhinn and Larissa to bring the prophecy to fruition in the way they wished, they needed to sever the bonds of love. But I had to prove that I would sacrifice anything for those I loved. Not just my mate and my friends, but the pack and others who fought valiantly against those who wanted to rip our world apart for power.

The magic binding us fractured, fire blazing through the lines on the floor to paint the trinity knot in silver flames.

Shadow wolves swarmed the space as I sent one last message to my mate through our mind link, trying to pour every ounce of love through it so he knew how much I would have given to have a lifetime with him.

*Save Craig.*

Luke was shouting but his voice was distant, as if I was floating away in a dream. Black spotted my vision as the witch twisted the dagger in my heart. The bond pulled taut as the magic binding us swelled, as if it was a living entity within us as it fought to keep me tethered to my mate.

I memorised the lines of his face, the way silver moonlight bloomed in his hazel eyes. My heart broke for him as he stared at me as though I was his entire purpose.

The blade wasn't silver, but I knew a blow to the heart like this would be fatal. A quiet acceptance settled as the darkness wrapped around me, an enticing warmth pulling me under.

"Eve."

My eyes snapped open to see Kate standing beside the witch

as power coursed through the dagger into me, mingling with the pain.

Her eyes were glassy, her signature blue hair billowing in the wind as magic surged, whipping through the cavern. "I need you to hold on."

"I can't," I whispered, my fingers flexing around the dagger. My knees threatened to buckle as a chorus of screams bounced off the cavern walls. Both the witches' and mine as the silver blade drew on their power, sapping it from them and pumping it into my chest, while the dagger embedded in my chest came for my life.

Kate reached out, her fingers closing over mine to push the dagger deeper into the witch's chest. "Yes, you can. You've always been stronger than you think."

"It hurts too much."

The pressure built, my heartbeat growing sluggish. I wasn't a true witch, just a descendent. I possessed enough magic to make me the target for the prophecy thanks to my lineage, but my body wasn't prepared to harness so much power.

"I know, just hold on a little longer." Kate's expression softened as she kept my hand clamped over the blade, and gently brushed the hair back from my face, just like she used to. Always looking after me.

"I'm not able to hold onto their magic." Tears stung my eyes, goosebumps rising on my flesh in the wake of her touch. It was light like a ghost, but I could feel her as if she were really here. I so badly wanted to release the dagger to hug her. Even if it was one last time. "It's going to kill me."

Another figure appeared to my right. A woman with long brown hair that hit her waist and piercing blue eyes. "It's not your destiny, darling, but it is hers. It's time for my sister to join me."

"Cadhla."

She nodded, a sombre smile tugging at the corner of her lips as she placed her hand over Kate's while the other touched the hilt of the blade embedded in my chest.

Magic stormed, my feet leaving the ground as it lifted us into the air. Luke and Craig faded as ancient magic swelled, the moonlight blinding as it flared.

The power called to me, tendrils of shadow licking at my skin like flames as they begged me to embrace my darkest desires. I could taste the magic in the air, energy skittering across my skin like electricity. Light poured through the web of fissures in the witch's skin as the dagger sapped her magic. It was there at my fingertips, just waiting to be claimed.

"This much magic isn't meant for one person. It needs to be released back into the earth. Balance must be restored." Cadhla pulled the blade free, only to turn it on herself. "Hold on to what lends you strength, release the power, and fight."

"I'm not ready."

Kate cupped my cheek, her chestnut eyes filled with love. "You are ready, Eve. I'll stay with you every step of the way."

"Promise?"

I turned my head to press a kiss to her palm, tears streaming down my cheeks as her hand tightened around mine on the hilt. Somehow, I knew this was our final goodbye.

"Promise."

Kate tightened our grip around the dagger and twisted at the same time Cadhla drove the blade into her stomach. The ancient witch's spirit doubled over, her image shimmering.

The wind howled, the crescent moon on my back burning as she severed the link to her bloodline.

Béibhinn threw her head back with a sickening crack, her body bending to an unnatural arch as her hands fell to her sides. Suspended in the air, magic seeped from her fingertips into the shadows gathered. In the distance, I could see Luke and Craig battling to get to me.

The dagger clattered to the ground as Cadhla's presence faded, her spirit leaving our plane while her evil sister's mouth gaped. One final scream spilled from her, an agonising wail as the white mist swirling in her irises cleared to reveal lilac eyes wide with fear.

Luke's voice was in my head, my mate tightly gripping the bond as he fought his way towards me. He called my name over and over, chanting it like a spell.

Magic called to me, ancient and powerful, as it rolled over my body and threatened to consume. It whispered such sweet promises in my ear, the sensation of it washing over me an intoxicating high.

I took one last look at Luke before letting the power sweep over me, magic searing through my body. My mate's voice echoed, calling to me in tandem with the magic as the ground beneath me fractured.

Whispers were carried to me on the wind, promises of power and immortality begging me to claim it. But power was never something I yearned for. Life was a cruel mistress, but all I'd ever wanted was to belong. I had everything I needed to navigate whatever the fates threw at me right there.

I stood on the shoulders of all the women who came before me as I tore the blade from Larissa's chest, severing my link to her power. Tears streamed down my cheeks as Kate's pride-filled face faded, and I felt her spirit cross over the veil.

The blade hovered between us, moonlight glancing off the symbol carved into the hilt that matched the one scorched on the earth beneath us. It shattered before my eyes, shards of raw power bursting from the blade.

Larissa shrieked as her own magic sliced through her like a thousand blades, carving deep wounds coated in power. The shadows seeped into the cracks in the earth, and the magic that had been suspending us in the air released us. I hit the ground, pain radiating through my body. The stench of burning flesh filled the air, the witch's shrieks piercing my ears.

My last image was of Larissa writhing in pain, and my eyelids drifted shut as the very thing she craved destroyed her.

# CHAPTER 37
## LUKE

"**E**ve!"

Fear froze my heart as the mate bond throbbed. Eve's body fell limp while Larissa's final screams rebounded off the cavern walls. I fought my way through the snapping jaws of undead hounds, willing to walk through the fires of hell to get to my mate.

"No," I gasped, sprinting towards her the moment the set of rotten jaws clamped around my arm released me.

I kept repeating her name as I fell to my knees at my mate's side. Panic choked me when I rolled her over, her delicate features set in the same sense of calm as my dad's when he passed.

"Eve," I whispered, my hands trembling as I tried to stem the blood flowing from her chest. The bond stretched between us, faint but still there. Her heartbeat faint. "Stay with me. I can't lose you, not after everything."

Craig joined me as the zombie wolves retreated, becoming thin wisps of shadow that sank between the cracks in the earth.

A loud rumble came from below us, rubble spilling onto the ground as the cavern began to shake.

"We need to get out of here." Craig dropped down beside us, his throat bobbing.

The shadows receded, flooding the cavern in moonlight. Magic pulsed in my chest, and I lifted my hands from Eve's chest to see the muscle slowly knitting back together.

Tears spilled down my cheeks as her eyelids flickered open, those bright blue eyes that had stolen my heart sparkling.

My hands were sticky with blood, but I didn't care. I cupped her jaw and brought her lips to mine in a gentle, tentative kiss. I could taste the salt of our tears as she kissed me back. When I pulled away, a kaleidoscope of emotion poured down our bond.

"I really thought I'd lost you," I whispered, tears catching in my throat as I nuzzled her cheek. She smelled like light rain on a spring morning—life. "I love you so much."

She reached up to touch my face, her body still trembling in my arms as she healed under the light of the moon that bound us. "It was the only way."

Craig reached out to squeeze her hand. "Don't ever do that to me again."

Her laugh turned into a cough as she clutched her chest. Her gasp sent a bolt of dread through me.

"What is it?"

"My powers. I can still feel my wolf side..." She palmed her chest, a smile spreading across her lips. "I thought I'd lose it when I released the power. I was so scared. I didn't want to lose that part of me, but I trusted Cadhla."

"You saw her?"

She nodded, wincing at the action. "She broke some sort of link."

I followed her gaze to where the dagger we'd thought was a fake lay on the floor, the bone hilt singed black in places.

Warmth spread through my chest at the happiness etched into her features. When I met Eve, she'd have happily given up her abilities out of fear. "Maybe the prophecy didn't mean unleashing the magic that created werewolves and vampires. It meant finally putting an end to the origins of the curse, the connection binding the sisters."

Craig swayed as he picked up the dagger, glancing up as more rubble fell and the walls began to crack. "This place is going to come down. We have to go."

Adrenaline overruled my aching muscles, and I rose to my feet, hoisting Eve into my arms bridal-style. A shower of rocks collapsed behind us as we raced back towards the entrance to the cavern, the torches lighting our way.

I looked back over my shoulder to see Larissa's dead body lying at the centre of the trinity knot carved in the cracked earth. The walls of the cavern crumbled just as we reached the entrance of the tunnel, burying the witch with the spirits of her ancestors.

Shocks radiated throughout the ground, the walls of the cavern collapsing behind us. I didn't even realise we'd reached the veil of magic marking the hidden entrance until I stepped back into the rift passage. Craig stepped through behind us, the last stretch of the tunnel caving in behind him. Where the veil once stood was now a wall of rubble, sealing away the secrets behind it.

It took some time to get Eve out of the cave. She still had her hybrid abilities, but she was too weak to shift. I crawled out first, seeking out Maya to help us carry my mate out with magic.

I turned as another magical signature caught my attention, expecting Gabi's parents. But it wasn't them I found.

Cassandra was blasting spells, green eyes meeting mine as she raced towards us. Behind her, the Crescent wolves were forcing the Faolchúnna pack and remaining vampires to retreat. My shoulders sagged with relief when I spotted Alice's shaggy coat, Dylan and Josh working alongside her. Darius and Jonas worked on the Lars' vampires, meanwhile I couldn't see any trace of their coven leader.

"Lars fled after you killed Damien," Cassandra said, as if reading my mind. She'd changed her appearance more than usual, at least a foot taller with broad shoulders and blonde hair that stopped around her shoulder, a full glamour in force. "I'm sorry I couldn't get here sooner. I've had to lie low lately."

I shook my head, a real laugh slipping from my lips as she pulled me into a tight hug. "You showed up, that's all that matters."

"Of course I did, alpha." Unspoken words shone in her eyes as she patted my back and released me from her embrace. "Larissa is dead? I felt one hell of a release of magic."

Eve joined us, supported by Craig on one side.

"I'm really glad you found a way to stop the prophecy." Cassandra's expression softened, only smearing blood around her face as she rubbed her forehead.

"We didn't. We brought it to pass, just not in the way Larissa expected," Eve explained, shuffling closer and allowing me to slip an arm around her waist to replace Craig's.

"I'm impressed." Cass arched an eyebrow, the amusement sparking in her eyes becoming curiosity as her gaze snagged on Craig's hand. "May I?" She motioned to the dagger, gasping when he handed it over. She marvelled at the blade while she twirled it between her fingers. "Holy fuck, I think this is Cadhla's blade."

Eve's mouth popped open. "What? Is that why it didn't kill me."

"That would explain why we felt magic from it. I always felt like it called to me." I stroked her side with my thumb, needing to keep her close. "You're her descendent and I'm bonded to you."

Cassandra nodded, her fingertips glowing as she traced over the delicate carvings in the bone hilt. "All witches are gifted a blade when they come into their magic. It's an age-old tradition. Do you mind if I keep this? I want to bring it to a friend in Cambridge, it needs to be locked away safely."

Eve shrugged. "Sure, I'd be happy to never see anything to do with the damn prophecy again."

"Well, you can't avoid the moon, but I can take care of the dagger."

I had a feeling Cassandra meant the sphinx that had helped us find the *Liber Umbrarum*; it was only fitting that it ended up alongside the book detailing the prophecy.

"Your eyes are fixed." I pointed to Craig, his irises having shifted back to their golden depths.

He nodded, rolling his shoulders with a groan. "I still feel like shit, but I'm no longer the dying kind of undead."

Eve thumped him weakly in the ribs, tiredness creasing her brow as she leaned into me.

Mary walked over to us, wrapped in a parka coat that someone must have taken from the car. Her hair was matted, blood streaking her hands.

"I'm so glad the two of you are okay." She pulled Eve into a one-armed hug, reaching out to pat my cheek like an aunt would. "Your dad would be so proud."

Emotion stirred in my heart. His spirit felt closer than ever.

My mate stifled a yawn and looked up at me, her own glowing pride coursing down the bond. "Can we go home?"

"You go ahead," Mary said, looking over at where wolves from the Faolchúnna pack were cornered and beginning to shift back into their human forms. "I need to go sort something that I should have done twenty years ago."

Dylan and Josh bounded over, still in their wolf forms, racing the blurred outlines of Darius and Jonas. But it was Alice who won, the air shimmering as she shifted and threw herself at us.

"Easy," I warned with a laugh, gripping Eve tightly to keep her upright as Alice pulled us into a hug.

"You guys head back to the pack house," Cassandra said, a sombreness creeping into her tone as looked out at the rolling fields. Burial sites were now littered with the dead, less than I had feared, but every soul lost was a tragedy.

"No." The bond tightened around my chest as I scooped Eve into my arms. My dad's teachings rang in my mind, the importance of respecting those who have laid their life down to protect the pack. "First, we see to the dead and give them the burial they deserve."

The others nodded, and as we dispersed. A black cat crawled out of the entrance to Oweynagat, its green eyes following us as we made sure each and every soul, friend or foe, was sent across the veil with dignity and respect.

# EPILOGUE
## EVE

"**Y**ou're going to kill me."

My head fell back against the pillow as Luke dragged his tongue across my clit, his fingers playing me like a musician mastered in his craft.

"What was that, Love?" Luke looked up at me with a wicked glint in his eyes to match his devilish grin.

"I said, I'm g-going to—" My words cut off as he hooked his fingers to press on that sweet spot that made me clench around him.

My vision blurred, and I couldn't tell if stars were dancing in my eyes or if it was the skylight above the bed, the moon glowing above us as he drove me to another climax. I came apart on his fingers, my trembling legs hooked over his shoulders as he licked me through every single aftershock.

A thump came from outside, followed by Max's voice screaming bloody murder about wanting food.

My mate ignored them, drawing a gasp from my lips as he sucked my clit into his mouth and hummed.

"Luke, they're right outside," I hissed, gritting my teeth as I rode out the waves of pleasure.

"So?" His voice rumbling against my clit was torture. "I'm busy."

Another knock came and Luke groaned, fisting his cock as he added a second finger. "I'm busy. Come back in ten." He ground the words out, the lust in his hooded eyes setting my body alight once again.

"Helena said you've five minutes, or she's sending a search party," Dylan's voice filtered through the door, followed by a titter of laughter that sounded a lot like Alice and Josh.

"Fuck off," Luke growled, tossing a pillow at the door before returning his attention back to me and showing me exactly how much he could achieve in a time crunch.

My legs were still shaking when we headed downstairs, even after a shower that made us late because neither of us could resist round two, or three. A blush crept into my cheeks as Luke stole one last kiss before striding into the kitchen without a care in the world.

"Your food's in the oven." Helena kissed my rosy cheeks as she passed, rolling her eyes in Luke's direction.

The pack would join us to hunt tomorrow, but Helena wanted to head up early to celebrate before everyone else arrived.

My heart swelled, the bond humming with contentment in my chest as I looked around the faces gathered at the table. Luke's family were gathered there, along with some of our closest friends. Darius and Jonas sat near Helena, in deep conversation with her and Josh about some of the vampires they'd rescued from Lars. The Royals had stepped in to help mitigate any fallout in terms of exposure to humans, but they blamed most of it on Larissa. Though the ancient vampire was under tight scrutiny, or so they claimed.

"Max, you're going to spill it," Alice warned, wrestling with her brother who was trying to drown his dinner in gravy.

Alec was squeezed in beside her, trying and failing to play referee.

Luke plated up the meat Helena had held back for us in the oven, and I dropped onto a seat beside Craig, a smile curving my lips as he pulled me into a hug. He'd dyed his hair back to black, living out his emo boy band dreams now with his pale skin and molten eyes.

The lights dimmed, and Luke turned to face me with a wide grin, carrying a crescent-shaped cake. Tears sprung to my eyes as everyone burst into a rendition of "Happy Birthday", the bond in my chest throbbing with a deep sense of belonging.

He set the cake down in front of me, his hazel eyes brimming with emotion.

"Time to make a wish, birthday girl."

I used to dream of fairy tales, but that's not what I wanted anymore. My happy ending was raw, real, and beautiful. We'd loved and lost, and we were still standing.

So as I closed my eyes and blew out the candles, I wished for a lifetime of moments like this, surrounded by friends and family, happiness, and love.

) ) ● ( (

AUTUMN LEAVES PAINTED Stephen's Park a collage of red, orange, and yellow, swirling in a frenzy as the wind whipped around us. I clutched Luke's arm, snuggling into his side on the bench where we sat sipping coffee while the world moved around us.

"Do you think we'll hear something soon?"

Luke chuckled, his thumb stroking the back of my hand. "I'm no expert in the field, but I'm sure we'll hear something soon."

Darren had called in the early hours of the morning to tell us Paula had gone into labour a week early. He'd joked that they weren't getting the Halloween baby they'd hoped for, but I could hear the worry in his voice. Werewolves weren't immune to birth complications.

They'd opted to go to the hospital in Dublin City were Tom used to work, so a werewolf on call could keep an eye on them. I was so excited; I thought my heart might actually burst from my chest. Luke had confiscated my phone to stop me checking for messages every two seconds.

"Mary said that Fiona started her new job this week."

I took Luke's distraction bait. "Yep, she's got a job as a pastry chef. It's near here actually. She thinks she might go to culinary school."

After Damien was killed, Mary had challenged Ryan for leadership of the Faolchúnna pack. It didn't come to a fight; Ryan fled with his tail between his legs soon after. He was technically a rogue now, last spotted roaming somewhere around North America with Nadine. Both of them were outcasts and welcome to each other.

I stared around the park, sunlight glinting in the cloudless sky above us. It looked so different compared to the night Luke found me. Not just in the light, but so much had changed since then. We were both different people, growing together as we wound our way in the world.

"Do you ever wonder what would have happened if you didn't find me that night?" I glanced over to find him studying me with an unreadable expression, love and adoration coursing down the bond between us.

He shook his head. "Never. I was always going to find you."

"Yeah, but things could have been so different."

"How so?"

"We met in the club. What if I hadn't gone out that night?"

"Eve, I was always going to find you. Whether it was that night in the park, or at the club when I spotted you on the dance floor." His voice dropped low, the gravel in his tone sending a shiver down my spine. *Whether I'd taken you home that night and played out the many fantasies that went through my mind while we danced. It wouldn't have changed a thing.*

He used the mind link so the old lady sat one bench down couldn't hear, but her eyes were already popping out of her head.

"No matter what, we were fated to find each other. *Anamacha gealaí*, remember? You were written in the moon and stars for me." Luke leaned to brush his lips against mine, his warm hazel eyes fixed on me. "No matter how we met, we were always destined to end up here. I'm exactly where I'm supposed to be."

He leaned in and claimed my lips in a soft kiss, the bond binding our spirits humming.

I melted into his arms, smiling against his lips when the bin nearby rattled as he tossed his coffee cup inside. He cupped my jaw to deepen the kiss, my heart hammering as the intensity stole the breath from my lungs.

Something vibrated in his pocket, and he cursed, only pulling away when I started digging through his pockets.

He grabbed the phone before I could, grinning as he held it to his ear. "Yeah, she's here. I'll put her on."

"What is it? What?" I badgered him, my hands fumbling with the phone after he handed it to me.

Darren's voice came down the line. "It's a baby boy."

"It's a boy!" I squealed and leaped to my feet, bouncing on my tippy toes as I danced.

Luke joined me, and a laugh of pure joy spilled from my lips as he lifted me and spun us in a slow circle.

"Both Paula and the baby are doing well. Do you guys want to come meet him?"

"Of course, we've only been drinking so much caffeine all day waiting. I'm afraid Eve might turn into a coffee bean." Luke set me down, pressing a kiss to my cheek.

"Head straight over. I know Shane can't wait to meet you."

I froze, my bottom lip trembling as I clutched the phone. "Shane?"

"Shane Tom Donohoe," Darren said proudly. "Named after two of the best werewolves I've ever had the privilege to know."

My mate pulled me close, his glassy eyes mirroring mine as a surge of emotion squeezed my heart.

"I can't think of a more fitting name," I whispered, tears thickening my voice. "We're on our way."

Luke brushed his lips against mine again, taking my hands in his.

"Let's go meet the newest member of the Crescent pack."

# AUTHOR NOTE

Writing "The End" for the last time in *The Hybrid Wolf Series* was a bittersweet moment. *Wolf Bait* was born from a love of reading and the dream of being an author. It was the beginning of the most magical journey, and I've loved every step of the way. Although I'll be moving away from wolves for a while, this series will always be where the adventure started.

I've changed so much since writing *Wolf Bait* five—*OMG five?!*—years ago. I've grown both as a person and as a writer. I've met other incredible authors, amazing readers, and learned lots about the industry. Most of all, I found my voice, and nothing is ever going to take that away from me.

A reader once described HWS as "home" to me. Honestly, I nearly burst into tears because that's all I ever wanted to give readers—somewhere to escape to. That's was what reading was to me for so many years.

I really hope I've done Eve and Luke's story justice. These characters have given me so much. They're the reason I'm an author, the reason you guys took a chance on me. This series will forever have a special place in my heart.

Thank you for reading my books, I hope you enjoyed HWS as much as I did. Hearing from readers is one of my favourite things, and I'm online far too much, so you can always find me in the places below!

**Newsletter:** www.ciaradelahunt.com/newsletter
**PNR Book Club:** www.discord.com/invite/dWCFbYGZFz
**Reader Group:** Ciara's Book Coven

# ALSO BY
## CIARA DELAHUNT

**THE HYBRID WOLF SERIES**

*Lone Wolf (Prequel)*

Wolf Bait

Blood Moon

Truth Bites

Fated Pack

# Acknowledgments

I'm not sure where to begin. *Fated Pack* should have been finished sooner, but you were so patient and understanding. *The Hybrid Wolf Series* is complete because of my wonderful readers. Your support for these books, and a new author like me, means the absolute world to me.

Writing is my passion, my dream, and my escape. I give my books everything; I skip events with family, I write on my weekends, and even my holidays. It's a labour of love to build the life I dream of, where I can spend my days writing, meeting readers, and being a part of such an amazing community. But these stories would not be here without my amazing support system.

The biggest thank you goes to my fiancé—if you're reading this after May 2025, then he's my *husband*, ahh! Thank you for your endless patience and for encouraging me every step of the way. You give me the courage to believe in myself, and you're always the first person I tell when I've finished a book. You never complain when I wake you to write early on the weekends, or when I slip into bed at three in the morning on a deadline. It's not just the reminders to sleep, minding the cats when they misbehave, or cooking when I'm on deadlines. It's your unwavering support, the way you talk me down when I'm stressed, listen to me vent, and hold me when I cry. Thank you for always encouraging me to embrace myself, quirks and all, and never failing to hold space for me. Our love story is my favourite one of all.

Alyssa (Cats & Bookstacks Author Services), I am so damn

glad to have you. Thank you for editing this book, and making it a worthy finale for the series. You work your magic on everything you touch, and it's incredible to see things coming together. You're a dream to work with, and your enthusiasm for the series is infectious.

My cover designer, Anna, you never fail to get it right. I don't know how you create such beautiful concepts from my ramblings! It's always a pleasure working with you, and you really helped bring *The Hybrid Wolf Series* to life.

To my author squad as always, thank you for supporting me and listening to my rants. To my street team, thank you for hyping this series. A lot of you have been here since day one and I'm so grateful to have you!

Once again, to my readers, thank you for taking a chance on me. The Hybrid Wolf Series wouldn't be the same without your support. Your messages make me laugh, you check in on me, keep me motivated, and are truly the best bunch of readers an author could ask for. I'm not sorry about any cliffhangers or pain I caused, because I always piece your heart back together in the end!

This isn't goodbye. It's the end of an era, but an exciting new beginning in other ways. I'll be dabbling in witches next, so there will be more magic and mayhem coming soon! But first, I need to take moment and give this series the send off it deserves.

# About the Author

Ciara writes paranormal romance with dark twists, spice, and a heavy dose of sarcasm. Her books feature strong women, morally grey love interests, suspense, and found family. She lives in the Irish countryside with her boyfriend and their two cats. When she doesn't have her head stuck in a book, you will find Ciara walking in the parklands nearby, in the gym, passed out on her yoga mat, or screaming at a rugby match.

A book-dragon from birth, her love of reading bled into writing when she was a teenager, and the rest is history. Ciara can't write without music and loves nothing more than to be curled up with her laptop and a mocha in her favourite coffee shop, writing to her heart's content.

amazon.com/author/ciaradelahunt

tiktok.com/@ciaradelahuntbooks

instagram.com/ciaradelahunt

facebook.com/authorciaradelahunt

threads.net/@ciaradelahunt

bsky.app/profile/ciaradelahunt.bsky.social

bookbub.com/authors/ciara-delahunt

goodreads.com/ciaradelahunt

www.ingramcontent.com/pod-product-compliance
Lightning Source LLC
Chambersburg PA
CBHW071134180726
48291CB00007B/2169